The Anointed Heir

By Janice Broyles

THE ANOINTED HEIR
By Janice Broyles

Published by Late November Literary
Winston Salem, NC 27107

ISBN (print): 978-1-7375561-6-9

Janice Broyles.
The Anointed Heir/Janice Broyles, 1st ed.

Printed in the United States of America

Scripture taken from the King James Version, public domain
*Psalm 22, King James Version
**1 Samuel, King James Version

Dedicated to

Every Godly leader—pastors, teachers, mentors—who led, encouraged, and corrected me by sharing Biblical truths.

~Janice

*And the time that David was king in Hebron
over the house of Judah was seven years
and six months.
2 Samuel 2:11*

*And as the ark of the LORD came into the
city of David, Michal Saul's daughter
looked through a window, and saw king
David leaping and dancing before
the LORD; and she despised him in her
heart.
2 Samuel 6:16*

Prologue

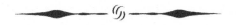

David

Northern Judean mountains

1012 B.C

I pushed the horse as fast as it could go. The terrain was rugged amidst the dense forest, but I could make out a path. Even without the path, this forest had been my companion for years. Branches slapped at us, but they were no match for me and my beast. As surely as the sun sets in the west, I knew my way, and nothing would detour me.

Eight years. Eight years separated from Michal. Eight years without her in my arms. Eight years on the run, trying to protect me and my men from a vengeful, mad king. And now? Now it was done.

My men were not far behind, but I did not wait for them. A part of me knew it came from the sheer joy of the reunion with my wife, but the larger part of me knew that I did not desire anyone to cite reasons as to why it was a bad idea. King Saul was dead, and even though I mourned him and his sons, especially my brother and friend, Jonathan, his death meant freedom. I no longer had to hide among the enemy. I no longer had to be separated from my Michal.

I heard my name faintly to my left but did not cast a glance.

There was still too much ground to cover if I planned to see her before nightfall.

"David!" The voice grew slightly louder. Whoever called out to me was catching up.

My horse jumped over a fallen tree and kept running without breaking its stride. *Long gone are the days of trying to ride and steer a donkey,* I thought to myself while patting the horse's mane.

"David!" Closer yet.

It was Benaiah. He was the only one who could outrace me on a horse. I told myself it was all those formal years of training under Abner, King Saul's commander, but really, Benaiah was simply good at anything he put his hand to do.

"David! We have news!"

The unstable path led to a clearing, and I grimaced. This was all Benaiah needed to take the lead. The dense forest was more my terrain, but sure footing was all his. The clearing consisted of rolling hills. I could feel the horse slow as it ran uphill. "No slowing now," I commanded it.

"You have to stop!" Benaiah yelled just beside me. "The Benjamite's garrison are positioned along their borders."

"I am king now!" I yelled back without turning. "I do not *have* to do anything!"

Our horses started the descent down one of the last hills. Something on the horizon glinted at me, reflecting the sun. Benaiah and I must have heard the horns at the same time. He yelled, "David!" but it was too late. I was nearly upon Hebrew soldiers.

I yanked back the reins, but my horse could not slow in time. Just as I saw the drawn arrows and spears, I turned him to the right and plunged into a field of tall grass. "Whoa! Whoa!" The heavy grass nearly covered the entirety of the horse and aided in our stop. The horse panted, and I patted him again. "Sorry about that, my friend."

By the time I maneuvered out of the thick grass, Benaiah was already waiting for me at the edge of the clearing.

"What are they doing here?" I asked.

"That is what I was trying to tell you. We heard this morning that Abner has stationed Saul's tribesmen around the entire Benjamite area. They expected you."

"But I am the anointed king."

"And as such, I advise not leaving your men at the break of dawn."

"I will take that under advisement, but the decision is mine."

"How can we protect you if you are not around for us to protect? Remember, my king, not everyone sees you as theirs." Benaiah indicated the large mass of men positioned to attack me at the command.

Irritation stewed within. "Enough of this. Saul is dead."

"At least wait for more men."

"Would that not come off as threatening? These men are my soldiers or soon will be."

"They may not see it that way, and even if they do, they may be following orders."

"Who would make those orders? *Saul is dead*," I repeated the words, allowing the frustration to slip out.

Benaiah pointed across the field. "Him."

My gaze followed where he pointed, and my heart dropped. "Abner."

Abner, Saul's commanding officer, sat on his horse, yelling at the men in the formation.

I gave a humorless laugh and shook my head. "Never-ending."

"It will end, but we need to make smart moves. Let us wait for the others."

I closed my eyes, took a deep breath, and sought the Lord. *Should I go forward?* Without waiting for an answer, I flicked the reins and told the horse to move. Benaiah sighed.

As I approached, Abner's attention landed on me. I lifted both hands to indicate a peaceful greeting. He ordered his men to stand down.

"Abner," I said, contemplating a bow. But that indicated submission, and as king, I needed to establish authority. So instead, I kept my gaze on his.

"David."

All those around us seemed to hold their breath. I needed to handle this correctly, but impatience fueled my frustration. "My men and I grieve with all of Israel over the death of King Saul and our brothers-in-arms. We weep with you."

Abner gave a slight nod. "Is that all which brings you here?"

"We are en route to retrieve my wife. Gallim is in this direction."

Abner raised an eyebrow. He seemed to weigh his words before saying, "That cannot happen. The king's edicts are still in place until the new king establishes his throne. You can take up your cause with him at that time."

My mouth opened in surprise, but I quickly shut it and steeled my countenance. "I am anointed king of Israel. You know this. Now is the time to put an end to this madness. Israel needs to heal. You and I were once allies. Let us be allies again."

"You are not Saul's son. He cut you off when he gave Michal to another. And you know that blood rules before marriage anyway. Ishbosheth is next in line. *He* is the rightful king. We can be allies as soon as you and your men accept this reality."

I glared at Abner, my frustration leading to fury. "You mean to divide a kingdom?"

"No. All of Israel should be under one king. The son of Saul." Abner paused, then asked, "Do *you* mean to divide a kingdom?"

"Ishbosheth as king is not God's design."

"According to who? Who decides Yahweh's design?"

"According to Samuel! God's prophet!" I yelled. "Now I demand my wife!"

"Samuel's dead," Abner said through gritted teeth. "Turn around David, and go back to where you came from. You are not king here."

"And if I refuse?"

"As I stated, King Saul's edicts are still in place until the new king is established. That means we have orders to kill you and your men immediately. You are still an outlaw and not welcomed here."

"What a way to thank us for years of dedicated service to the kingdom. We are not done with this."

"Why the anger?" Abner asked spitefully. "We could kill you right now, and yet, out of deference to our past relationship, I have ordered the men to momentarily stand down. And is that not Benaiah just off in the distance? He is a wanted man. He disgracefully ran from Saul's army. I could order him captured this moment."

I did not move for some time. My hands held the reins so tightly, the hide burned against my skin. My jaw hurt from being clenched so hard. My entire body became taut, and I thought of the many ways I could jump from my horse onto Abner and snap his neck.

"Leave, or Benaiah is ours."

Knowing I had little choice, I turned the horse and made my way to Benaiah. I understood the reason for him staying several stones away. He ran from Saul's army to serve under me. I cleared his name, but not Saul or Abner. Until I was king over all of Israel, Benaiah could not be exposed, and yet, that is exactly what I did. I swallowed back the shame.

"I take it things did not go well."

"We need to leave, or they take you."

"I would like to see them try."

I did not doubt that Benaiah and I would cause massive damage to the troops, but this would not help my cause with the Hebrew people. "We cannot kill these men. It would look poorly upon us."

"Then let us leave before Abner changes his mind."

The two of us stayed on the edge of the tall, dense grass to quickly hide into it if necessary. We heard the thundering hooves before we saw a band of our men descending the hill toward Abner's blockade. Would Abner think this was planned and consider it a threat?

I waved my hands to draw their attention to us. "Please Yahweh, let them see me."

But the horses had already turned toward us as if my men already knew.

"They had scouts tell them of our whereabouts." This did not surprise me. My men were good. They would never run toward Israel without making sure there was safe passage.

"Of course, they did. If you had waited, you would have known about this blockade, and it would have been avoided."

I did not answer because there was nothing to say. My haste in seeing Michal would earn a sound tongue-lashing from them. And I deserved it.

"I see an opening into the forest up ahead," Benaiah said. "Head there, and I will lead the others to follow."

I saw it and pressed the horse to go faster. Shame heated my face, and I refused for others to see it. My urgency in retrieving Michal led to a rash decision that could have ended badly. As I traveled the trail, hours passed, and the day turned to dusk. The horse needed to rest, but I was close to the one place in Israel where I would be safe. "We are almost there," I said to the beast. "We are almost to Judah."

Of
Kings
and
Kingdoms

1

Michal

King Saul's Palace, Gibeah

1012 B.C

I slowly moved through Merab's old chambers, desperately desiring her to scold me for being in her room. But my older sister was dead, as were my father and three oldest brothers. I stopped and admired the small marble vase that held a group of parched, withered flowers. I had given them to her after one of my long walks around the palace gardens just days before she married Adriel. And here they still were, over ten years later.

Dinah, my maidservant and best friend, quietly approached. "I knew I would find you here. Come, you need to eat. The boys are asking for you."

Merab's five sons had come with me to the palace for the mourning period, but then again, where else could they go? With Merab gone, Adriel seemed to be taking his grief out with him to the battlefield, which left me raising their children. Not that I minded. They were remnants of my sister, and I loved them fiercely. Too tired to engage in conversation, I nodded and left Merab's chambers.

"Rizpah stopped me again and asked to see you." Dinah walked alongside me.

"I am not ready for company or conversation."

"I have expressed that to her, but she told me just last night she must see you."

Rizpah had been my father's favorite concubine. She and I had always been friends, but my mother, Ahinoam, loathed her. But just like with everything else, time changed situations. She and my mother had formed an uneasy alliance now that their futures were uncertain. Both insisted they had every reason to be nervous, but I could not comprehend their fears. Even though David was no longer my young-and-somewhat-naïve husband from eight years ago, I struggled with understanding their fears. But maybe I was naïve. Maybe David really changed, and my family *was* in danger. I longed for reassurance, for normalcy. Strangely enough, when I lay awake in the night, tossing and turning, it was no longer only David I desired. I also missed my horses and the beautiful vineyards of Paltiel's land. "Fine. We will stop by her chambers before meeting up with the boys."

The two of us continued walking through the halls of my father's palace. It was still his. At least in my mind. Would David demand it to be his?

"Any word from David?" I asked.

"No."

"He better not send his misfits. I refuse to speak to them. If he wants me, he can come get me."

Dinah pressed her lips together as if to stop her from speaking.

"What? What is it you desire to say? Out with it."

Dinah gave me a sideways glance before saying, "I do not think it is a good idea to antagonize David or his men. They are quite fierce and have an aggressive reputation."

"I am not afraid of David or his men."

Dinah stopped and reached for me. "You should be."

"I think I can handle my husband."

"He has not been your husband for over eight years. You have

10

been living with another man. David could have you and Paltiel killed if he desired."

"You know I had no control over that! Besides, David could have retrieved me at any point."

"Do you not remember your father's animosity toward him? King Saul's men were stationed all around Paltiel's countryside. They were waiting for David to show up. Rumor is they have reinforced their stations. There are blockades all along the Gibeah and Gallim countryside."

"David has conquered many enemies," I said, not masking the hurt behind the words. "Yet, he never showed up. He did not try. I waited and waited, and if my husband desires me now, he will push past the blockades and show up at my doorstep. I refuse to see anyone else." I marched away from Dinah, my insides shaking.

I arrived at Rizpah's door and knocked, trying to even out my breathing. I couldn't. My breathing was ragged as the ache in my heart intensified.

She opened it and yanked me inside.

"I have news," she said quickly. She took my hand and brought me to her sleeping chamber. The concubines were never given spacious dwellings, but Rizpah fared better than other concubines because father actually loved her. Just the same, the chamber was small in comparison to mine, and it did not contain a balcony. Taking one look at me, she quipped, "You have seen better days, my friend."

"As have you," I snapped, not desiring to hear how lousy I looked. Rizpah appeared strong and beautiful, just as always. It irritated me. Was she not grieving? "I was told it was urgent to see me, so what is it? I would like to get about my business."

Rizpah raised her eyebrows but never broke her gaze. "Careful, Michal. Learn to suppress those negative feelings, or you will become bitter and vengeful. Like your mother."

"And now a lecture. Anything else?" I made sure to have a bite to my words.

Rizpah gently touched my arm. "Michal," she said, her words gentler. "Talk to me. You always used to talk to me."

I pulled my arm away and lowered my gaze. "Is this why you summoned me here? To pressure me with your questions and suppositions."

"It is evident that you are handling recent events in isolation rather than grieving together. You have completely ignored your mother, and she has requested meals with you every day since you arrived back at the palace. You ignore me and nearly everyone else, other than Dinah, and rumor has it you have become unbearable to her too."

My insides quaked from raw emotion, and I felt as if my skin crawled with insects. I took in shallow breaths and broke out in a cold sweat. "I cannot breathe."

"Sit."

I felt her push me down to a sitting position.

"Place your forehead upon your knees and try to even out your breathing. I need to find a damp cloth for your neck."

Sobs erupted, and I clutched the silk of my skirts, as I sobbed into them. I longed for Merab. I longed for the life I use to love. I longed for the husband of my youth. I longed to see Jonathan and to hear him calmly guide me with his advice. I longed to be anywhere but here.

I felt the cool cloth upon the back of my neck. Rizpah stroked my head, and before I knew it, she was beside me, and my head was on her lap.

She let me cry until my tears were depleted. My breathing was still shaky, but my insides felt cleansed. Eventually, I sat upright, took the cloth, and wiped my face.

"Nothing like a good cry to make us feel a little better."

"I did not think I had any tears left."

"Michal, I have not seen you cry the entire time you have been back. During the funerals, you said nothing to no one. You have kept to your chambers."

"My pillow is wet with tears every night. Trust me, I cry."

"You need to eat something."

"I am not hungry. And I am on my way to eat with the boys. They will want me to be at evening meal."

"Of course. You are their mother."

"No, I am not. And at the moment, I am a poor replacement for their real one, but that is the way of this life. Pain and heartache burden our shoulders like sacks full of wheat. The quicker the boys learn it, the better they will be for knowing it. Maybe it will protect them from making foolish decisions."

"I know you miss Merab. She was a good sister, but you are their mother," Rizpah repeated. "Say it until you believe it. Those boys are lucky to have you. And life is full of a lot of wonderful moments. Revel in those. You cannot keep pain and heartache as bedfellows, or they will suffocate you in your sleep."

I surveyed her chamber. I felt embarrassed at my meltdown. "Is that all you needed from me?"

"I did want to check on you, but that is not the only reason I needed to see you. I spoke with Abner."

"Abner?" It struck me as odd that Rizpah would speak with Israel's commander.

She looked down and her face turned flush. "Yes, well, we talked occasionally when Saul was alive. We both were concerned with his mental state. Abner proved to be a good listener and friend."

"I am still unclear as to why you want to talk to me about Abner."

"He is encouraging your brother to take Saul's place as king of Israel."

"Ishbosheth? As king?" I gave a humorless laugh. "I highly doubt that will go over well. He is nothing like father, and besides, David is anointed king. Samuel declared it when David was just a boy."

"Yes, and Samuel's dead."

Rizpah's calloused words surprised me. "So is my father, my sister, and my brothers. Does that mean we forget about them too?"

"That is not what I meant." Rizpah grabbed my hand. "Men's hearts and ears are fickle. They are easily swayed. With Samuel gone, many feel David is trying to usurp the throne. That the throne belongs to a son of Saul."

"David is my husband, which makes him a son of Saul."

"Blood sons take the throne first. You know that. And with Paltiel, technically alive and married to you, the people may not see you as David's wife anymore."

"Paltiel is not married to me. We never even consummated the relationship."

Now Rizpah acted surprised. "You mean you never…"

"We did not. David sent Paltiel his bloody sword with a promise to avenge my honor should consummation happen. So, I am married to David, not Paltiel. My father had no right to do that, and my life would be much more different if he would have let me stay with him." I turned slightly to hide the pain from her. It was there, and it throbbed nearly as intensely as when it first happened. I used to fantasize about life on the run with David. What it would have been like with me at his side.

"Will you stand by David, or will you stand by Ishbosheth?"

"How can I stand by David? We are married, but we are not together."

"He is coming for you, Michal. If for no other reason than as a political pawn. He needs you to establish his throne."

"Can he not come for me out of love? Can he not come for me because I am his wife?" The words angrily flew out of my mouth. "Is that all I am? A political pawn for his gain? Then he is no better than my father." I stood up and paced the room.

"Men are not like us," Rizpah explained. "They are arrogant, carnal creatures who may occasionally perform good acts, but overall, they are selfish, spoiled individuals who hold the power."

The bitterness and frustration in Rizpah's words echoed into my soul. "We take care of the family. We handle the household. And they run off and marry other women. You are right. We do not have the power."

Rizpah came and stood next to me. "I am the other woman." She gave me a small, understanding smile. "Saul married me when I was only fourteen, and your mother hated me. And honestly, I understood why. I knew she was the queen. I knew that my sole purpose for existence was for the king's pleasure. For the first few years, I was miserable. I thought of ending my life nearly every day."

"My father loved you, which only made my mother more jealous."

"That was my choice." Rizpah shrugged. "When I was nearing my eighteenth year, I stumbled upon a realization. Men wanted me. I was aware of the glances as I walked by, but I did not realize that it gave me a small amount of power if I played it right. So, I did everything I could to make your father love me. He had dozens of other concubines, but it was not hard. I learned to be for him what he needed most at that moment. As Queen Ahinoam became more bitter and angry, he took solace in his harem. I made sure that he eventually sought solace from me alone."

"That does not exactly help me," I said. "In my story, I am the jealous queen. I am the one who watches as my husband marries other women."

"It is the way of our people. The fact that David reciprocated your love for a time is a blessing many women never experience."

"Once again, you are not helping."

"I am not trying to soothe you. I am trying to reason with you." Rizpah's words carried an edge to them. "You cannot change this world, Michal. I thought you would have embraced that more fully. You have somewhat, but you still have this little girl dream of having your warrior king all to yourself. That was never going to happen."

Tears threatened again. My face warmed with shame at showing any vulnerability to Rizpah. How had I not noticed how calculating she was? According to her, she purposefully came between my father and all the other women, including my mother. "I need to leave."

She grabbed my hand again. "Do not be angry at my honesty. I am trying to help you whether you believe it or not."

"Help me how? How does telling me that David loved me once and I should be happy with that help me?"

"I am trying to show you how powerful you can be in this situation. If you continue to think you are powerless, you will fade into nothing more than a shadow in David's memory. He is going to have other women, Michal. He is potentially future king. I heard from Abner that Judah chooses to break away from Israel and claim David as chosen king. You knew that when you married him, so do not act shocked that a powerful, ambitious man married other women. But if you learn how to utilize yourself in a way that gets his attention, you can still have the man you love."

I did not stay to answer. Instead, I left Rizpah in her chambers. As I shut the door behind me, I saw Dinah still waiting for me. "Do you speak ill of me behind my back?"

"No, but that does not keep the palace from gossiping."

We began walking in the direction of my father's library. "It seems that there are those who say I treat you unkindly."

"No one has said a word to my face. And if it makes you feel better, they said that before you ever left the palace. Where are we headed? This is not in the direction of the children's chamber."

"I want to see Abner. He has been at the palace for an extended period, and I now know why." When I saw Dinah leaning in to hear me, I whispered, "Rizpah said that Abner is pushing Ishbosheth to take the throne."

"That imbecile?" Dinah covered her mouth. "I am sorry. I should not speak so openly here on palace grounds."

"True," I answered. "To both your statements. Yes, my brother is an imbecile, and yes, you should refrain from such words here where not everyone sees you as their equal. Some think you no longer have a tongue, remember? We should try to keep up appearances until we leave."

As we turned the corner that led down the king's main hallway, Abner's voice carried into it. "You have nothing to fear. He will not harm you. I am certain of it."

"How can you be certain? He and his men kill men, women, and children with no thought. If he so much as hears of me considering Israel's throne, I am as good as dead."

"He did not touch Saul. You are Saul's son and Jonathan's brother; he will not touch you either."

I stepped into the room, foregoing all decorum. Ishbosheth was not king yet, so I figured it mattered little. "You are also my brother, and David is my husband. I doubt he will kill you. He will want peace between the kingdoms."

Both men turned to me in surprise.

"You speak out of line, princess," Abner said. "Although what you say is correct, you should not presume your presence is welcomed."

"Do not enter this room without an invitation!" Ishbosheth's pale face turned red. He lacked the confidence and stately demeanor of my other brothers, as well as any brotherly affection toward me. Just the sight of him made me ache for Jonathan.

I ignored both of their comments and continued, "However, have both of you forgotten that Samuel anointed David's head? Is he not the true king?"

"You may take your leave, princess," Abner said in warning.

Addressing Ishbosheth, I added, "Our father pursued him for over eight years and was not successful. Consider that."

"And you betrayed our father, did you not? You chose the murdering shepherd over our family. So, I will not hear another word from you. As far as I am concerned, you are not welcome in this palace. The grieving period is over. Take your leave."

"I will leave," I said between gritted teeth. "But mark my words,

I will not shed a tear for you when you meet your end."

Both men stared at me in apparent shock. Neither had probably ever been addressed in such a way by a woman. I no longer cared. Ishbosheth began sputtering over words. "Out! Guards! Get her out!"

I stepped back into the hall without a formal departure and began marching toward the front entrance of the palace. "Dinah!" I called out, knowing she had waited for me outside the room.

"I am right here, beside you," she said, moving quickly to keep up.

"We are leaving immediately."

"I gathered as much. What of the boys?"

"Go, and fetch them. They will return to Paltiel's home with me."

Dinah left to do my bidding while I marched through the hall, down the stairs, and past the main foyer. I ordered the doors opened, and the servants scrambled to accommodate. As I made my way outside and demanded passage to Paltiel's, my insides shook once again, and my skin crawled. I stood and waited, taking in deep breaths. *Do not lose control*, I told myself. *Do not show emotion.*

So, I kept the brewing emotions under the lid of my clamped mouth.

2

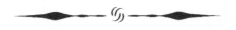

David

Judah

1012 B.C.

The Judean mountains towered before me. With their peaks and gentle slopes, I marveled at how the sun seemed to rest upon them as if tired from a hard day's toil. I also knew the cruelty of those mountains. The extreme temperatures and brutal terrain. But I couldn't hate them. Those same mountains had protected me and my men. When we had nowhere else to go. When Israel turned her back on us, the mountains were there to hide us.

"My king?" Joab, my nephew and newly-appointed commander among my men, stepped beside me.

I kept my gaze on the mountains, not sure if I deserved to be called "king." My rash decision to leave ahead of my men to retrieve Michal could have ended much differently. It reminded me that I still had much to learn about being a leader. What had Samuel seen in me? I still remembered the sensation of oil being poured over my head when I was a boy and the prophet's declaration that I would be king. But that was long ago, and a lot had happened in the eighteen years since that day. Knowing Joab waited for me to answer, I said, "You found me. I thought this would be a good hiding place for a few moments."

"It was not difficult. You enjoy rooftops."

The two of us stood on the rooftop of one of our allies. It reminded me of the nights Michal and I would sleep on the rooftop of our home and gaze at the stars and whisper our dreams and promises to each other. My heart immediately began to ache. "She's not with you?"

When Joab didn't answer, I turned to him. He seemed to find his sandals fascinating.

"Nephew? Where is she?"

"From what we have been told, she is still in mourning with Ahinoam and the rest of Saul's family."

"Of course." Hebrew mourning would last thirty days for the loss of Saul and his sons. It was naïve of me to think Michal would be running to me after the news of her father's death. Even though he was the one who forced our separation, going so far as to give Michal to another man, Saul was still her father. "And the borders?"

Joab paused before saying, "They are fortified. Hebrew soldiers line city gates. All information comes from our allies within. They come and go from their cities freely, which aids in our cause."

Eleazar, Jashobeam, and four others of my mighty men climbed up onto the rooftop and now approached us. I watched them with a mix of frustration and gratitude. These men had sacrificed for me time and again, so how could I be annoyed that they had failed at bringing my estranged wife back to me? Even I had been unsuccessful, but that did not alleviate the frustration.

"He's not happy," Joab announced to them. "I told you he would not be happy."

"I can tell," Eleazar said. "David's never been one to hide his emotions."

"First of all," I said in defense, "I hid among the Philistines twice and was successful, so I think I can hide my emotions when truly needed."

"Ha!" Eleazar laughed. "You were spotted the first night and had to kill the guy to keep the secret. And the second time we walked right into King Achish's palace. We were not hiding anything."

"Eleazar's right." Jashobeam shrugged. "Your face is an open book."

"Then it's a wonder I have stayed alive all these years." I did not hide the sarcasm.

"We had a little to do with that." Eleazar placed his arm around my shoulder. Changing the subject, he tried to encourage me. "Give this time."

"It has been eight years." I pushed his arm off me. "I want her here now. It makes no sense that Abner would keep her from me."

Eleazar stepped in front of me. "David, stop."

"Let me pass."

"Listen, even with the borders being patrolled, Michal is still grieving her father and her brothers. You cannot throw aside her grief. Give it time."

"There is the matter with the other women." Benaiah's words fell to the ground as if sunk by the heavy weight of the other men's glares. "Never mind. It is no matter."

"He needs to know." Jashobeam continued, "Her name is Maacah, the daughter of Talmai, King of Geshur. She has been offered as a gift of peace for the new king of Israel."

"Another one?" Abishai, Joab's brother and another one of my nephews, asked with his eyebrows raised. "How many does that make?"

Jashobeam shushed the young man, but I agreed with Abishai's assessment. "I have all of these women, and yet, not the one that I desire."

"We need to remain steadfast to the plan. You need to claim the throne, and the people of Hebron are willing for us to establish you here. An alliance with King Talmai is prudent, and I heard his daughter is a beauty in the land. With her comes gold and jewels, chariots and horses, not to mention many servants."

"It helps establish your throne," Benaiah said in agreement.

"Yes, I know," I muttered. "Is that all?"

Jashobeam added, "We have more news."

"Out with it," I grumbled, clearly showing my displeasure.

"Men from Jabesh-Gilead traveled through the night and retrieved the bodies. Word has it they are burning them and then burying them. We are unsure if they were able to retrieve Saul's head. It was not with the bodies fastened to the wall of Beth Shan. The Philistines set it on a pedestal in Dagon's temple."

I rubbed my temples and took a deep breath. Once again, I would have to set my desires aside. This news demanded my attention. "I am glad they honor their king. The men of Jabesh have always been loyal to Saul and his kingdom."

"Speaking of kings," Jashobeam said. "The men of Judah found a stretch of land here in Hebron that will work as your military base and home. Since they have anointed you as their king, they take it upon themselves to offer the land and resources as a tribal gift."

As soon as we arrived in Judah, we were received warmly. My tribesmen had ignored Abner's orders of securing the borders to keep us out. Instead, they waited for me, hoping I would make my way to them. Within days, they had anointed me their king. "It is a humbling gift," I admitted. "And I gladly accept. We will work at once to help in completing any necessary tasks to finish the property before we move in."

"Do you want to see it first?" Eleazar asked. "You don't have to just accept the gift. As king, you can demand better land."

"Is it unfit for a king?" I asked. "Then again, I have slept under the stars and in caves most of my life. I have low standards."

Eleazar smiled at that. "Rest assured, it is a great piece of land and will work well as the central location for you to build your kingdom. I only wanted you to remember that you can take time to consider the gift and see the land for yourself."

"Yes, I will see it. Let's set out today."

"There is the other matter." Benaiah stopped others from

speaking. "Abner was successful in grooming Ishbosheth as king."

"So, we have a split kingdom," I spoke the words to myself as guilt grew.

All Israel should be under one king. The son of Saul. Do you mean to divide a kingdom? Abner's words repeated in my head.

"You are king of Judah," Eleazar explained. "Israel should not break away from Judah, but there are those who are Saul sympathizers and believe that the throne should go to a son of Saul."

"Which is why securing Michal as my wife would be for the betterment of our kingdom." I did not add that having her with me was also for the betterment of my sanity. "With her at my side, I am a son of Saul."

"If we go and take her, Saul loyalists may take it poorly. Some see your men as unruly and barbaric." Benaiah gave a pointed look to Jashobeam.

"Why are you looking at me?" Jashobeam asked in a huff.

"I doubt you take your weekly bath," Benaiah said under his breath.

Jashobeam took a step toward him. "Have the guts to say that to my face."

"Fine. You stink. There."

Jashobeam smiled tightly, glanced around at the rest of us, then without warning, unsheathed his sword and expertly swung it at Benaiah.

Benaiah just as expertly dodged it. "Getting a little slow in your old age."

"Enough," I said. Benaiah and Jashobeam were often at odds. I could normally deal with their banter and brawls, but not right now. "If you must fight, we have plenty of enemies."

I walked back to the edge of the roof and studied the mountains again. *Why does everything have to be a struggle?* I thought. Michal continued to be just out of reach and even the kingdom wasn't fully mine. "So, I am king of Judah, and Ishbosheth will be king of Israel? This is not what was promised to me."

"As soon as Saul died, Abner went running back to Ishbosheth. He probably had this planned all along. Maybe not for the kingdom to go to Ishbosheth, but definitely to Jonathan." Eleazar added, "He is Saul's cousin, so I understand him wanting to use Israel's loyalty in placing Jonathan on the throne. But Ishbosheth? He does not have a strong reputation."

"Abner's foolish rush back to Ishbosheth weakens the kingdom," I agreed. "We will examine the land in Hebron today, but I need two of you to relay a message to Abner."

"I will go to him," Joab said. "What is the message?"

"Ask him how there is to be peace in our land if the tribes stay divided. Tell him I request a meeting."

"Will it be peaceful?"

"That relies solely on him, but I hope so."

3

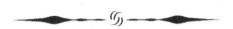

Michal

Paltiel's Vineyard, Gallim

1012 B.C.

I walked Eglah back to her stall, combed her, and fed her. "I missed you," I told her. She nudged me in understanding. "I could not take you with me. You understand?" She snorted and nudged me again. I wrapped my arms around her thick neck.

"Princess?" Dinah called out to me from outside the stall. "Paltiel is asking for you."

I released Eglah, promising we would ride again tomorrow.

Leaving the stall, I asked, "Does everything seem in order?"

"He has prepared an evening meal."

"I am not hungry."

"Michal, please eat something. You are wasting away in front of my eyes." Dinah's words became choked on emotion.

I studied my hands and thin wrists. I was not oblivious to my body's response to my lack of appetite. My bones were more pronounced, my tongue and mouth suffered from dryness, my reflection showed sunken cheeks, and I had not had my monthly cycle in nearly a year. "I am not hungry," I repeated. "Grief and despair feed me a bitter potion."

"And they are slowly killing you."

I nodded, knowing her words were true. "I will try to eat something."

We walked out of Paltiel's stables, and for a moment, I stopped and admired the rolling hills of the vineyard. The last time Jonathan visited me before his death, he mentioned the beauty of this land. I was too angry to see it then, but I saw it now.

"Jonathan had it right," I murmured.

"How so?"

I shook my head, not wanting to recount Jonathan's last visit with me before his death. He showed up at Paltiel's out of concern for me. I had not taken Merab's death well, and he reminded me to see the good in this life. And I had tried. Until I heard of his death, along with the deaths of my father and two other brothers. Now, it felt like I was drowning in grief. Dinah and I followed the path to Paltiel's house. Servants lit the lanterns as the early evening light waned.

Laia, Paltiel's first wife, stepped off the veranda and approached. There was a time when we avoided each other. We had made peace recently, and I was glad for it. Hostility and contempt were exhausting to endure. Thankfully, Laia and her children enjoyed the horses, which led to calm waters between us. "He is waiting in his private chambers." She then motioned in the direction of the stables. "I finally have my children resting for the evening. I thought I might go for an evening ride. If that is agreeable?"

"Of course. Do you desire Paltiel's horse or mine?"

"Until I get one of my own, I do prefer Eglah. She is a sweet beast."

"Yes, she is. Go then, but take a lantern. She sometimes spooks in the dark."

"As do I."

The two of us shared a smile before Laia walked past us to the stables. "It is interesting how time changes enemies to friends, friends to enemies, and lovers to haters."

"Do you have someone you hate?" Dinah asked.

But I did not answer. My heart was confused and heavy with hurt. Instead, I left my maidservant and moved through Paltiel's home to his private chambers. His invitation did not worry me. When I first arrived here eight years earlier, I would have been fraught with anxiety over the invitation to private chambers. But now, I saw Paltiel differently. He had honored my marriage to David and still provided a home for me, Dinah, and eventually my sister's sons. This had somehow become our home.

I knocked gently on the door. "Paltiel? You called for me?"

"Yes, come in," he said from the other side.

I entered the room and saw the savory meal spread across a low table. He sat among the cushions, sipping his wine.

"Come, come. The servants prepared us a great feast. The children are fed and warm, and now all that is left is you." He patted the cushions beside him.

Memories surged of the times I sat on cushions beside David, our arms around each other as we ate our meals. Eating together with David had been intimate and a lovely experience. But now, I felt nothing but a void in my heart. My imagination turned to him eating with his other women.

"Michal?" Paltiel's voice brought me back to the present. "Please, sit and eat."

I nodded and moved beside him, sitting down and making myself comfortable. "The meal smells delicious." Interestingly, my stomach rumbled in agreement. This was the first time I felt hunger in several moons.

Paltiel broke bread, gave thanks, then handed it to me. He served me a plate of stewed lamb, and I dipped the bread into the juices and bit into it. As I ate, Paltiel watched me with relief on his countenance. "It is good to have you home. I did not expect you for some time. Your mother sent a message that you required more time at the palace."

"She did not give my brother that message," I said simply while taking another bite. Paltiel seemed to wait for me to continue, so I added, "Ishbosheth ordered me to leave. I thought it best to oblige his wishes."

"You angered your brother? How so?"

"I overheard Abner trying to convince him to take control of Israel. That the throne is rightfully his. I stepped in and reminded them that David was anointed king. He is already king over Judah. Ishbosheth did not like that comment and called me a traitor to the family and the throne. I was ordered to leave immediately."

Paltiel watched me for another moment before saying, "Ishbosheth is a surviving son of Saul. I can see why Abner feels justified in offering Israel to him."

"I know. I feel torn because Ishbosheth is my brother, but David is my husband."

Paltiel looked down at his cup. "Maybe if Ishbosheth is king, you can stay here. It has not been too horrible, I hope."

"It has not been horrible. You have been kind and understanding of my...complicated situation." Once again, memories flashed of Paltiel forcing a kiss upon me at Merab's marriage feast. I had been so repulsed that I threw up on him. A laugh escaped my lips. It sounded foreign to my ears.

"What is it? What is so funny?"

"I am remembering when I drank too much wine at my sister's wedding, and how it all came back up and onto you."

Paltiel grimaced but laughed. "I will never forget that. The lesson learned was to not force a kiss upon a drunk princess."

Another laugh escaped, and before I realized what was happening, laughter filled the room. Both of us held our stomachs as we laughed, paused, then laughed again. When we eventually stopped, I wiped at my eyes. "I have not laughed until I cried since...never mind. It has been a while. I will leave it at that."

We finished the meal and drank our fill from the wine pitchers.

"I did not realize how hungry I was. Thank you for an enjoyable dinner."

"I am glad it pleased you. We will have to do it again soon."

"Laia and the children should join us," I said, thinking of his other wife. "I do not want to exclude her."

Paltiel hesitated before answering, "Or it could just be the two of us. I do enjoy your company."

I swallowed, suddenly feeling the effects of the wine. My eyes drooped, and I told myself that it was exhaustion I felt, not the awkwardness of the unmasked desire permeating from Paltiel. "I must leave. The food and wine have made me quite tired." I stood up and walked to the door. Before leaving, I stopped and said, "Thank you, Paltiel. I needed this."

"Wait."

I heard him move toward me. I felt his hand touch my elbow.

"Michal."

I did not turn to him. I kept my hand on the door handle.

"Is there any way you might desire to stay here? I cannot bear the thought of him coming for you. I do not know what I will do. I...I cherish you and the boys."

"I do not know what is going to happen. David is preoccupied at the moment, and he has other women now. Chances are he wants nothing more to do with me."

Paltiel took a step closer. I could feel his breath on my neck. "Then he is a foolish man. Who would not desire you?" When I did not respond, he continued, "Could there ever be a possibility of you truly being my wife? In every way?"

I could never give Paltiel what he longed for. Even though I understood the blessings Paltiel bestowed upon me while living under his roof, I did not love him. Not in that way. But I could not hurt him, so I simply said, "As long as David is living, we are still pawns in a treacherous game." I quickly opened the door and left him in the room alone. Once again, my heart felt heavy, but this time, it was not the heaviness of grief but the heaviness of guilt.

4

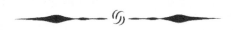

David

Judah

1012 B.C.

I walked outside and took one last look at the large compound that would be my home in Judah. The mountains were scattered just beyond the southern walls with rolling hills to the east. It did not have the scale and vastness of Saul's palace, but it still boasted numerous chambers in separate wings with airy entrances and several expansive courtyards. "This will work. Thank you."

"We have work to do, but Judah's people are willing to help." Jashobeam approached.

"There are many rooms to furnish."

"Marriage to Princess Maacah will help with that. The message arrived that her entourage have begun their journey. It will take several moons to arrive, but they are en route."

"And the rest of my family? How are they?"

"Your wives and children are awaiting word. They are situated among our people with their caravans ready."

"Bring them first. Let my wives and children set up their respective places before the princess arrives." I thought of Michal. "The queen gets the east-facing chambers. No one touches those."

"You are referring to Michal?"

"Who else would it be?"

"I am merely verifying. You do have other wives now, plus a princess on the way."

"And none of them are my queen."

Jashobeam did not push further. "Then we need to work quickly. As I stated, the princess and her entourage are already on their way."

"How long?"

"Within a full moon's passing."

Both of us turned to the sound of a running horse, heading toward us. "Why is Eleazar in such a hurry?"

He slid off the horse before it had fully stopped. "We have a problem."

"What is it?"

"Joab and his brothers."

"What of my nephews?" I asked. Joab, Abishai, and Asahel were all three sons of my sister, Zeruiah. They served in leadership positions since they joined my men years earlier.

"They are playing war games with Abner and Hebrew soldiers."

"What kind of war games?"

"The killing kind."

Anger mixed with annoyance flickered in my veins. "Why would they agree to such a thing? Abner and his men are highly trained."

"As are we," Jashobeam said defensively.

I rephrased. "Killing Israel's soldiers will not help our cause."

"No, it will not. Much of Israel already consider us a bunch of brutes." Eleazar shook his head.

"We have had to kill to survive all these years." Jashobeam crossed his arms across his chest. "Israel sings a different tune when we are fighting to protect them."

"We are not fighting to protect them at the moment," Eleazar answered. "That is why I am here. Our men are fighting Abner's men. To the death."

"Who is winning?" Jashobeam asked.

"We are, but the body count increases. Mostly on their side, but we do suffer some casualties."

I rubbed my hand over my face. *Joab*, I thought. *What has your hothead gotten into now?* I loved all my nephews, but Joab had shown leadership abilities as soon as he joined my cause over eight years ago. He was charismatic and passionate about me being the rightful king. The men listened to him and respected him, which was why it made sense to make him my commander. But he was quick to make decisions and quick to fight, especially when he felt offended or slighted. "Jashobeam, go with Eleazar. End it. Order Joab to stand down."

"Joab does not respond well to anyone who is not you."

"Tell him it is an order from his king. He is to come to me immediately."

"I agree with Jashobeam." Eleazar studied me closely. "You should probably go and diffuse the tension. Let Abner see you as wanting peace."

"I cannot go. I am waiting for Benaiah to return from his assignment. I trust you two to convey my message and put a stop to the war games."

"Surely, Benaiah's assignment does not represent the same magnitude of importance." Jashobeam narrowed his eyes at me.

Eleazar too watched me with suspicion. "You sent him to Michal."

"What if I did? I have nothing to hide. Besides, it is simply a message so that she knows I desire to retrieve her."

"Did we not decide to wait until after the fourteen days of wedding celebration before trying to contact Michal? I do not think having your first wife here, newly reunited with you, is the best wedding gift for Princess Maacah."

"What do I care of this princess? She is not Michal. It is a peace contract between two kingdoms. Nothing more."

"Exactly. A peace contract. Just how peaceful is it going to be with Michal here while you are consummating your fourth marriage?"

I flinched. "I only sent a message, but trust me, if there was a way to take Michal and keep the peace, it would have already been done."

"Is not Benaiah wanted by Israel? If they capture him, that is on your conscious."

"It was his idea, and he volunteered to go. You and I both know that Benaiah can handle himself. His skill is unmatched."

"Be that as it may, the days of you being happily married to Saul's daughter are over." Jashobeam stepped toward me, his voice slightly elevated. "You are king. You have duties as such. Chasing after some heart-broken, weepy girl is not part of them."

"Watch your words," I warned. "Michal is my first wife and queen. And I can and will have her here while still fulfilling my duties."

"David." Eleazar was my oldest friend. He gently rested his hand on my arm. I saw the concern behind his expression. "Jashobeam may need to learn some tact, but what he says is true. Gone are the days of your wedded bliss."

"We are not young as we once were, but neither are we old. We can pick up where we left off, or at least try."

"You need this alliance. If the king gets word that you are snubbing his daughter, or that the union was tainted by your affections toward Saul's daughter, what then?"

"That is not going to happen."

"King Talmai hated Saul. Are you going to jeopardize this marriage contract on account of Michal? One word to him that you are in love with Saul's daughter, and this alliance is over." Jashobeam had yet to lower his voice.

Eleazar motioned for him to call down. To me, he said, "You are king. You have to consider the ramifications of every decision that you make."

"And Michal is my queen. She needs to know I have not forgotten her. Now I am done discussing this. Are you two leaving to stop Abner, or am I calling for someone else to take your place on this mission?"

Neither Eleazar nor Jashobeam said anything for a moment. Both watched me in either anger or frustration. But it mattered little. I was determined to retrieve Michal.

I leaned against the entrance of one of the outer chambers that would house my family. The entire compound was sectioned off with three distinct courtyards. These chambers, along with several others, surrounded the smallest of the courtyards, but it was still larger than any courtyard I had ever seen outside of Saul's palace. It would do well and provide a safe, private space for the women to do their duties and raise their children. I paused. *My* children. I thought of Amnon and Daniel and smiled. I would see them soon. It would not be long before they were ready to begin their studies of the Torah. I envisioned them riding horses with me when I was home and playing sword-fighting with each other. Even though I had brothers, I never had the camaraderie that I longed for in them. But Eleazar and others had been my best friends and brothers. Out in the fields with our sheep and slings, we would run and play, using sticks as pretend swords.

"Master David?"

I turned to see Cush, my newly assigned butler, bowed low. "Cush. I am glad to see you have arrived safely. What do you think of this compound?"

Cush stood straight but kept his eyes downcast. "My master is blessed indeed. Your messenger said to report to you upon arrival."

I studied the Egyptian young man. We had found him nearly dead after the Amalekites had ransacked our belongings in Ziklag and kidnapped our families. Cush aided us in finding the

Amalekites, and he followed us back to Judah upon hearing the news of Saul's death. We decided I needed a butler, and this young man offered himself to me. Still, I rested my hand on his shoulder. "Cush, you are not a slave. Do you understand? I know the Amalekites treated you harshly, but I am not an Amalekite. Your service to me is appreciated, and I want you comfortable."

"Your kindness has blessed me. My devotion is yours. It is a privilege to serve you as King of Israel."

"King of Judah. Israel is under Ishbosheth for the time being. But thank you."

"There is favor upon you, my king. It will not be long until all of Israel is under your reign."

The sincerest of this Egyptian's words encouraged me more than I cared to admit. "The reason I called for you is that I am expecting my family to arrive soon. The rooms surrounding this courtyard are for them. Largest goes to the mother of my firstborn, and then in order of marriage."

"Sir, forgive me for seeking clarification, but you want the queen to live among the concubines?"

"No," I said sharply. "The queen's chambers face the east on the other side of the compound."

"My apologies. I assumed she was the mother of the firstborn."

"You assumed incorrectly."

Cush bowed low. "Consider this done."

"Most of their belongings have already arrived and are labeled at the nearest stables."

"And the queen's belongings? I assume they are separated elsewhere?"

"They have not arrived." I swallowed hard. "It will take longer to retrieve Michal than I originally intended. You will be among the first to know when the queen and her supplies are en route."

"Yes, my king."

"Before the queen arrives, there will be a marriage."

"What shall you have me do?"

"A princess is coming and should be here before the next full moon. She is to be married to me as an offering of peace. We need a wedding tent erected on the outskirts of the property, closest to the mountains. Arrange that, and make sure it is stocked for the fourteen days of consummation. Of course, there is a wedding feast to plan. We have other servants who traveled with us and are here. You are to assign tasks and direct them as needed. You report directly to me."

"Has the princess sent her belongings ahead of her?"

"Yes, or so I have been told. When they arrive, allow her entourage to direct with where items go within her assigned rooms."

"As you command, so it will be done."

I left Cush, desiring to be alone. I had already walked the compound's grounds and through all the rooms, so I took the stairs to the roof. The compound's design provided strong fortified walls just shy of a man's chest, spanning the entirety of the roof. The design allowed soldiers to see the entire expanse of the grounds in any direction. I leaned against the wall now, taking in deep breaths of the warm afternoon air.

What was bothering me? There was the dilemma about the war games, and the situation surrounding Michal's retrieval, but it was more than that. "It still remains out of reach," I said out loud. I closed my eyes and thought of the events that transpired leading to me standing here in this expansive compound. "But it still is not what was promised."

I opened my eyes to the sound of a wagon approaching. Tall banners occupied each corner, the same color and emblem as the last time he visited. "Samuel?"

Leaving the rooftop, I scrambled down the stairs, questions stumbling about in my mind. The most important one was with Samuel dead, who is coming with his banners raised? Someone from the House of Samuel was the obvious answer. My heart beat faster at the thought. Maybe they come with a message for me.

I ran down the halls and barreled out of the entryway doors. As I caught my breath, a short man with a long, dark beard stepped out of the wagon. His dark beard contrasted his white cloak and tunic. The apparel of a prophet. Dropping to my knees, I bowed three times as he approached. "Anyone from the House of Samuel is welcome here."

"It is good to see you, King David."

I sat back on my feet and appraised the man as he dropped the hood of his cloak. "We have not met, yet you know who I am."

"Of course, I know who you are. David, son of Jesse, of Bethlehem. Anointed by God through his servant Samuel as the next king of Israel. You are also the giant slayer and the defier of great odds." He paused, then asked, "Do you know who I am?"

"You are of the House of Samuel, and you are most welcome here."

The man smiled and his brown eyes twinkled in apparent delight. "Yes, my name is Nathan. I am of the House of Samuel, and God has sent me to you."

I bowed again three times, touching his feet. "You must stay here. Not only for a visit but to stay and speak words of life to me."

When I sat back again and met his gaze, his smile had grown even more. "Oh, I shall, David. I shall."

5

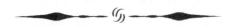

Michal

Paltiel's Home, Gallim

1012 B.C.

Ashvi frowned and brought his hands together. "Please? I can ride your horse alone."

I bit into a grape to hide my smile. Ashvi looked so cute with his pleading expression. Merab's eldest son was still a young boy, but he was smart and handled Eglah well. "There are a lot of things that can spook a horse, and I do not know if you would be able to handle a large beast should that happen."

"I will stay near the stable. Papi would let me."

I tousled his dark, curly hair in need of a trim. "Oh, would he now? Yet, he is not here for us to ask. He is still in town."

"I saw him outside," Ashvi said. "I am going to ask him. He will say yes."

Ashvi began to run.

"Wait!" I called, knowing he would not obey. Paltiel had a kind heart for children and spoiled them too easily.

I followed Ashvi to the entryway and saw Paltiel standing with a small piece of parchment in hand. He did not appear pleased.

"Papi!" Ashvi called. "May I ride the horse?"

Paltiel looked up, startled. He quickly shoved the parchment into a pocket of his tunic. "I am not able to ride this morning."

"I go alone," Ashvi explained. "I am good at horse riding."

"I told him he is still too young to ride alone. He can wait for me to finish with my obligations," I said to Paltiel.

"Listen to your mother," Paltiel said to Ashvi. "You can go riding this afternoon."

Paltiel's words affected me, as they did anytime he referred to me as their mother. Ashvi frowned and crossed his arms. As he stomped his feet out of the room, I said, "At least he is now upset at you and not me."

He smiled but seemed distracted. "I have to check the eastern vineyard. I will return by this evening."

"Is everything all right?"

"Just a lot to do now that many of the vines are ripe."

"May I inquire about the letter you held in your hands? It has seemed to upset you."

"It is nothing," he said quickly. "Now if you excuse me, I have plenty of work to do."

I watched him leave, curious as to what caused his agitation. Eventually, I went searching for Dinah, finding her with Merab's toddler twins. "Do you have any idea what Paltiel could be upset about?" I picked up the youngest and kissed his neck. Adriel, their father, had yet to name them.

"No. His vineyards are ripe and ready to harvest, and you are back from the palace. That easily lightened his mood."

"That has faded. He had a message in his hand just now, and he was so distracted by it, that he nearly snapped at Ashvi. He shoved it in a pocket and left me standing there."

"He is not usually short with any of the children."

"I know. Do you think it was a message about me?"

"Why would it be?"

I gave Dinah an exasperated look. "Because at some point David is coming for me. I am the daughter of Saul. Even if he no longer loves me, he needs me to secure the kingdom."

"Will you go?"

"Do I have a choice?"

"If you did have a choice, would you go?"

I thought for a moment, then said softly, "Yes, if for no other reason than to look upon him."

"I venture Paltiel understands this. It is an inevitability."

"So, the message must have been about me. He barely looked upon me, as if it pained him."

Ashvi came stomping into the room, his arms still crossed. "No one will let me go riding."

"Come," I said, making a quick decision. "My obligations can wait. Let's go riding together."

His countenance changed immediately, and he began running around the room in excitement.

"Is this for him, or to satisfy your curiosity?" Dinah asked. "If I know you, you will be riding through the vineyard, spying on the master of the house."

"I have no idea what you are talking about." I feigned innocence, grabbing Ashvi's hand and leaving the room.

———

Ashvi held the reins but was not moving Eglah fast enough.

"Here, let me hold the reins for a little while." I grabbed the leather and immediately urged Eglah forward. Ashvi laughed and shouted in glee as we blazed through the vineyard paths.

But as the day's sun became hotter, we were beginning to run out of places Paltiel could be. I could not locate him. We stopped at the creek that often watered the vineyard, so Eglah could rest. Ashvi played in the grass while I tried to figure out where Paltiel had disappeared to.

"Look," Ashvi said and pointed past us to where the pasture began. "It's Papi's soldiers."

My gaze followed to where he pointed. I saw two Hebrew

soldiers sitting on the king's horses atop the hill. "Those are not Papi's soldiers. Those are your grandfather's men."

I continued watching them. This was the first time I had observed them so close since I first moved here over eight years prior. "They know he is coming," I said to myself. My heart betrayed me and leaped in excitement. Could it be? Could David really be coming for me?

"No, they are Papi's. He told me that. I met them."

"How? When?"

Ashvi shrugged. "When I went riding with Papi. He came out past the vineyards and met with soldiers. He gave them coins. I saw it."

It should not surprise me that Paltiel would do something like this, but it irritated me. Did he think he could keep David from me? Then again, it had worked. I was confused. Had David not come for me? Or had he been blocked from coming for me? "Come now. We need to head back."

Moments later, we were on Eglah, moving through the vineyards back to the stables. My mind replayed multiple scenarios as to why David never came for me. I knew my father had his men throughout this entire region while he was alive. I doubt Ishbosheth had stopped that order, but where did Paltiel fit into this madness? Had he paid for additional protection?

Making a quick decision, I rode past the stables and stopped just outside the back veranda. "Ashvi, run inside. I need to check on something."

"Let me go with you," he whined, but I had already helped him off the horse.

"Not this time. Now go inside. Tell Dinah to wash you before evening meal." I clicked my tongue and snapped the reins. Eglah took off. Thankfully, she was a high-spirited girl and enjoyed our fast-paced rides as much as I did. This time, we sprinted along the outskirts of Paltiel's land. There were easy paths that led up the gently rolling hills to the forests. From the tops of some of those hills, I could see his entire valley.

Once far enough away, I slowed Eglah and let her catch her breath. I studied Paltiel's vast lands, searching for any more men. It did not take long to find pairs situated at higher elevations encircling his property. I glanced around me, suddenly aware that a pair or two would be in this location or close to it. But I could not see anyone within several stones throw of me.

A high-pitched whistle startled me. I held my breath and turned slightly in the direction I heard it. The trees.

I heard it again. And again. It sounded human. I stared right into the trees and wondered…and hoped…Before I could tell myself no, I clicked my tongue and ordered Eglah toward the trees. Maybe it was because Paltiel was hiding something from me, or maybe it was because I needed some answers, but whatever the reason, I needed to find out who was making that sound.

Once cloaked in the trees, I told Eglah to stop, and I listened again.

There it was. The whistle.

I moved toward it once more, exhilarated and nervous at the same time. I turned in my saddle, trying to uncover the mystery. The sound of movement came from in front of me. I suddenly froze, sensing fear for the first time since following the whistle. Could it be one of the bandit groups we were warned about? Or one of the king's men who wanted to lure a woman to a place where they would be alone?

The person came closer, and soon the tree branches and dense brush revealed one of my father's horses emerging. But the man atop it was not wearing Hebrew soldier's garb. He was large in height and build, his well-defined form pulling against his tunic. His tunic had no sleeves revealing arms laden with taut muscles. His cloak hung low over most of his face, but his bronzed skin reminded me of someone from my past. Someone close to my sister.

"Benaiah?" I whispered.

He slowly pulled the cloak's hood off his head. Benaiah gave me a small smile. "Tis I."

Eglah brought me to him, and after pausing a brief moment, I leaned over and hugged him. If he had any hesitation, he did not let on, for he quickly hugged me in return. When we released, I said, "It is good to see you."

"You too." He scrutinized me, then asked, "Have you been unwell?"

"Alas, one's appetite disappears when one must bury her sister, her father, and her brothers within several moons of each other. Other than that, I am well."

Benaiah's face turned grim. "I still grieve over her. I will never feel toward another woman the way I felt toward Merab. I know it was not meant to be, but you cannot change who your heart loves." He stopped and gave me a guarded expression, "As you well know."

"Yes, I am well aware of what it is like to love someone without reciprocation."

"He loves you, Michal. Dearly. That is why I am here."

"Can he not retrieve me himself?" I asked, trying to hide my offense, but failing miserably. "And why can you not come to my house and retrieve me properly?"

"Because we cannot retrieve you presently. If I were to be caught, it would not be good. I ran from the army to join David. Abner says I am still a wanted man."

"Then why would he send you?"

"I volunteered. No one can capture me unless I want them to capture me." Benaiah gave me a confident smirk. He pointed behind him. "Just ask those guys."

"Who?"

"The soldiers assigned to this post. There are pairs surrounding the land. Not to mention the blockades at every entry point leading to Gallim."

My mouth dropped. "Why?"

"Because your surviving brother and Abner know that David wants you. They want him to breach Israel's line. That is why I volunteered. To give you a message. Paltiel did not seem too pleased when his servant gave it to him. I saw it in his eyes. He was not going to give it to you. So, I have been hiding, waiting for you to ride this horse of yours."

"How did you know I would take this path?"

"Because this is the path you normally take when you want to be alone."

"How do you know that?"

"Your father's men were always on the lookout for David, but we are very good at infiltrating wherever we need to be." Benaiah smiled sadly at me. "David has watched you through our eyes this entire time."

My stomach fluttered just knowing David sent men to be his eyes and ears, but it was not the same as doing it himself. "What is the plan?"

"The plan was for you to get that message. It was a note from David that you are in his thoughts, and he wants to come for you as soon as Ishbosheth allows it. He wants to keep the peace. No civil war between tribes."

"Is this not an Israeli horse?" I noticed my father's crest on the horse's armor.

"Yes, I took it from one of the soldiers I knocked out. They are not dead. They are back the way I came. I need to retrieve the other horse and put on one of their uniforms. It will help me travel this region easier." Benaiah paused. "I need to return to David. I have been camped out for days waiting to lay eyes on you. David will want to know that you are well."

"Where are you located? Judah, I presume?"

"Hebron. Judah's elders have already anointed David king. Abner is interfering with the other tribes, making it complicated."

"Are you still living in tents?"

"A large property has been bestowed upon David and his

kingdom. It is a nice compound. His men are stationed around it. Some have more permanent dwellings; some stay at the soldiers' barracks since they travel so often."

"I look forward to seeing it. However, I do not look forward to having to face this very different David."

"In some ways, he is still much the same, but as king and leader of his mighty men, he is no longer a boy. He makes decisions for the good of the people."

"Such as marrying other women and fathering their children?"

"Yes," Benaiah said simply. "A king must have multiple children, and he must provide resources for his men and their families. Without the marriages, we would have starved."

"My head knows that, but my heart struggles to accept it."

"Michal, he endures marriage proposals often. Many men offer their daughters and bountiful resources. It is the way of the land. Even as we speak, a princess and her entourage are en route. She brings shields and spears of gold, chariots, horses and sheep, dozens of servants, and furnishings for the new compound."

"He is marrying again?" I felt faint at the thought. "And a princess? Like me."

Benaiah pressed his lips together as if realizing what he said and wanting to take it back. "I should not have said anything. Forgive me."

"He is marrying again?" I repeated. "Is she beautiful?"

"Michal…"

"Answer me."

"She is Maacah, the daughter of Talmai, King of Geshur."

I had heard of the princess, and she was of famed beauty. "My father and King Talmai were never on good terms."

"Yes, we hope this will bring peace between kingdoms. David desires to strengthen our kingdom through allies."

I barely listened to what he said. I was stuck on him marrying again. Suddenly, my hurt turned to anger. He had moved on from me. It was time I do the same. "Seeing he has a new wife, he does not need me. Tell him to keep me here." I turned the horse and directed it to leave.

"Your stubbornness will not change the fact that he is coming for you, Michal. Take this time to come to terms with the fact that your husband is king. Even though he is the same in many aspects, he is the ruler of Judah and soon the ruler of Israel."

I did not answer. I left Benaiah without so much as a backward glance. I refused for him to see how much the news of David and the new princess just shattered my heart all over again.

6

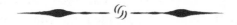

David

Judah

1011 B.C.

"**K**ing David?"
My shoulder shook, rousing me from a deep sleep. I blinked into the sunlight, then brought the blanket over my head. "Not yet."

"Sir, the princess and the remaining entourage have arrived."

I sat up fast, demanding my tunic. Cush handed it to me, along with a pitcher of water. I guzzled the cool liquid, then handed it back to him. "Order my bath and a new set of clothes."

"Already done, sir. Everything is awaiting you in your chambers."

I stood up and requested he fold the bedding but keep it on the roof. "Bring a chest here for my bedding and create a cover to protect it from the elements."

"As you wish." Cush followed me down the stairs and through the hall.

Servants hustled from one point to the next, but everyone moved out of my way as I approached. Ever since the princess's entourage arrived two days ago, the halls had been busy. To say she brought enough furniture and manpower for the entire compound would be an understatement. I did not mind the bustle of people with their arms full. It had been quiet and vacant in this compound for too many moons.

"Do you prefer sleeping on the roof?" Cush's question brought me back to the present.

"Sometimes I enjoy sleeping under the stars. It reminds me of when I was a boy." We entered my chambers. Steam moved off the tub of water, and I could smell the pleasant fragrances infused in it. Two young maidservants from a local Judah elder also arrived as tokens of loyalty not quite a fortnight ago, and they now lay out clean linen and a brush of horsetail. "Everyone out. Leave me to my bath. I will call when I am ready to dress."

"I am right outside the door," Cush said, bowing low. He showed the two girls out and closed the door behind him.

Once alone, I stripped down and stepped into the water. I sank into it and allowed myself a moment to enjoy the warm water on my aching muscles. I was sure there would come a point when sleeping on the rooftop could no longer be an option if for no other reason than my back would not allow it, but not yet. For now, my muscles were soothed from the hot bath. I took a clay pitcher beside me and began pouring the hot water over my head. Knowing the princess waited to greet me, I did not take long to soak. I washed quickly and dried myself off before calling Cush and the maidservants back to the chamber. Throwing on an undertunic for modesty, I allowed them to dress and groom me. It felt odd. I was perfectly capable of doing this myself, but my men advised me to start thinking and acting like a king.

"Is the throne room finished?" I asked, as one of the girls brushed my hair and pulled it back with a tie.

"Yes, my king," Cush said as he arranged a heavily jeweled cloak around my shoulders. "We have arranged your collection of helmets and shields around the room, per your directions, and the high priest, Abiathar, gifted your throne and your counsels' chairs just yesterday. They are made of the finest cedar, outlined in gold, and handcrafted with your emblem on each. They are very fine indeed."

"I would like to thank Abiathar and his fellow priests for these gifts. Please arrange that meeting."

Someone knocked at the door. Cush opened it and allowed Eleazar in. He raised his eyebrow in my direction.

"Too much?" I asked. "This cloak is heavy."

"Not at all. You look like a king."

"I still feel like David, the poor shepherd from Bethlehem."

"Good. A humble king is a wise king."

"Have you seen all the furnishings that were delivered with Maacah's entourage?"

"That is not the half of it. King Talmai delivered on his end. We will need to build more structures to house the chariots and weaponry." Eleazar gave me a satisfied smile.

"This pleases you," I said. "I am glad. We have overcome much."

"That we have. It seems far away from our beginnings."

"Dodai should visit," I said, referring to Eleazar's father. "It has been too long since I have hugged his neck."

"Travel is hard on him, and he still looks after your father's sheep. I do see him when I can. He is proud of you."

Someone else knocked at my door. Cush opened it and ushered in Jashobeam.

Eleazar and I both glanced at each other in surprise. "Jashobeam, my friend. You look clean."

"Why do you act so surprised? I bathe." Jashobeam acted insulted, but the offense did not last long. "It is not every day that I get to witness a marriage contract between royalty."

One of the girls held a looking glass before me. My brow furrowed at my reflection. The man staring back at me looked every bit a king. Still, I waved the looking glass away. "I am done."

I exited my chambers and my men followed me. We set up my throne room at the front of the compound, and there I found the rest of my most trusted men waiting for me.

Uriah stepped forward with his arms extended. "There he is. My king." He then bowed, touching my feet, before standing and kissing both sides of my face.

"You are back from your new marriage. You look happy and well," I said, patting his back.

"Ah, yes, my new bride is young and kind. And quiet," he added with a wink. "I hope you can meet her soon."

"I look forward to it." I turned to the rest of my men who greeted me warmly. I had said the words repeatedly, but I felt to say them again. "We have been through too much for you to bow. I appreciate your reverence, but without you, I would not be here."

"Princess Maacah awaits in there." Uriah wiggled his eyebrows at me. "The rumors of her beauty do not do her justice."

We all turned toward the sound of footsteps. Benaiah walked down the corridor to where we stood. Everything else faded away, and my thoughts turned to Michal. "How is she? Did you deliver the message? How did she respond?"

I heard Jashobeam sigh in frustration. To Benaiah, he said, "This conversation needs to wait."

Benaiah nodded in agreement. "My king, may I have permission to clean up from travels before our conversation?"

"How is she?" I repeated.

Benaiah glanced at Jashobeam, then said, "She is well."

Eleazar stepped between me and Benaiah. "David, please, let us complete this transaction and meet the princess. You can have this conversation afterward."

My heart yearned for Michal and to learn of Benaiah's message to her, but my men were right. It needed to wait. "Go, wash and rest. I will call for you later this evening."

After Benaiah left us, Cush entered the throne room and introduced me. I entered with my mighty men behind me. As we

entered and took our places, the princess and a crowd of her
entourage bowed low before me. For just a moment, I felt
butterflies in my stomach. But I quickly shook off any nerves and
stood confidently before them. "Princess Maacah, it is an honor to
finally meet you. You are most welcome here." When none of them
moved from their low bow, I remembered that I needed to release
them. "Please, you may all look upon me."

Princess Maacah and her host stood with heads still low. "The
honor is mine, my king."

Her voice was gentle, but for a moment, I did not respond. The
rumors were true, for she had dark, wavy hair cascading down her
back and creamy skin with a slight blush to her cheeks. For a
moment, I could only look upon her in admiration. Eventually, I
asked, "Were your travels pleasant?"

"Pleasant enough," she said with a smile. "But we are glad to
have arrived."

I enjoyed listening to the lyrical quality of her voice. So much
so, that I desired to ask her more questions if for no other reason
than to listen to the response. "And your father? I pray King Talmai
is well and prosperous."

"My father is well and sends his blessings to you and your entire
kingdom. We bring gifts and our sworn alliance to your kingdom."
She motioned for her servants to step forward.

Two eunuchs approached setting one large bag each of gold
coins and jewels at my feet. Another handed me a sealed
parchment. I opened it and saw King Talmai's mark on the
marriage contract.

"Your gifts are gladly received. Our marriage contract begins
tomorrow at sunset, but please, spend some time relaxing and
making yourself at home."

Maacah's smile only grew, as if she found humor in my
statement. "I have much to do in preparation for tomorrow, but I
thank you for your kindness."

"Would you have a few moments to walk the grounds with me?"

I was not ready to end our time together, and I found myself hoping she felt the same.

Her eyes lit up as she smiled widely. "I would be honored to join you."

I closed the space between us and extended my arm. She placed her hand inside my arm, and boldly looked directly at me. My breath caught. Together, we left the throne room. As we left, Benaiah walked past us, freshly washed and changed. He stopped to bow.

"Benaiah, allow me to introduce you to Maacah, daughter of King Talmai. She is to be my wife. Maacah, this is my dear friend and one of my trusted commanders, Benaiah of Kabzeel."

"I am humbled to make your acquaintance," Benaiah said without looking up.

Maacah did not reply.

"Yes, well, we are on our way to tour the grounds," I offered after an awkward pause. Benaiah stayed in position, and I realized he waited for me to release him.

"Forgive me, my friend, you are released."

Benaiah stood straight, gave me a wink, nodded at the princess, and left us.

"Pardon my forwardness, but are your men always that familiar with you?"

"My men are my friends. Many gave up prosperous lives to follow who they felt was the anointed king. I am forever in their debt."

The princess acted surprised. "My father always said powerful men must demand boundaries, lest they be overtaken."

"All power comes from Yahweh Himself, and I can treat my men kindly while still keeping boundaries. Come, let us start with the flower gardens."

The conversation stayed lively at first, for the princess was quick-witted and sharp-tongued. It did not escape my notice, however, that she would not speak to or look upon anyone else unless giving an order. I could easily read her discomfort at my camaraderie with my men. From Joab to Jashobeam, she lifted her head and slightly turned it when they approached us with news. It made me think of Michal. She too was a princess and was used to getting her way, but there was a kindness and approachability to Michal that this Princess Maacah did not possess.

I sighed, suddenly weary of the conversation. Even with the lovely princess beside me, my thoughts wandered off to Michal. Still, I escorted her to her chambers where several servants furiously worked at setting up her furnishings. "I hope these rooms will suit your needs."

For a brief moment, her smile waivered, but it was so quick that I almost didn't see it. "I have more furnishings than rooms, but I will make it work."

Before another word was spoken, I left her in the chamber and moved quickly through the halls, searching for Benaiah. I found Cush and requested a meeting with my returned commander, then went to my own chambers where I could take off the weighty cloak and put on something more comfortable.

"Out," I ordered to the two maidservants, cleaning the room. "Please," I added, trying to undo the cloak. "I need some privacy."

They bowed and left. I tossed the cloak and started in on the heavy sleeves. I couldn't get it off fast enough. Eventually, I was free of most of the garb. I took in a big gulp of air and remained mostly naked for another moment.

The knock at the door had me reaching for the closest tunic I could find. It was silky and smooth, and my mind took me back to the days of the rough shepherd's clothing. "Those days are gone," I said to myself, slipping into the tunic. To the person on the other side of the door, I called out, "Enter."

Benaiah stepped inside. "King David." He bowed and then stood erect. We decided that my closest men did not need to bow to me when not in public. I found it ridiculous, but several of them did so even when alone with me.

"What have you learned? Did Michal receive my letter?"

"No."

"So, it is as we thought. Has she received my communication?"

"None."

"That vile, little man. I will rip him apart limb from limb." I seethed, thinking of the years he must have been intercepting my letters to Michal. "Did he dare touch her? Have they consummated a union?"

"I do not believe so, but I am not sure. She left before we could continue a conversation."

"You laid eyes upon her?"

"Yes. I tarried in the area, after hearing that she had left the palace and had arrived back in Gallim. She enjoys her horse, taking excursions out past the vineyards. In a few days, we made contact."

"I wish I could lay eyes upon her. It is as if we will never see each again."

"You can and will. Eleazar likes to say, *Give it time.* I agree with him. We are almost there. I can feel it."

"What is it you feel? Because I often feel like I am climbing a mountain, and no matter how far I climb, the summit is just out of reach."

"Look around you," Benaiah said. "Look at everything you have already been given. You and your men no longer have to go to sleep with empty bellies. We no longer have to kill as mercenaries for our enemy."

"You are right. But I made a promise years ago, and every day that I do not deliver on that promise, I feel that it only deepens the divide between me and my wife. I have already been in Judah for nearly a year, and nothing has changed. Other than the addition of another wife. I doubt that will work in my favor."

Benaiah paused before speaking as if weighing his words. "You have other wives now. You are on the cusp of another marriage contract. Your marriage with Michal does not exist at the moment."

"That is why I need her here. When she is here, nothing else will matter."

"Until then?"

I thought of how I would explain the marriages to Michal. Surely, she would understand. The marriages were needed for a multitude of reasons. But Michal would always be my first love. My queen. "God will make a way. I have to believe it. As soon as I can find a way to bring her to me that will not upset the precarious balance between Judah and Israel, then I will make my move."

"I hope and pray that you are both reunited soon, and that the reunion is everything you hope it to be."

I heard Benaiah's measured tone. "There is something more you desire to say." When Benaiah made no move to speak, I continued, "Benaiah, please speak openly. We are brothers."

"She did not take the news of your marriage contract well."

"How does she know?"

"She heard rumors of a marriage to an ally's daughter. When she pressed, I tried to answer diplomatically. I told her that you desired her alone, but she became visibly upset and left soon after."

"What does she expect me to do? I am *king*. If another king presents his daughter to me as a gift, it would cause an all-out war to refuse the girl."

"I am not a woman, nor am I an expert on women, but it seems as if she views it as a betrayal. Women do not see things the same way as men."

"I will make her see reason," I said, not knowing how I would accomplish that. "But it will not happen until we are face-to-face."

"Until then?" Benaiah asked again.

I thought of the young princess and of the wedding feast and celebration that would begin at sun-up. "Until then, I do what I have been doing. I continue as king."

7

David

Judah

1011 B.C.

Three days into our marriage union, I was ready to be anywhere but with Maacah. Her beauty was resplendent, but her treatment of servants mortified me. Being with her day and night revealed too much arrogance and cruelty for my taste. I had only one other experience with a princess, and Michal outshone Maacah on every front.

When Cush rushed in, bowing low and apologizing profusely for interrupting, I nearly hugged him. "My king, there is an urgent matter. Joab has returned and has pressed me to request a meeting."

"Is all well?"

Cush would not look upon me, only saying, "My king, Joab is not himself. Please, come. He is at your spot on the roof."

Maacah approached behind me. Cush kept his gaze on the ground. "We have barely been married. Is it not Hebrew custom for a fourteen-day marriage celebration? Are we not to be celebrating privately?"

"It is our tradition, yes, but a king's duties are never paused for long. Cush, go and tell Joab I will be there momentarily."

After Cush left, I found a day tunic and belt, hustling to leave the confined chamber.

"Why are you leaving?" she whined. "And why are you dressing yourself?" She snapped her fingers to one of her maidservants and pointed at me. "Dress him."

"No," I said firmly. To the maidservant, I tried to be gentler. "I dress myself. Thank you."

Maacah crinkled her nose and frowned. "The ways of Hebrews baffle me. You are king, yet you behave like a peasant. Lower than that even. You behave like a—"

"Like a shepherd?" I asked. She already knew the answer, so I gave no further reply. Instead, I left her standing in the chamber staring after me.

I ran from the private wedding chamber, assembled on the opposite end of the Hebron fortress, to the rooftop where Joab waited for me.

Only it was not just Joab, but Abishai too, and my innermost circle of men. All of their tunics were rent, and ash had been smeared on their faces. My heart sank. "Who?"

Joab's normally composed face crumpled, "Asahel."

"No." I looked to Abishai, then to Eleazar and the others. "No. Not my nephew."

Abishai openly wept. Joab failed at blinking back his own tears. Their brother—my nephew—dead? "By Abner's hand," Joab said the words, heavy with bitterness and anger. He turned to Abishai, "I swear I will avenge our brother's death." The two hugged, clinging to each other in their grief.

The grief bubbled up from within me too, and I too ripped my tunic and let them apply ash upon my face. I went to my two nephews and threw my arms around both of their necks. Eventually, we would have to discuss what happened. Eventually, decisions would have to be made. But not in this moment.

We numbered in the hundreds. It would have been more, but I

ordered my men not to overwhelm the town of Bethlehem. Still, they stationed themselves in the valleys throughout the area, mourning the loss of not just Asahel, but of the 19 others lost to war games against Israel.

The women lamented, sobbing loudly, then Abiathar led in a song of the hurting heart. I kept my eyes on the family sepulcher where Asahel had been laid to rest. Even though I grieved with my nephews and sister, my thoughts roamed elsewhere. Asahel's death complicated things. Joab made it clear that he was out for Abner's blood. And I knew my nephew. Abner was as good as dead. But that would not help our cause. If my men killed Abner, who was loved and highly favored since Saul's death, it would only prolong the war between Judah and Israel. It irked me that Asahel's death, along with the others who died, was preventable. Why the war games? Why would Joab approve such an unwise pastime? But another thought slipped in: *Where were you?* I could not entirely place the blame at Joab's feet.

Eleazar and Jashobeam had encouraged me to go and handle the situation, but I refused. I was too busy waiting to hear from Benaiah. If I had gone and put an end to the war game myself, my nephew and the other men would still be alive.

The prophet, Nathan, stood by himself away from the crowd. He had kept to himself since my celebratory feast announcing his arrival many moons ago. I slipped through the crowd and approached him. Surely, he would have a word for me.

I greeted him, and he nodded in my direction, only to turn and continue singing the song of lament. I questioned myself on how to best bring up the subject. With Samuel, I was completely open and honest, mostly because Samuel always seemed to know the truth anyway. But with Nathan, I was unsure if I should approach him in the same manner.

Before I could find the words, he stopped singing and said, "You are here because you are facing a situation that becomes more entangled with each passing day."

"Yes," was all I could say.

"Joab seeks vengeance, which will halt any peace you seek between kingdoms."

"Yes."

"Do you need me to illuminate Yahweh's design?" When I did not immediately respond, he clicked his tongue in mild annoyance. "My king, what would the Lord have you do? Seek vengeance or seek peace?"

"I have fought so many battles that I question the correct answer. No matter how much I have longed for peace, battles rage on, and I must fight or die."

"Yet, that is not the case here. When Yahweh tells you to fight, you fight because it is the Lord who fights your battles. With Him, you are ensured victory. But this is not the Lord's battle to fight, David. This is the result of stubborn arrogancy in the hearts of Hebrew soldiers on either side. So, what should the king of Judah do? Seek vengeance or seek peace?"

I nodded in understanding, then turned my attention back to the funeral. Together, with Nathan, and those surrounding us, we lifted our voices in song, grieving the unnecessary loss of Hebrew lives. I vowed silently to seek peace with Israel above all else. No more unnecessary bloodshed between the Hebrew brethren. But it would be a daunting challenge to persuade Joab to such a resolution.

Another moon cycle passed, and the borders between Israel and Judah became more and more hostile. Family of the fallen soldiers decried the war games, laying blame at my men's feet. I ordered soldiers not to slay another Hebrew but to seek peace by any means necessary.

Joab entered my dressing chamber. "You needed me?"

I had given Joab space to sufficiently grieve, but with the Philistines continued threats and weakened land contracts from the

Jebusites, I needed Joab to do what he did best. Negotiate and fight for our growing kingdom. "We need a set of troops to spy on the Jebusite territory and the land surrounding it. King Talmai sent word that it has potential for us."

"Potential for what exactly?"

"Us. This Hebron compound is a blessed gift, but the time is coming when Israel and Judah will unite. We barely have room as it is with the Judean soldiers. Can you imagine all twelve tribes with this as our fortified location?"

Joab gave a humorless laugh. "I doubt there will be any union of kingdoms any time soon, especially with that dog as commander."

"That may be so, but I have been advised to search it out anyway. So, assemble a small group and see what is happening there."

"With all due respect, uncle, my services are better served at the borders."

"Are they? Or is that where you have positioned yourself for a better chance of seeing Abner?"

"Do you blame me?"

"Why tempt yourself? I told all soldiers to stand down. We will not have a repeat performance of the ill-advised war games that cost nearly four hundred Hebrew men."

"We lost twenty, and it was Abner's idea! He and his men mocked us. Should we have ignored it?"

"Yes, you should have, and you should have ordered Asahel to stand down and not continue pursuing Abner and his men."

"I did. I ordered all of our men to retreat, but you know Asahel. He had him right there. He probably had the glory of killing Saul's commander in his sights."

"And now he is dead."

"Because Abner came back and killed him!"

"What choice did he have? That is what happens in a war game. Kill or be killed. Which is why I do not condone nor encourage it.

We have enough enemies trying to kill us. Why make a game of it?"

Joab pressed his lips together, took a deep breath, stretched his neck, then said, "I will assemble a special force to spy on Jerusalem and the land surrounding it. That is where the Jebusites now occupy."

I watched my nephew and could see he was done with the previous conversation. I could push it but resisted. Keeping Joab busy would hopefully calm the tempest within him. "Make sure Abishai is a part of the group. I do not want him anywhere near Israel's borders."

Joab nodded stiffly, bowed quickly, then left the room. I felt the prick of foreboding. I sensed that I only delayed the inevitable.

8

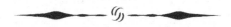

Michal

Gallim

1011 B.C.

My head throbbed. Too much wine last night, and the night before last, and the night before that one. I had been out of sorts since the surprise visit and conversation with Benaiah. David was getting married again. My David.

But was he mine anymore? He must not think so because I had been back at Paltiel's home for well past several new moon cycles, and David had yet to retrieve me.

It hurt. It hurt my heart, my head, and my digestion. I longed to numb the pain. I longed to forget all about him, but my heart betrayed me, for he was constantly in my thoughts. And that made me angry. Why think of him when he thought little of me? Why give him space in my heart?

"You have barely touched your plate," Dinah complained, bringing me out of my thoughts.

"If I do not eat, then maybe I will die."

"Stop that."

I refused to look at her. "Make sure new vessels are filled and brought to me."

Dinah stood over me. She was silent, but only for a moment. "What about riding? That always excites your senses. You have not taken Eglah out since…"

"Yes, I know. I do not want to go riding. What I want is to be left alone. Stop badgering me with incessant questions and suggestions. It is annoying, and it is unwelcomed."

"I am concerned for you," she said quietly.

"Silence!" I shouted, bringing my hand to my head. The throbbing intensified, making me crankier. Making sure to add bite to my words, I spat out, "I do not *need* your concern. I *need* you to do your job. Bring me filled vessels, and leave me alone." Dinah did not make a move to leave. I grabbed the brass plate, still filled with my breakfast, and threw it at her. It clattered against the floor, spewing food in all directions. "Out! Now!"

Dinah's hurried steps moved past me and out of the room. A part of me—the rational part of me—knew I lashed out at the wrong person. But that was a small part. A much larger part of me was losing my grip on any form of rational thought. I fantasized about running away. Just pack my things and leave. Move to some faraway country and start again. Maybe I could marry another powerful king to make David jealous. I even fantasized about taking my belongings and riding to David's rumored compound in Hebron. What would he do if I showed up at his doorstep? I wanted to believe he would take me inside and lavish me with his love and affection, but I no longer believed he would do that. The dark thought that interrupted my fantasies was to end it all. My entire family was mostly dead, and I was no longer sure that living in this unfair world was the better way. But I was too stubborn for that. There must be a better end to my story. That tiny sliver of hope kept me alive, even if I was drinking myself into a daily stupor.

Sometime in the middle of my despair, I fell asleep. I awoke to my hair and tunic sticking to me from midday warmth. My throat felt parched, but I saw new vessels filled with wine had been brought in. I lifted one and took a deep drink. Still feeling hazy, I listened to my surroundings. Rapid footsteps approached.

Dinah entered and in a clipped tone said, "You have a visitor."

"Tell them to go away."

"It is Rizpah. She says it is urgent."

"I don't care. Send her away."

"She has been kicked out of the palace."

I blinked away the lingering sleep and fully sat up. "What? How?"

Instead of Dinah answering, she asked, "Would you like me to still send her away?"

"No, provide her some refreshment. I will be there momentarily."

"Would you like to wash up before presenting yourself?"

The words stung. I understood Dinah was upset with me, but it was unlike her to hold a grudge for this long. This morning's outburst wasn't the first time I yelled at her, but something seemed different. "Are you saying I stink?" Before she could respond, I stood up and marched over to her. Face-to-face, I said, "Out with it then. Tell it to my face."

Dinah boldly returned my glare, and simply said, "You need a bath."

"Provide me water in the pitchers, then send Raja in to assist me. You can make yourself useful elsewhere."

"As you wish." Dinah turned and left the room.

"Are you not forgetting something?" I called after her.

She stormed in, grabbed my two empty pitchers, and left without casting another glance my way.

"And when you come back, you best have a better attitude!" I harumphed over to the looking glance and halted at my appearance. I barely recognized the woman looking back at me. My tunic was rumpled, and stained, with my sash askew and threads dangling. My face resembled a corpse I once saw lying on the street with ashen skin and dark circles under the eyes. Clumps of my hair were matted with strands sticking to my forehead.

I couldn't move. I stared at the reflection in horror.

Dinah marched in, carrying two full pitchers, and set them beside my wash basin. She turned to leave without a word.

"What have I become?" I asked.

Dinah paused but did not change course. "Raja will be in shortly."

I peeled the musty apparel off my body and stared at my reflection. Tears leaked from my eyes in response to the skeleton that stared back at me. Raja entered. She was a nervous girl who kept her hair in her face to cover a long scar made by her previous master.

"You called for me?"

"Lay out clean clothes. When I am done washing, I will need you to prepare me for company. And take these and burn them." I slid the dirty, rumpled outfit that had laid at me over to her.

She bowed, then picked up the clothing and left the room. I moved to the water pitchers but could barely lift them in my weakened state. Eventually enough spilled out into the basin, and I began to wash.

"Oh, mistress, allow me," Raja said in a heavy Egyptian accent. She rushed to lay an outfit across the chaise, then hurried to me. As she washed me, I couldn't stop the tears. "Am I hurting you?" she asked, as she rubbed my skin with a rag.

But I didn't answer. All I could do was wonder where my life went so wrong.

When I finally finished dressing, Raja informed me that Rizpah waited for me in Paltiel's courtyard. I entered to find her playing hide-and-find with three of my nephews. She smiled and laughed when Ashvi found her, but it did not reach her eyes.

"Rizpah, greetings." I closed the distance between us and kissed both her cheeks. "I apologize I kept you waiting. I was right in the middle of a bath."

"I enjoyed playing with your nephews." She kissed me in return, then scrutinized me. "How do you fair?"

"Let us not talk about me. What brings you here? Dinah shared some of your news, and I am disheartened if it is true."

Rizpah's face contorted into a mixture of grief and anger. "It is true. Ishbosheth heard word of Abner's friendship with me, and there were some heated words—"

"Why would Ishbosheth care about you and Abner's friendship?"

Rizpah pressed her lips together and broke eye contact.

"Rizpah? What is truly going on?"

"Abner and I have become...entangled." She quickly continued, "I never behaved unscrupulously when your father was alive, but now...now he is not here. I am terribly lonely. Abner has been a steadfast companion in these dark times."

"You and Abner?"

"Why is that so surprising? Why are you looking at me like that?"

"He's...He's...married!"

My dismay must have been apparent because, for a moment, Rizpah acted guilty, but it was only a moment. Then she stuck out her chin and defended herself. "I told you, Michal, that as a woman, we must use things to our advantage. Without the king here, Abner was more than a companion. He found housing for us so that we may leave the palace and set out on our own."

"But what of Ishbosheth? I am assuming that since you are cast out, he is not supportive of this relationship."

"I was your father's concubine. I refuse to let that weak man, Ishbosheth, touch me. Alas, he found out about my and Abner's situation, and now I have nowhere to go until I contact Abner. May you please request Paltiel for me to visit? Just until I contact Abner."

I tried to process Rizpah's claims. "I will seek permission. Do you know where Abner is?"

"He and Ishbosheth argued. It was loud, and then he was gone. Abner left. For good."

"He left the House of Saul?"

Rizpah acted near tears. She nodded and took a breath. "Saul's men have told me that he went to David."

My heart dropped at hearing my husband's name. "What of David? It's because of Abner that Ishbosheth is even king!"

"Abner has offered himself to David as an ally. Hebrew soldiers, those loyal to Abner, are joining ranks in Hebron."

"But what of Ishbosheth?" I found myself repeating the question. Even though I did not share a closeness with him, he was still my only surviving sibling that shared the same mother. "What of my mother?"

"They are both at the palace. Ishbosheth is still King of Israel, but I doubt that will last long. As you already know, David is beloved among the Hebrew people. Those loyal to Saul dwindle each day."

And yet, David still does not come for you, the voice in my head reminded me.

Rizpah seemed to know my thoughts. "Hebrew soldiers fortify lines around Israel daily. They have strict orders to capture David or his men."

I thought of the soldiers surrounding Paltiel's vineyards.

"Abner told me one evening that David was on horse heading toward the Gallim valleys. He was alone, traveling well ahead of most of his men. Abner ordered the troops to hold back, but only to warn David that Ishbosheth was taking Saul's place and that Saul's edicts were still in place."

My heart began to beat rapidly. Even Dinah stopped ladling stew in a bowl to make eye contact. I suddenly felt angry again, but not at David. "Why must everyone conspire to keep us apart?" My voice raised. "Even Paltiel hired additional men to guard the grounds. My father had no right to do this, and neither does

Ishbosheth or Abner or Paltiel!"

"We are pawns. You know this. We are at the mercy of men. It is why I do what I do." Rizpah's mouth settled into a deep frown. "My value is in my body. When that goes, I will have no value."

"What is my value? You at least have two sons. I am barren. What man wants a broken woman?" I looked from Rizpah to Dinah, but neither could answer the question.

Rizpah leaned to me and whispered, "Are you barren? You told me you had not consummated relations with Paltiel. Maybe when David comes for you, you can provide him a son."

"He already has sons."

"Not by you."

Could it be that simple? Could I have a child with David? "It is impossible to birth a son when we are not together."

"Is it that, or is it something else?"

"What do you mean?"

"I mean that you have longed for David all these years, and now you are afraid to admit you no longer want him."

"That is not true. I have desired my husband for years, but not like this. Not with other women and other children."

Rizpah reached for my hand and squeezed. "Then what you desire is the past, for those days are not in your future. Think of your father, and how busy and occupied he was. That is a day in the life of a king. A king who has dozens of servants, soldiers, and women at the ready. That is David's life now. Do you see yourself as a part of it?"

"I want to try. I want to believe that he loves me still and that he prefers me. You said so yourself. He has tried to come for me. That must mean something."

"Are you going to keep holding on to that romantic notion, while you starve yourself to death?" When I did not speak, she continued, "Or, could you make this your home? Could you choose Paltiel? Provide *him* a son?"

I frowned at the thought of betraying my heart. Not that my heart mattered in any of this. "As you said, I have no choice."

"Give yourself to Paltiel."

"David would kill him. He would kill me."

"Would he? I do not think he would. It is known throughout the land that he upholds the law. He is faithful to Yahweh. That means that if you choose Paltiel and give him all of yourself, David would uphold the law."

"But the law says I am married to David. He is still alive. That would be adultery."

"You know your father voided the marriage contract between you and David. As a usurper and traitor to Israel, the contract no longer stood."

"My father cannot absolve a contract made before God."

"Yes, he can. He absolved contracts all the time." Rizpah paused as if contemplating her next words. "Why do you hold onto him so? David has moved on. Do not misunderstand. He is coming for you. If for no other reason than you are Saul's daughter, but it is no longer motivated by love."

I stared at her in disbelief. "This coming from the one who encouraged me to not give up hope in the giant slayer. You practically pushed us together."

"Years ago! And you enjoyed what many never do: young, passionate love. Most girls are handed off to a man for property or possessions. They never experience the pleasure that comes from truly loving a man."

"With that pleasure is pain," I muttered.

"I warned you even then that it may not last forever. With David as king, he would naturally increase his kingdom and subjects with numerous wives and concubines. At least as many as the law allows. It is our way of life."

I shook my head and tried to walk away, no longer interested in the conversation.

"Michal, you cannot leave when the conversation becomes uncomfortable."

"Yes, I can. It is my home, and I do not have to hear another word."

"And there it is. *This* is your home. Paltiel's home. He welcomed you, and now even your nephews, to enjoy his land and possessions, and you withhold from him the one thing he desires most. *You.*"

I stopped at the doorway, the truth hitting me between the shoulders like a spear.

"Most men take from women." Rizpah approached me and gently rested her arm across my shoulders. "I wish you could see how blessed your life has been. I am in awe actually that Paltiel has behaved in such an upright manner. Those men are few."

"I realize that I am blessed, and I am genuinely grateful to Paltiel. But…"

"But…what? But…David is going to come and rescue you?" Rizpah turned me to face her. "Michal, even if David comes for you, are you sure you truly know for what you wish?"

9

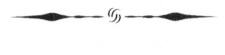

Michal

Gallim

1011 B.C.

altiel acted delighted with Rizpah. He insisted on dinner in the courtyard with all of us, but the entire meal, he lavished attention on my father's former concubine. Then again, Rizpah still had the talent of flirting with every male from servant to lord. Throughout the meal, he would occasionally make eye contact with me, only to turn his attention back to Rizpah.

I sat and ate quietly, my mind racing from our earlier conversation. If Rizpah was correct, David would be here soon. That nugget of truth summoned up an entirely new anxiety. There was so much to do to prepare, and I was not ready for him. For the rest of the day, every morsel of food Dinah set before me, I ate. No more skipping meals. No more drunken stupors. Even Dinah had put my ugly behavior behind her, as we discussed my grooming and exercise schedule.

"The outdoors always brings color to your countenance," she said earlier in the evening.

"I agree. I will awaken and break my fast, then I will exercise Eglah and myself."

My emotions still tossed me to and fro. I reasoned that if what

Rizpah said was true, then David desired me and pursued me. Even my conversation with Benaiah told me as such. Yet, my thoughts would turn to his other wives and who may currently be in his bed when it should be me. The internal battle was strong, so much so that I had ignored much of the dinner conversation and focused on eating the prepared lamb. I did not have much of a plan other than to strengthen myself, but it was a good place to start.

"Michal?"

I stopped the inward battle momentarily and glanced at Paltiel. He still sat amidst cushions at the head of the long table, but most others had already left. "That was delicious," I said, knowing I had been caught daydreaming.

"I am gladdened that you enjoyed the meal. It has been several days since we broke bread together."

"I have been unwell, but I am better now." I left out my recurring drunken state since my conversation with Benaiah.

"Is it the visit from Rizpah that has you in happier spirits? Or is it something else?"

I searched his features, wondering if I heard a bite to his words, but he seemed to be genuinely smiling. "It has. She and I were close, and it is good to reminisce about our younger years."

"If it is not too much trouble to tear you away from her, would you please follow me back to my private chambers?" He must have observed my hesitation because he quickly added, "Just for a quieter atmosphere. The servants need to clear this space."

He approached me and held out his hand to assist. Knowing I had few options, I took his hand and allowed him to gently pull me up until we stood face-to-face. I saw the yearning for more flash in his eyes, but it was brief. He gave another smile and placed my hand on his arm.

We walked down one hallway and turned into another. Eventually, Paltiel said, "I too have been busy."

"Yes, I am sure the vineyards keep you occupied."

"Mmm," he murmured then opened the door to his chambers,

ushering me in. He shut the door behind us. I immediately noticed the candles lit throughout the room and two goblets amidst the cushions near his bedchamber.

"What is this?"

"It is for you. Please sit. Let me pour you some wine."

"Wine has not been good to me these last several days. I should probably not partake."

"Nonsense. Wine is good for our constitution. The key is to avoid drinking in excess." He took my hand and pulled me to where the cushions lay. "I will make sure you limit yourself."

I studied Paltiel and for a moment questioned his intentions. Yet, in the eight years I have lived under his roof, he had only ever acted nobly. Then I thought of new revelations about him. Had he been acting nobly or selfishly? Before I could stop the words, they tumbled out of my mouth. "Have you been paying for security around the vineyards?"

"Yes," he said simply. "I am protecting you."

"Protecting me? Or keeping me from David?" Before he could answer, I continued, "And what of messages that were to be relayed to me? I have not heard from him in over eight years, and yet, I was notified that he has tried to stay in contact. What say you to these things?"

"I do not deny them. Your father's edict was clear. Any communication between you and the fugitive would lead to punishment. I not only have you to think of, but I also have my other wife and our children. I did not dare bring the wrath of the king upon my household. So, yes, I have kept silent of all communication."

My mouth must have hung open at his complete confession. He did not even hide it! Did he truly feel so justified in his actions? Finding words, I sputtered, "That was not your decision to make! These long years he has tried to reach me? I thought he had forgotten about me. I thought he wanted nothing more to do with me, but all this time, he has been *kept from me*. And not just by my father or Ishbosheth or Abner or their men, but by *you*."

"And if you had known? Tell me you would not have tried to send a message back to him."

"Of course, I would!" I yelled. "He is *my husband*! I have been robbed of him for all these years! By you!"

"By me? Have you gone mad? Have you forgotten that I have been a pawn all these years? I have been forced to take care of you, and now your five nephews, with no benefit to me. Half the time you are withdrawn and sullen. Yet, have you ever lacked food, clothing, or horses?"

His words were like a slap across the face. I needed to get away from him, from everything. "There is nothing more to say. I will take my leave."

"No. I do not release you. We are not done having this conversation that *you* started." His nostrils flared in anger. "What would your father have done, Michal, if he found out that you were in communication with the fugitive?"

"His name is David, and my father would have never found out unless you went running to him."

"You would have been imprisoned, and my entire family would have been slaughtered." Paltiel visibly shook. "I would have been killed. My children. My servants. My entire household. Gone. That might not mean anything to you, but it has terrified me. So, you do not get to hold a grudge against me. I will not allow it, and I do not deserve it. He made me promises…"

"What promises?"

"It does not matter because he is no longer alive to uphold our deal, and Ishbosheth has his own struggles than to worry about our marriage."

"Our marriage? We're not married, Paltiel! I cannot be married to two men. You know this!"

"I *know*!" he bellowed. "I am reminded of it every day! From the bloodied sword delivered to me to the dejection and angst that is upon your countenance from sun-up to sun-down."

The words hurt. I told myself he was angry and the words were meant to be ugly. I opened my mouth to respond, but no words came.

"Years ago, I was promised that the fugitive's death had already happened. Then, after the marriage contract, when I learned the truth, it was promised that his death was imminent. Yet, he still lives, and you are still here as a daily reminder of what we are not."

At first, I said nothing. Even in my anger at Paltiel for keeping messages from me, I understood what a dangerous situation this was for him and that he was a pawn too of this political game. I studied Paltiel as he paced before me. I took in the scene he had created with the candles and cushions. I asked, "What was your intention this evening?" I indicated our surroundings.

He stopped pacing, glanced around, and sighed. "Last time we ate a meal in here, we enjoyed ourselves. It is not often that we are alone, and I wanted to change that. So, I hoped that we could drink some wine and enjoy each other's company again. Our conversation took an unexpected turn." He approached me, paused, then gently took my hand. "You may think of me as selfish, and maybe I have been motivated by selfishness, I do not know. There is a part of me that sincerely wants you to be happy, and I understand that your happiness is not with me, but there is another part of me who has worked so hard to care for you, hoping that one day you will see that I have been faithful for all these years. I have not taken from you what you have not been willing to give." He acted as if there was more to say.

And at that moment, I remembered Rizpah's words. *Why do you hold onto him so? David has moved on.* Paltiel desired for me to choose him because he too realized that David as King of Judah would want Saul's daughter by his side. If I chose Paltiel instead, then there might be a small chance David would act honorably and accept my choice. "I do not hold that power," I said just as much to myself as to Paltiel. "I am property. Nothing more. And I am King Saul's daughter and Ishbosheth's sister. David will take me if not out of love, then out of necessity, of that, I am sure."

"Would you want to stay?" Paltiel said the words quietly, but there was hope in them. "It has not been so terrible here, has it?"

"Not at all," I said truthfully. "I have built a home here, and you have allowed me that. I am grateful. Truly. And I understand why you keep me from any form of communication with David, even though I do not agree with that decision."

"There, with him, will you shine? Or will you be another woman among many?"

"Am I not another woman here? You too are married to another."

"I was young and foolish when I married Laia. Of course, I care for her and our children deeply, but with you...*I love you.*" The words filled the air. It was then I noticed that Paltiel had yet to let go of my hand. I now felt his nearness. Years ago, it would have repulsed me. He used trickery and blackmail against my mother to secure a marriage with me, and yet, he had grown into more. So much more. He was a constant and faithful provider, and he practice self-control. Most men would have simply taken what was not theirs, yet he honored our delicate situation and my marriage to another.

"I care for you," I began, not quite able to declare love. "And this land, and home, is mine because you have allowed that."

"It can be yours completely. You can stay here and live in comfort. All of your days." He brought my hand to his lips and brushed his lips against it.

"We do not have a choice. As you said, we are pawns, and the game is not over."

"But it could be. It could be over, Michal."

"How?"

Paltiel wet his lips, and his breathing became heavy. "You could let me have you, in every way a wife gives herself to her husband."

My body surprised me and released butterflies inside, filling me with a warmth and tenderness that I had not expected. For a moment, I wondered what it would be like to have a man hold me again. Could I? Could I give myself to Paltiel? "If I lie with you, David would no longer want me."

"We would be one." He took a step closer to me, closing what little distance there was. "And I would give you anything you wanted. Anything your heart desired."

"If he killed you instead? How could I live with your blood on my hands? I know of the sword he gave you." I stepped back because I needed to breathe…and think. For the first time, I was tempted to betray David. "Please allow me time to think this through."

Paltiel appeared pained. "What is there to think through? I am offering myself and all that I have to you."

"Please." I walked backward to the door. "To consider the offer, I need to think. This cannot be a flippant decision. If I choose you, Paltiel, I will choose you. Heart and soul."

He gave a brief nod, then turned from me. "Go. I fear we do not have a lot of time for thinking, but I refuse to take you without your consent. I want, once and for all, for you to desire me above him." He grabbed a goblet and poured wine into it. He drank it greedily. "Come to me at any time, and I will receive you."

I left Paltiel's private chambers and leaned against the closed door. My heart pounded. Was I truly considering stepping back inside his private chamber? My internal battle felt like a shouting match.

Just make the decision.

David betrayed you long ago, and here is a man that has provided for you and sustained you in some of your darkest days.

But it's Paltiel. He's kept David's messages from me. He's hired additional security with the sole purpose of keeping David away from me.

Do you desire to live amongst David's wives? I shuddered at that thought. *At least here, you already live in comfort. You have your horses. You have Merab's sons. And you have a man who desires you above all else.*

I rested my hand on the door handle, contemplating opening the door and being with a man who loved me. Still, I hesitated. This decision would change everything. David could refuse me. I would be tied to Paltiel.

My brain kept coming back to what worried me more than anything: *What would David do when he found out?* The answer to the question hurt me more than I cared to admit: *What if he did nothing?* And that scared me more than anything.

10

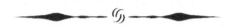

David

Hebron

1011 B.C.

I left Maacah's chambers and walked down the corridor of my family. Maacah requested my presence nearly every evening. All my advisors encouraged me to make her happiness a priority, but truth be told, I found it only exacerbated my loneliness. My wives fulfilled fleshly longings, but there was so much more I desired. My thoughts turned to Michal, but they were filled with more despair than hope.

My thoughts were interrupted by someone's whispers. I followed the voice and saw Abigail already awake, feeding Daniel in the courtyard.

"Good morning," I said, approaching them.

Daniel struggled to thrive, and even in his fourth year, was much smaller than his older half-brother, Amnon. Yet, he was a happy child and always enjoyed my visits. Now, he ran at me and hugged my legs. "Papa!"

"There is my Daniel-boy." I ruffled his hair. "Why are you up before others?"

"Mama likes the quiet." He skipped back to Abigail.

"My king, to what do we owe the early morning visit?"

I leaned down and kissed her cheek. Abigail was the most even-tempered of any woman I had ever encountered, including Michal. She had a gentleness in disposition that I respected. Just the same, I withheld the information of coming from Maacah's chambers. "I often walk around the compound to collect my thoughts."

She provided a knowing smile and patted my arm. "You have a young, new bride. There is no need for excuses with me. Would you like to join us?"

"I would like that." I sat and let Daniel climb in my lap. "So, what wakes you up so early?"

"The courtyard can be quite crowded," she said simply, handing me a bowl of porridge. "I prefer the quiet of the mornings before the noise disturbs my thoughts."

"We are searching for a different location. This compound is too small to house so many."

Abigail once again smiled gently without saying a word. The three of us ate, conversing about ideal locations for a potential move. Cush found me there.

"Good morning, Cush. How did you sleep last night?"

Cush always seemed surprised by my inquiries into his life. I tried to put him and all the servants at ease. This would not be a household where they would be in fear for their lives. Still, my manservant acted perplexed at such questions. "I slept well...thank you."

"What news do you bring?"

"You have a visitor, sir. Abner, commanding officer of Israel, is at our gates with twenty men."

I stood up so fast, I startled Daniel. I kissed him and then Abigail before leaving them in the courtyard. "Do they seem hostile? What is the nature of their business?"

"He says he comes in peace, desiring to bring the two nations together."

"Two kingdoms," I corrected. "We are one nation, but we have a split kingdom." Cush still needed occasional help in understanding our way of life.

"I understand, sir. I apologize for the confusion."

"No apologies necessary," I said as we made our way through the halls. "I am going to clean up and change. Let them into my throne room. I want full coverage. Just in case."

Cush paused outside my chamber door. "Consider it done."

I rushed inside, already peeling off my previous evening's attire. Water and pitchers had been readied per my directives. I preferred to bathe and dress alone, but I did enjoy having everything prepared for me ahead of time.

As I washed, I prayed. I was intrigued by Abner's visit. Could it be that he truly sought peace? I remembered Nathan's words to seek peace and not vengeance.

Three knocks sounded at the door.

"Enter." I finished tying my belt around my waist.

"Why do you continue to dress yourself?" Eleazar teased.

"Old habits, my friend."

Eleazar shook his head. "I would have servants waiting on my every whim."

"You would not. Your father taught you better than that."

He shrugged. "Yes, but it would be tempting."

Changing the subject, I asked, "What do you think of our visitor?"

"He is a filthy dog who killed your nephew."

"You sound like Joab and Abishai."

"Because of him, Ishbosheth became King of Israel, and we became a nation divided."

"Yes. He has made matters difficult."

"If Joab or Abishai were here, he would already be dead."

"I told them to stand down."

"You also sent them on a mission away from border walls. You know that order is going to be difficult for them to keep."

"What do you propose? Go in and shove my sword in his heart?"

"No, that will not bring you favor with Israel or with Judah."

"Exactly. Peace is the only way."

"He comes in peace. Even left his weaponry at the gate."

I paused and raised my eyebrows. "In all of my years, I have never seen him without his sword."

Eleazar shrugged. "It is strange. I supposed we should hear what he has to say."

I pulled my hair back into a tie and moved toward the door. "I am ready."

Eleazar stopped me. "You look like a glorified shepherd. You do not meet the commander of Israel's army or any commander from any army wearing a tunic and leather belt."

"Last I checked I *am* a glorified shepherd, and I like wearing this. It is comfortable." As I opened the door, I asked, "Did Jashobeam send you to check on me and make sure I looked kingly?"

"No. Why would Jashobeam care?" Then Eleazar grinned. "It was Benaiah."

"Maybe Benaiah should not be in the room with Abner. Last time, Abner threatened his life."

"Which is why Benaiah is insistent on being in the room."

I chuckled. "Yes, I remember that."

Once at the throne room, Cush confirmed all was as it should be.

"That is what you are wearing?" Benaiah approached behind Cush. To Eleazar, he said, "You failed."

"When has David ever listened to me?" Eleazar defended himself.

"Instead of worrying about my apparel, let us go and greet the commander of Israel's army." I patted Benaiah's large bicep. "This should be interesting."

"Abner," I said, entering the throne room and taking my place on the throne. I considered greeting him warmly, but my men stood about the room on edge, and I did not blame them. My nephew was dead by this man's hand. "I am surprised by your visit."

"King David." Abner bowed low, and the men with him followed suit. "Greetings in the name of our Lord. Thank you for allowing us this conversation."

"Considering you have no weapons, it seemed peaceful enough to allow you a few moments of my time. But that is all you get. So, please, tell me why you are here."

Abner stood and looked me square in the eye. "It is time we set aside differences and bring the two kingdoms under one king. *You are that king.*"

I tried to hide my surprise. "This coming from the man who propelled Ishbosheth to the throne. The same man who told me that I was not the true king of Israel. The same man who refused for me to collect my wife. The same man who unwisely participated in war games and whose hand killed my nephew."

"Yes, I am that man. Forgive me for driving a wedge between Judah and Israel. I blindly placed my faith in Saul's son because of my loyalty to Saul and his kingdom. It was self-preservation, but it was an unwise move. Just as the war games were an unwise move."

I met Eleazar's gaze, but he and all the other men were stone-faced. I felt the tension in the room. They did not want his apologies. They wanted his life. Yet, I could hear Nathan's words as clear as when they were first spoken: *My king, what would the Lord have you do? Seek vengeance or seek peace?* "And what says Ishbosheth of this change of heart?"

"He is frightened and fears for his life."

"I will not touch him just as I did not touch Saul. But what of you? What do you have to give me other than words? How do I know you are not trying to gain trust only to give our secrets away?"

"I have approached the leaders of the tribes and urged them to turn their allegiance to you. They have agreed."

The energy in the room shifted to that of shock and disbelief.

"You lie?" I asked, not wanting to believe it myself. "You dare step into my throne room and lie to my face?"

"I do not lie. I truly come in peace. Many of the tribesmen have been dissatisfied with Ishbosheth. They see him as weak and you as strong."

"I *am* strong."

"I know. We are better under you. I am sorry it took me so long to see it." When I did not say anything immediately, Abner continued. "The elders desire to meet with you. Give the word, and I will arrange it. I will do whatever it is you would have me do to show my loyalty to the throne of David."

An idea started to form, and I sat at the edge of my seat more hopeful than I had been in years. "There is something I desire. Something you must do before we move forward."

"Anything."

"Bring me Michal."

11

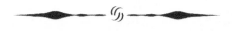

Michal

Gallim

1011 B.C.

"Queen Ahinoam is here to call upon you," Dinah said, picking up one of the crying toddlers.

Rizpah jumped up and we made eye contact. "Do not tell her I am here," she whispered.

"Why not? You are welcome here. She has no say in my life."

"Please, do me this favor. I will go make myself scarce, and you do not tell her I ever came." Rizpah's eyes pleaded with me.

"Fine, but we will discuss why after she leaves."

Rizpah hurriedly left the room. I nodded to Dinah.

Mother entered just as regally as she ever did before. With my father gone, she handled all palace matters, including heavily influencing Ishbosheth, which suited her just fine. "There is my daughter."

I rose to meet her and kissed her cheeks. "Mother, what a surprise."

She stepped back and raised an eyebrow. "Poor Michal. I thought there was no way you could look worse than when you were first grieving your father, but alas, I was wrong."

I practically growled and quickly moved away from her.

"Starting the conversation on a high note, I see. What shall you desire to assist in your verbal attacks against me? Sword or javelin?"

"Such a martyr. Now, where are the rest of my grandsons?" She petted the one Dinah held and then stepped away.

"Out with Laia's children. Probably running around the vineyards."

"Laia?" Mother said the name like it had a bitter taste. "Who is that?"

"Paltiel's wife."

"You are Paltiel's wife. That other person is nothing more than another woman vying for your husband's attention. Do not let her."

"I do not care. She can have his attention." I thought of Paltiel's offer from three evenings past, and my face warmed. Now that I had some time to think, I realized that as long as David was alive, I could never love another man. In that regard, David had ruined me. My heart still belonged to him, even though he obviously did not feel the same way.

"It is evident you do *not* care. One glance at your appearance settles any doubt."

"Why are you here? Were you bored? Had you already finished yelling at your maidservants?"

"I am here, dear daughter, because your husband reached out to me to solicit help."

"David?"

"David! Why are you bringing him up?"

"Because he is my husband. I am so confused." I pinched the bridge of my nose. When Mother did not immediately respond, I glanced back over at her. Her mouth hung open as if in shock. Then it dawned on me. "Paltiel? Did he reach out to you? Clarifying would have been helpful."

Mother's shock turned to anger. She approached me and grabbed my arm, holding it so tightly, I nearly yelped. "What is wrong with you?" she seethed. "How dare you speak that

90

shepherd's name in the house of your true husband, the man who has been devoted to you for nearly a decade."

I yanked my arm from her, but she reached and grabbed it again, even tighter than before. "Let go of me," I said in anger. "You seem to forget that my first husband is still alive. That has made this entire situation complicated."

"There is nothing complicated about it. The traitorous usurper does not want you. You know the law. You are already one with another."

"Interesting how you had many male companions while married to Father, and yet, now you bring up the law. What again are we to do with adulterers? What does the law say about that?"

"Do not talk to me that way. I may no longer be queen, but I am still your mother."

"If David is king, then that makes me queen. Funny how life can turn so suddenly."

"*David does not want you.* When you give yourself in a marital union, you are one with your husband. The contract with Paltiel will stand." She lifted her chin as if winning the argument.

I smiled tightly. Before I could think about any ramifications, I blurted, "Then it is good that I never gave myself to Paltiel. I am still wholly and fully David's."

The blood drained from Mother's face, and I gloried in it for a moment. "No. No. This isn't right." She released me and motioned to Dinah. "Bring me Paltiel. Immediately."

"Mother, you hold no power in this home. You cannot demand to see Paltiel as if he is beneath you."

"What have you done?" she lashed out at me. "If David retrieves you, then what will happen to your brother? To me? He cannot be a son of Saul. You must consummate this union with Paltiel! I insist. It is no wonder he reached out to me. He understands the direness of this situation."

It irked me that Paltiel would reach out to my mother. Did he think that would help in my decision-making? "What did he say in his note?"

"That I needed to speak to my daughter about doing her wifely duty and giving him a child. There are special remedies to help with fertility; I know a herbalist who can help." She paused to scrutinize me. "But it matters little if you withhold yourself from him."

Now it was my turn to be shocked. Paltiel went behind my back to *tattle*?

Mother was still talking. "I do not understand why you continue to hold out hope that the glorified shepherd will come back for you. Look at this place. And the vineyards. And your horses. Oh Michal, you could have fared much worse."

My mind reeled. Irritation bubbled underneath the surface, I heard the truth of Mother's words, the same truth that came from Rizpah's mouth days earlier. And had I not also concluded with the same assessment of Paltiel's home and land? Not that my mind was currently rational. I thought about leaving my mother momentarily to find and confront Paltiel.

"Do you not desire one of your own?" Mother held one of the twins. He patted her face and gave her a toothless grin. I watched them, surprised at the tenderness my mother bestowed upon the boy.

"That one is Ramsi," I said, my irritation momentarily forgotten. "Adriel finally granted them names. The other one is Ramah."

"He is delightful." Mother tickled Ramsi while he squealed in delight.

"Yes, both of the twins are full of sunshine. It makes caring for them easy."

"Merab was the same way. She rarely cried and always entered a room with a smile on her face. Everyone in the palace adored her. She broke one of your father's miniature vases that he had been gifted from a neighboring ally. It was one of a collection. Your father bellowed at the servants, blaming them. But Merab, the little cherub, patted her father's leg and confessed to it. Then smiled her smile, and that was that. Your father's heart melted."

"I broke the vase," I said quietly, remembering the scene. It was one of my earliest memories. We had been running around the palace chambers hiding from each other, and I ran into father's library. I smacked into a display stand and the vase hurled to the floor.

Mother looked at me thoughtfully. "I am not surprised. She always protected you."

The two of us sat quietly lost in memories of time past.

"There are only two of you left." Mother handed Ramsi to one of the servant girls. "Sometimes I find it hard to breathe. It does not seem right that I live on while four of my children are dead."

"I miss them," I said simply. "I miss the life I had."

"You have a good life now."

I fiddled with one of my bangles, tracing the oasis pattern etched in it. "I do not even know who I am anymore, let alone what I want."

"What I want for you is to be content and happy and to continue the bloodline of your parents. I do not understand you, youngest daughter."

"I was content and happy with David. Wait—" I held up my hand before she could interrupt. "I know you want me to forget about him. Paltiel does too. But I cannot forget about my love for him. It is still there. I wish it was not. I wish I could choose Paltiel and give him everything he desires, but my heart does not belong to him. Think of how much you loved father. Did that love go away when you knew he was with other women?"

"No, it did not," she admitted. "I will love Saul until my last breath."

I watched my mother in shock. I had never seen her be vulnerable like this. She always placed a wall between her emotions and others, even her children.

"If David comes for you, which is going to happen because he still claims to be a son of Saul, it will break Paltiel's heart. You need to prepare yourself for that."

"I know." I once again fiddled with my bangle, my thoughts on Paltiel and how crushed he will be should the time come for me to leave.

"And you need to prepare yourself." Mother reached over and took my hand. I almost pulled it away from her, shocked at her tenderness.

"I have been eating and bathing regularly. I will be ready when he returns."

"That is not what I mean." Mother watched our intertwined hands, then she brought my hand up to her lips and gently kissed it. "Michal, you need to prepare yourself to be queen."

"I observed you for years. I think I can manage—"

"You think you can manage being queen?" Mother's mouth twitched in a humorless smile. "So, then, how will handle it when your husband chooses to dine with a concubine? How will you handle the fourteen days of a wedding feast, knowing your husband is consummating yet another marriage? How will you handle running into his children? Not your children...*his*? And what will you do if, God forbid, he prefers another woman over you? You think you know loneliness? Oh Michal, you have no idea."

Once again, I found the words ripping open old wounds. I thought of Rizpah's warning, *Are you sure you truly know for what you wish?* In need of comfort, I rested my head on Mother's lap. "I do not know what to do."

And for the first time since I was a young girl, my mother ran her fingers through my hair and comforted me, if only for a moment.

12

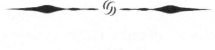

Michal

Gallim

1011 B.C.

Rizpah waited for me outside my private chambers. "How did it go?"

"Have you been waiting here the entire day?"

"No, just until I heard the entourage leave. Did everything go all right? She stayed for hours, which is surprising. You normally dismiss yourself from her company before noonday."

"It went...well." The word surprised me even as I said it. "At first, it was as it always is. She yelled at me, and I yelled back."

"That sounds like the Ahinoam I know."

"Yes, she came because she received a note from Paltiel, but then something shifted between us."

"What?"

"Merab." I smiled at Rizpah. "We reminisced the entire afternoon and into the evening about my sister and our childhood antics."

Rizpah gave me a strange expression. "Never in a thousand generations would I think that Ahinoam would *reminisce* with you."

"It happened today, and we plan on seeing each other before the next full moon." I paused, thinking about the surprising events of the afternoon and evening. "It was a good visit. I needed my mother, and for once, she acted like a mother." I moved past Rizpah to enter my chamber.

"What of Paltiel's note to her?" Rizpah seemed to have some desperation in her voice.

"We talked about it at first. Well, we argued mostly, but then we did not bring it up again. And I am glad for it. All these years, I never realized how exhausting it is to be at odds with my mother." I smiled again at Rizpah, not even registering her confused expression. "Now, if you will excuse me, I ate with Mother, so I will stay in my private chambers until Paltiel returns. A good nap will do me well in preparation for our meeting."

Rizpah's expression changed, and she gave me a knowing smile. "Yes, rest up, Michal. That is good news indeed."

Now it was my turn to act confused. "What is good news? My meeting with Paltiel? It is simply to discuss why he would go to my mother with a message."

Rizpah's smile faltered. "Oh no, do not bring that up. Men do not like to be questioned."

———⚜———

I once again found myself outside of Paltiel's chamber door. I planned to demand an explanation for writing a note to my mother. He could not have possibly thought that sending a message to her would do any good. He knew of our strained relationship. Even though the day spent with her turned out surprisingly well, it was a first-time event in my adult life.

But Mother's words, coupled with Rizpah's, churned in my brain, and I did not know what to think anymore. Why was it so difficult to forget about David and move on? Why did I continue to hold back from Paltiel?

Suddenly the door flew open, and Paltiel stood in front of me.

"Michal? Is everything all right?"

"I heard you were finished with your evening rounds of the southern vines, and I thought I would come and tell you about the visit with my mother."

Paltiel shifted slightly, and I noticed Laia behind him.

"Oh, my apologies. I did not realize you had company." I stumbled backward, embarrassment heating my face.

"No, it is fine. Laia was leaving." Paltiel turned to her, touched her elbow gently, and ushered her out the door. "I will do everything I can," he whispered to her.

She nodded but left us quickly, not once looking in my direction. "I will come back," I said. "That was an intimate conversation. I should not come to you unless invited."

"I told you the invitation is always open, and it is. Please, come in. I have yet to eat my evening meal. I would not object to the company."

I wanted to point out that he just had company, but I refrained. Entering his chamber, I shut the door while he made himself comfortable on the floor with dinner's spread on a tray beside him. "Is Laia all right? Is she unwell? It is none of my business, but I overheard a small portion of the conversation."

"Her mother is gravely ill, and she requested to visit her and potentially stay in the family home for the duration of the grieving period."

"I had no idea."

"She requested I accompany her, but my duties here overwhelm me. It is not feasible, so I will send her and the children off at daybreak."

"I need to say goodbye. She may be gone for several moons. The boys will miss her and your children. Ashvi reveres your eldest."

"That is because Uri lets him ride the horse alone when we are not looking." We shared a smile. Uri, Paltiel and Laia's eldest son, was nearing his twelfth year, four years older than Ashvi. The two were often inseparable.

"Ashvi will want to see them off too." I thought about leaving the conversation to go speak to Laia. I had been too consumed in my own negative emotions that I failed to see that she had struggles too.

"There is no need to worry. They will return soon. Should you still be here, you will see them again." Paltiel swallowed a mouthful of stew. "Did you say something earlier about your mother? I pray all is well."

It took me a second to switch topics so quickly. "My mother? Yes, she visited today."

"I am sorry I missed her. Did she stay for the evening meal?"

"No, she is particular about what she eats and the way it is prepared." The two of us shared another smile. Mother complained so vehemently at Paltiel over the way the food was cooked and served the last time she stayed for a meal, that she developed quite the reputation for being loud and contentious among Paltiel's servants. "I am curious why you wrote her a note. You know my relationship with her is strained."

Paltiel stopped eating and glanced at me curiously. "What note? I am not sure I have ever written a woman, let alone the late king's queen."

I was not expecting his response. "You did not write a message to my mother about fulfilling my wifely duty to you?"

He brought his goblet to his lips, only to suspend it at my words. "Why would I write a message to the late king's queen? I would never write to a woman. Most know not how to read."

"She said that she received a message from you to talk to me about performing my wifely duty. How would she know that? Have you mentioned it to laborers or those in your circle?"

"It would not be advantageous for anyone to know anything other than we are husband and wife. That is all anyone knows unless you have spoken to someone about it."

"My sister knew, but she is no longer here, and there is Dinah, but she cannot read or write. She would not do something like this even if she could write a message." I paused, thinking about recent conversations with Rizpah. "Rizpah knows, but she cannot read or write either."

"Laia can. She was taught by her father when she was a girl, but reason does she have to do so?"

I thought of Laia leaving Paltiel's chambers and not making eye contact. She and I made peace several moons ago and got along quite well. "The primary motive must be for me to stay here…with you."

Paltiel washed his hands in a small bowl beside his cleared dinner plate and dried them before arising and heading over to me. "Michal, I want nothing more than for you to choose me and my home as yours, but I would not risk upsetting you by undermining you. It was not me."

I searched his countenance, and my gaze met his. "I believe you."

"There is something you should know."

"What? You can tell me."

"The evening I brought you here to drink wine? The evening that did not go as planned?"

"Yes, what of it?"

"That was Rizpah's idea."

"To bring me to your chambers? She had just arrived."

"She sought me out before our evening meal and said that you confided in her how much you desired to stay here and to truly be my wife. She suggested that I let you know that I desired it too, which I do. More than anything."

"Why would she do such a thing?" My words came out harsh, so I rephrased. "I have contemplated whether to stay here and be fully committed to you and the household, but she overstepped her bounds in seeking you out."

"I realized as much when the evening did not go as planned." Paltiel frowned. "I should have told you, but I was embarrassed.

Forgive me?"

"Of course." I reached for his hand and squeezed. "You and I are being played by several people, and it is cumbersome. I will speak to Rizpah directly."

"What did you say to your mother? After she inquired about our unique situation?"

"Everyone is telling me the same thing. That I have it good here."

He had yet to release my hand. "And what say you?"

"I am leaning toward agreement." I gently pulled my hand from his. "I am hesitant to move forward without speaking to David."

"You wish to speak with him? That does not bode well for me. He will surely persuade you to his side."

"I do not think he will," I said, believing the words even as I said them. "I love him, and I always will. But I love the David from ten years ago. I love the young shepherd turned giant slayer. I love the man who defied the odds and married the king's daughter. All these years, while you took care of me and now my sister's sons, he was marrying other women. He did not honor our marriage contract. I understand that men are allowed multiple relationships, but I do not agree. Did not Yahweh Himself make one man for one woman? To go to him now and share him with others. I cannot imagine what that would feel like, and I do not want to find out." I took a breath and concluded, "It is time I let him go."

Paltiel blinked back tears and tried to hide his emotion. "My words fail me," he eventually said. He reached out and tenderly rested his hand against my cheek.

I wanted to feel something like the passion I would feel with David, but even though I was not repulsed, it was not the same. *It does not matter,* I told myself as I smiled at Paltiel. *You are taken care of here. You are preferred. You are friends with the women here. This is your home. And this is the man who is willing to give it to you.*

He hesitated briefly then leaned in to kiss me. He paused, "You are not going to become sick, are you? Last time I tried this, it did not go too well."

I laughed. "You are safe."

Paltiel brought his lips to mine, and I had to suppress the urge to cry. Not because I did not enjoy the closeness, but because it meant burying my feelings for David, once and for all.

———⟨⟩———

After I left Paltiel's chamber, I did feel sick. And I hated myself for feeling that way.

So overwhelmed with the most recent events and my volatile emotions, I marched right past Laia and Rizpah whispering in the hall. It was only when Rizpah called out to me that I noticed them. I immediately scowled and asked, "Did you send a message to my mother?"

"Yes, but only because all my other plans did not work. If you would have simply chosen Paltiel, I would not have to resort to such measures."

"You are justifying your deceit by laying the responsibility at my feet." I huffed in frustration. "And after I allowed you in as a guest! You had no right, Rizpah!"

"I do apologize for the deceit, but not for trying to help you see what is right in front of you."

"What does it even matter to you?"

Rizpah broke eye contact. "Until I hear from Abner or my sons, I have nowhere to go. I have no family in this region, other than you. You have always been a sister and a friend. If you go to David, then I will not be allowed there. Not unless—"

"—He takes you in as a concubine."

Laia looked from me to Rizpah. "Why is that?"

"The next king can reject the previous king's concubines, in which there is nowhere for them to go unless a family member pities them," Rizpah said quietly. "Or, the new king can choose to keep the concubine as his own."

I grimaced at the thought of David touching Rizpah. "You thought that if I stayed here, I would have mercy on you."

"I have not heard from Abner, and I doubt I will. I have been cast aside. I could go to David, but I do not want to do that to you."

"You seem to think he would not reject you."

Rizpah met my gaze again and raised her eyebrows. "I have my ways, Michal. I have yet to have a man say no to me."

My cheeks burned, and it was I who looked away.

"Forgive me for being motivated by selfishness, but I felt we would be safer here."

"That is not your decision to make. It is mine, and I weary of those who try to manipulate me to bend to their will."

"Do not be solely angry at Rizpah," Laia said quietly. "I penned the words for her." My face must not have hidden my surprise because Laia continued, "I too was led by selfish motives. I do not want you to leave. The children have become close, and I enjoy riding the horses. You have become family. Now that I have to leave to take care of my mother, I worry that you will not be here when I return."

The anger dissipated at Laia's heartfelt words. *We were a family.* "You do not need to worry. I just left Paltiel's chambers where I told him of my decision. I choose to stay here." Both Laia's and Rizpah's faces lit up. "We are wanting to celebrate the occasion with a feast. You will miss the feast, but at least when you return, all will be as it should be."

Laia threw her arms around me. "You have rejuvenated my soul. This makes me happy indeed." She released me and gave me a half-grin. "Who would have thought that the two of us would become friends?"

"Well, I am glad for it."

"I am too."

I excused myself, suddenly exhausted from the full day and the decisions made. In the quiet of my chamber, Dinah moved about, preparing my night bathing ritual. "I have decided to stay."

Dinah stopped pouring water and gave me her full attention. "Do you have that choice?"

"If I consummate my relationship with Paltiel, David will need to uphold the marriage union."

"Or he could kill Paltiel and his entire household for defiling the queen."

"David has left me alone for years. I cannot continue to live my life holding my breath that he will return to me. He is gone, and Paltiel is here."

"Is it what you want?"

"Nothing is as I want. Not since I helped David escape through our window. But here, I am valued. They have become family, and it would hurt them if I chose to leave with someone who has cared little about me."

"I am not of that opinion. We now know that David has tried to communicate with you. It is Ishbosheth that still holds his father's edicts that keeps David from you."

"Please," I said, bringing my hands to my face. "I cannot continue to hold onto hope. It has already stolen years of my life. I have made my decision. Now, I can only hope that David respects it."

Dinah and I stood across the room, watching each other. I saw the worry on her countenance with her furrowed brow and deep frown. I doubted she believed the words, and I was not entirely sure I did either.

13

Michal

Gallim

1011 B.C.

Dinah finished braiding my hair and wrapped it around my head like a crown. "These flowers will do nicely," she said, taking the assortment of blooms and arranging them in my hair. She eyed me curiously. "Are you sure this is what you want?"

"Yes," I said, meeting her gaze. "I have made my decision. This has been my home for several years, and now, it is home to my sons. Merab would want her boys to feel wanted and secure. Here, that is accomplished."

"But do you love him?"

"What is love? Is it passion or is it comfort? For me, it has been sleepless and agonizing nights and a broken heart bruised and trampled on by who I thought loved me in return." I picked up a delicate flower petal and played with it with my fingers. "Paltiel has been good to me, and at the end of the day, I shudder at the thought of being amongst numerous women all vying for David's attention." I shook my head. "No, I refuse that life."

"What life do you refuse?" Mother walked into my chamber, and Dinah pressed her lips together as if to remind herself not to talk. Mother still thought Dinah could not speak. Dinah asked me to not share the secret, and after Dinah's loyalty all these years, it seemed like an easy request, so I agreed.

"A life where I am not valued or appreciated."

"I have something for you." She held out a corded necklace with a small vial attached and a black gem cut like a raven with its claws holding the vile in place. "It is a tincture to open up your fertility. It has been gifted upon you by the Ashtoreth priestess."

"Thank you. Do I drink it now?"

"No, wait until after consummation. Now, turn around and let me help with its clasp." She fiddled with it for a moment. "What is this other necklace? Is it new?"

My hand instinctively reached for it. "It was a wedding gift. From David. I vowed I would never take it off."

"Do you think it fortuitous to be wearing a gift from your first husband?"

"I made a vow, and it is a good reminder."

"A good reminder of what?" Mother frowned.

"To never again be led by my heart." Still, I fingered the single pearl and allowed myself to briefly reminisce of when David gave it to me.

Mother muttered something about it being "foolhardy and a bad omen."

Rizpah rushed into the room. "It's time." She stopped when she saw Mother. "Ahinoam. Lovely to see you. I did not realize you were here."

"Of course, I am here," Mother snapped. "I am here to celebrate with my daughter. The question is why are you here?"

"I am visiting Michal."

Mother turned to me. "Is this true? Why did you not tell me?"

"I do not turn away family, and I did not say anything because I did not know I needed to."

"You turn me away all the time," Mother huffed. "And she is not family."

106

"Her sons are my half-brothers, so yes, she is my family. And turning you away is different. I know you have a palace to go back to."

"Ah, that is right. You were turned away," Mother said to Rizpah. "Ishbosheth kicked you out, and your love affair with Abner did not reap the results you desired."

Rizpah lifted her chin in defiance. "I am waiting for Abner. He is finding a dwelling for us."

Mother snorted. "You are starting to sound like Michal. Waiting for a man who is never going to come."

"If you truly think David is not coming, why did you rush over here to practically push me into Paltiel's arms?" I teased. When Mother opened her mouth to respond, I hurriedly continued, "I am teasing, Mother. My choice in Paltiel is all my doing."

"You will be happy with your decision," Mother said, throwing one last petulant glance at Rizpah.

"On that, we agree," Rizpah said. "Choosing this comfortable life will be good for you and the boys."

Mother scowled again. "I would like a moment alone with *my* daughter."

Rizpah turned to me, and said, "You look beautiful, Michal," before leaving the room.

"Seriously, Michal. Give me a warning before the shock of seeing that concubine seizes my heart."

Rizpah ran back into the room. "Someone is coming. An entourage with royal flags."

"I told Ishbosheth about tonight's celebration," Mother said, waving her hand at the interruption. "Now, go."

"Why would Ishbosheth come to my dinner?" I asked, not hiding my displeasure.

"Because you are his only surviving sibling."

The commotion grew outside the door. Rizpah left my chamber, only to rush in a few moments later. "It is Abner! He has come for me." She pushed past Mother to me. Grabbing my hands, she kissed one cheek and then the other. "Thank you, my sister. I will never forget your kindness." Then she rushed out of the room to pack her things.

"Leave it to her to find a way to make today about her."

"I, for one, am glad that Abner is here to do the right thing. She should not be forsaken just because the king is dead. She has given him two sons."

Rizpah burst into the room again. This time she looked panicked. "Why does he bring soldiers? If it is to retrieve me, then he would not risk drawing attention to himself."

We made eye contact. From what Rizpah explained earlier, Abner was headed to David to seek an alliance. "Whose flags does he fly?" I asked as anxiety took hold of me.

"Saul's, but he would not come into this territory waving David's."

Mother must have caught on. "If he allied with David, you do not think—"

"Yes, I do," Rizpah interrupted. To me, she added, "He is not here for me. He is here for you."

"Why would David not come himself?" I asked, trying to keep my emotions in check. I could not tell what exactly I felt at the moment, but mostly, it felt like disbelief.

"He still cannot cross the borders," Mother answered, her eyes still on Rizpah. "It would not surprise me for David to order Abner to bring Michal to him."

"What are we going to do?" Rizpah asked Mother. Both women completely ignored me, as they left the chamber to see the arrival first-hand.

Dinah and I were alone. "What happens now?" she whispered.

My mind whirled. Could it be? My thoughts were interrupted by yelling.

We ran outside the room and leaned against the balcony that overlooked the main path. Rizpah was right. Abner had brought at least a dozen men with him. But it was not Abner yelling, it was

Paltiel.

"You cannot do this! You have no authority!"

"I can and I will do this. Now get out of our way. We will take what we need, and we will leave you in peace."

Soldiers moved past him and into the home. There were shouts and shuffling, as heavy footsteps headed up the stairs. They rounded the corner at the end of the hall, marching in this direction.

"What do we do?" Dinah asked, fear in her voice.

But I could not answer, nor could I move. I stood frozen in my place. As soon as the soldiers made eye contact with me, the last several years of pain, heartache, and loss came flooding back. And more than any confusion or disbelief, I felt anger.

"Queen Michal? You are to come with us."

Dinah and I exchanged a glance with Dinah raising her eyebrows and opening her mouth as if in shock. *Queen?*

One of them ordered Dinah to pack my things, then they were surrounding me. Two grabbed my arms, one on each side, and led me down the hall.

"There is no need to manhandle me," I said, but they did not relinquish their hold. Once down the stairs and out the main entryway, Paltiel and I came face-to-face.

He wore his ceremonial tunic, but his eyes were red from weeping. He took one look at me in my ceremonial garb and the tears surfaced again. "Tell them," he pleaded. "Tell them you have made your choice."

My heart broke, watching his anguish. "Paltiel, I do not think they will listen—"

"We have no time for this," Abner said. "Queen Michal, you have been summoned by your husband, King David of Judah. A set of soldiers will stay behind and oversee the entourage of your belongings and servants. Who among these is going with you?"

"You cannot come into another man's house and take what is his!" Paltiel shouted. "You cannot do this. Our laws forbid it."

"Our laws also forbid marrying a woman who belongs to

another man." Abner motioned to the soldiers holding my arms, and they practically lifted me and moved me toward a horse.

"The king made promises! And David is not king here!" Paltiel ran behind the soldiers. He grabbed my skirts and wept. The more of a scene he made, the more uncomfortable everyone became. My heart hurt for him, but there was nothing we could do. It was foolish to think I ever had a choice.

I thought of the children and tried to turn to see if I could see them. I needed to reassure them that everything would be fine. But they were nowhere to be seen, and I did not know if I could promise that everything would be fine. David could easily reject them.

It should not happen like this. "Wait," I called out, but no one heard me. Paltiel had rent his clothes and wailed so loudly that Abner had us moving out without wasting any more time.

"Michal!" Paltiel wept. "My love! Tell them! Tell them!" He ran after us, calling out to me, but I could not turn around. I could not look back.

Because decisions were made without consulting me, it hurt to think of the years Paltiel supported and cared for me only to have David order my father's man to retrieve me.

You are a pawn, a small voice whispered in my head. *You mean nothing.*

Paltiel's weeping followed us, but not once did I look back. It would break me even more than I already was. "I am so sorry," I whispered. I prayed that someday he would forgive me for not being strong enough to stand up to Abner, to fight for the life we had built together.

14

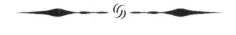

Michal

Gallim

1011 B.C.

A small, dark man waited for us at David's compound. He bowed low. In broken Hebrew, he said, "Queen Michal, it is an honor to greet you. I welcome you to your home."

I took a moment to scrutinize my surroundings. The land rested against the Judean mountains but with the masses of soldier tents scattered throughout, the backdrop was not nearly as breathtaking. The actual structure of David's dwelling was expansive enough, but it boasted little in comparison to my father's palace.

Before, none of it would have mattered as long as I was with David. I would have lived under the stars with him if he had ever given us a chance. But now, all I could do was compare it to my father's place and Paltiel's place. Just knowing that other women lived here too, women who belonged to David, made me desire to turn around. And where was David? Could he not so much as come out and greet me? With so many emotions and so many thoughts, I could barely make sense of what was happening. So, I said nothing.

When I was assisted off the horse, I said nothing.

When the manservant asked about my journey, I said nothing.

I needed privacy. I needed to collect and compose myself.

"Michal."

The whirlwind of thoughts stopped at the familiar voice. My gaze landed on Benaiah. I opened my mouth, but nothing came out.

He held up a hand, then turned to Abner. "The elders have already arrived. David waits for you in the throne room."

To the men that came with us, the little manservant offered refreshment after their horses were fed.

Once Abner and his men left, it was me, Benaiah, and the manservant. Benaiah offered an empathetic smile and greeted me warmly. "Michal, it is good to see here. Where you belong. David is impatient to be with you again. He asked me to come greet you, so you would know that he has highly anticipated this moment."

The manservant agreed. "We have prepared your chambers, which boast a large courtyard and a covered porch for your pleasure. As soon as your belongings arrive, we will set up accommodations per your directions. We are here to serve you, my queen." He bowed low again.

"Cush," Benaiah addressed the manservant. "Please make sure that refreshments are in place for the queen. She should want for nothing. I will escort her to her chambers momentarily."

Cush left us before I could gather my wits and say anything. When it was just me and Benaiah, I finally found some words. "I do not think I can do this."

"Yes, you can. You can and you will."

"Because of orders! Not of my own choices."

"You do not desire to be here? I thought you have done nothing but desire this day for years."

"Everything is changed. There are women in there—" I pointed to the entrance of the structure. "Who are married to my husband!"

Benaiah acted perplexed. "I do not understand. You married David, knowing he was the anointed heir. You knew based on your father's life and daily interactions that multiple women fulfill the needs of the king."

"I thought it would be different for us," I said quietly. "I wanted to believe that I was enough."

"Michal." Benaiah grabbed my hand. "I cannot imagine what it is like to be a woman in this culture, but I do know this. David loves you, and he has since I have known him. Please do not allow your displeasure to overrule your relationship with him."

I took a breath and slowly released it. "I will try."

The small voice whispered, *They give you no choice. You are one of many.*

The voice startled me. Even though it had to be in my head—there was no one around besides Benaiah—the voice sounded real.

Benaiah led me through the doors, and I followed, partly listening to him and partly listening to my inner dialogue.

Of
Pride
And
Power

15

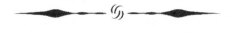

David

Hebron

1011 B.C.

"She is here." Abner stood before me with those three words echoing in my ears and my heart. "I also met with the elders of the eleven tribes, and they are willing to meet with you. They too tire of Ishbosheth's weakness against our enemies."

Even with Abner's success with the elders, I could not think logically. Just knowing that Michal had arrived and was in residence nearly undid me.

He seemed to wait for me to say something. "I commend you. I did not expect you to arrive so quickly."

"Let this prove my loyalty to you and your kingdom."

Those in the room looked expectantly at me, but my heart pounded in my ears. I needed a moment. Or two. I needed to see her. "This is an excellent start," I quickly said, "And your efforts deserve a celebratory feast. Cush, direct Abner to a prepared room and his men to their tents." To Abner, I said, "Please, go and refresh yourself. Tonight, we celebrate our alliance."

Abner bowed low, but he could not get out of the throne room fast enough. Finally, he and his men left.

"Where is she?" I asked Benaiah as soon as the opportunity presented itself.

"She is in her chambers. Her belongings and servants have yet to arrive. Cush assigned girls to her so that she wants for nothing."

I moved to leave, but Eleazar stopped me. "Before you go, we should discuss our next strategies."

I placed my hands on Eleazar's shoulders and planted a big kiss on his cheek. "My long-lost wife has returned to me, my friend. Allow me time."

Eleazar rolled his eyes and grinned. "Fine."

I ran out of the room, only to run back in. "Should I go to her? No, have her come to me. No, that is too pompous. I will go to her."

Benaiah stepped forward. "Go, and get cleaned up. I will escort her to your private chambers."

"Good thinking!" I called out, already running out of the room.

I ran to my chambers, not caring about what anyone thought should they see me act in an unkinglike fashion. My bride, *my queen*, was here.

Michal stood in front of me, just as beautiful and royal as I remembered. But there was no love in her eyes as in the days of our youth. No joy and adoration as she used to look upon me. No, now she stood reserved, as if unsure how to act.

"Michal." I stepped hesitantly toward her. "It is good to see you."

"Here I am. At your bidding."

I took her hands and kissed them. "Do you not want to be here? I thought you would want to be back with your husband."

"My husband? Which one?"

The words had their effect and stabbed at my heart. I dropped her hands. "The only one you have. The other was a counterfeit who stole another man's wife."

"Is that how you choose to see things? That counterfeit, as you call him, took care of me. While you were running around in the mountains, marrying other women and impregnating them, Paltiel kept me safe and provided a life."

"Running around in the mountains?" Was this what she thought? "Do you have any idea of the horrors my men and I have experienced? No, you do not, and I wanted to keep it that way. I could not see you half-starved as many of us were or be constantly on the move because Saul and his troops found us again."

"That does not change the fact that you promised to come back for me, yet you broke that promise. For the first couple of years, I walked to the same spot. Every day. And waited. And watched. I just knew that *my* David was coming back for me. But I was wrong. Even for this journey, you did not come for me."

"Through no fault of my own. I could not set foot in Israel before because of your father, and now your brother lays claim. I have been trying to keep the peace out of respect for you and your family."

"Is that your excuse? Is this the same David who fought Goliath? And you cannot find a way to see me?"

"Goliath was not a Hebrew. That is a key difference. And he was also not my king, which also happened to be my wife's father." I took a breath. "I do not want to bring up the sins of your father. I know his death is still hard for both of us."

"You have sins upon your head, as well," she said coolly.

"Of course, I am a sinful man, but of what sins are you referring?"

Michal acted offended, even shaking her head. "Did you not kill for the very enemy who robbed my brothers and my father of their lives? Were you not a mercenary for the Philistines? Pray tell me the rumor is false!"

Shame burned within, but I shoved it aside as anger flickered. I repeated, "You have no idea what you are talking about."

"So, you do not deny it?"

"*I had nowhere to go!*" I shouted. She flinched, and I felt immediate regret. "Forgive me for yelling, but Michal, I had nowhere. He hunted me down like a dog. My men and I ran out of options. Surely you can see that I did what I had to do to protect my men and their families."

"Maybe I would have a better picture if I had been there, but *I was not.* You found other women to fill my role and satisfy you." And there I saw the first crack in her armor. Her lip quivered, and she had to blink back the hurt.

"Michal..."

"Where are they now? Your other wives? I heard that you have acquired a few more. No doubt making you a busy man."

"It is not like that. There has only been you." There was pain in my words. "Please believe me that I thought of you day and night, but I was given no choice."

"So, you have honored our marriage and not consummated your marital contracts with the others?"

"Why are you doing this?" I demanded. "You know the duties of ruling and being a king. It was not what I wanted or what I expected, but I did what I had to do to survive. And none of them are you."

I desired my heartfelt words to reach her, but she showed no emotion. Eventually, she asked, "Are those words supposed to move me? *It's only been you, Michal, until it was not.*"

Anger and hurt rippled off her like waves of the tumultuous sea. "Please, do not do this. I have waited over eight years to hold you in my arms. I do not know what to do with your anger."

"Such contradictions! You love me so much, yet you could not even come to get me yourself. You had to send my father's man. I heard it was because you were too busy signing a new marriage contract."

"No. It is because your brother has claimed Israel, and I wanted to keep the peace. No more unnecessary bloodshed." I thought of Asahel's death but did not dwell on it.

Michal shook her head. "Listen to yourself! You do not want unnecessary bloodshed, yet you divide the kingdom."

I could not believe Michal's words. "I divide the kingdom?"

"Israel chooses Ishbosheth, yet you insist on being Judah's king. Why not tell Judah to follow their rightful king? A true son of Saul?"

Shock turned to anger. Michal knew of my anointing. She knew of my past and what the prophet, Samuel, proclaimed to me when I was a boy. Her words were meant to hurt. "Who are you?" I said so quietly I wasn't sure she heard.

She blinked back tears, and when she spoke, her voice shook. "If you would have never pursued being king, we would have never been ripped apart. Of course, my father would see your pursuit for the throne as a power play. What did you expect him to do? Lie down and let you walk over him and my brothers to the throne? If you loved me like you say you do, you would have chosen our love over your ambition and pride."

"You think I have not fostered the same thoughts? I did not approach Samuel and demand to be king. I never demanded it of your father, which is why I refused to lay a hand on him. It is why I refuse to lay a hand on Ishbosheth. But my destiny does not belong to anyone but the Lord. It does not belong to me or even you. I am His first." I released her. "You may go."

She bowed low, stressing the words, "At your command, my king."

"Go!" I ordered, desperately desiring to nurse my wounds in private. She moved quickly to the outer door of my chamber. "Wait. One more thing." When she paused, I continued, "We're having a banquet in honor of your return. Everyone needs to meet their queen."

Without so much as a backward glance, Michal walked out of my chamber. My body shook from a mixture of shock, anger, and guilt. I headed toward my balcony and drew in deep breaths. But I could not stop the anguish that bubbled up from inside. I clutched the railing of the balcony, as my vision blurred with tears. Everything I endured. Everything I lost. Every struggle and adversity reared its ugly head, and for a moment, I dwelt in that pain.

Michal's words cut so deeply, I wondered how I did not bleed. *If you loved me like you say you do, you would have chosen our love over your ambition and pride.*

"Ambition and pride?" I asked aloud. I needed to understand. "How can she see it that way?"

Why had Samuel anointed my head? And if I was destined for the throne, why have every step toward it be such a battle?

I walked back to my chamber and grabbed the parchment and ink. I didn't hesitate as the words poured out of me. All the anguish and rejection and frustration flooded out of my innermost being and onto the parchment. I could barely see past the tears, but it didn't matter. My soul's lament did not need my sight, and I was used to writing through the tears. This was not the first time I flooded pages with anguish and despair.

"David."

I paused briefly at Eleazar's voice. "I did not summon you. Go away."

"No."

I spun around so fast, the stool I sat upon fell over. "Get out!"

"No."

Fury ripped through me. I stormed to Eleazar and shoved him as hard as I could. He stumbled back but remained firm. "I am your king!" I shouted as I kept shoving. "You must obey me! Now go! Get out! Leave me alone!"

Eleazar grabbed my arms. "Stop this, David. I am not your enemy. I am your best friend."

I turned from him and covered my face with my hands. "She's gone," I said. "She's not...she does not love me."

"The situation forced upon both of you was horribly cruel. Yet, with her father's death, she probably struggles to place blame at his feet. Grief has a way of changing our perspective. Give it time."

"Give it time? You say those words repeatedly. I hate those words."

"If she loved you once, that love can grow again. But it takes time."

"So, you think she no longer loves me?" I watched Eleazar's expression become guarded. "Answer the question."

"I think eight years is a long time to be apart. She obviously adapted to life with Paltiel."

"I will kill him."

"I am not sure that will help your cause." Eleazar tried again. "We have a celebration tonight. We have truly been given a gift in Abner's allegiance to your kingdom. This will give Michal time to adjust to her new living arrangements."

"What choice do I have? I will prepare for the feast." I rested my head against an entry post. "Will she forgive me?"

"In time, I believe she will. Let her see you as the strong, confident king of Judah. Her heart will turn to you again."

———※———

The celebratory feast brought in more wine and dancers than the men knew how to handle. I stood and saluted Abner for his allegiance, and he and his men seemed pleased. My men, on the other hand, were inept at acting as if they approved the situation. Which was when I summoned the dancers. And I thought it could not end fast enough.

One dancer emerged from the group of women and approached me. She danced before me, making eye contact now and then. But my mind was elsewhere.

The men became intoxicated and the dancers more brazen, but my thoughts were far away. I tried to imagine how I could present myself to Michal in a more unassuming way. Eleazar's suggestion of presenting myself kinglier was not the way to her heart. She fell in love with the shepherd, not the king. Somehow, I needed to show her that I was still David. My titles changed, but my heart had not.

Festivities continued into the night, but I left as soon as I could.

I hesitated in the hallway, tempted to go see Michal. "Are you leaving so soon?" The soft voice surprised me. I turned to see the dancer from earlier slowly approach. She bowed low and kissed my feet. "I am available to provide you a private dance, my king."

Cush found me before I could respond. "Commander Joab is in your chambers. He has just arrived."

"You may leave," I told the girl.

"If you change your mind, the servants know where to find me. She bowed low and kissed my feet again before leaving us. She turned once and caught me staring. She smiled, turned, and kept walking.

"Sir?" Cush interrupted my wandering thoughts.

"He did not desire to wait until morning?"

Cush did not respond.

"He found out about the celebration," I said, already knowing the answer. I took the stairs to my chambers, feeling annoyed and grumpy.

Eleazar waited for me outside my chambers. His eyes warned me.

"Do I not get a reprieve?" I raised my voice, opening the door and coming face-to-face with my nephew.

Joab's face was stone. "Is it true? Pray, tell me what I heard about Abner becoming an ally is not true."

Eleazar skirted past me. "Joab, can this not wait until morning? We have had a busy day. The king needs time to refresh. We will reexamine this topic in the morning."

Joab's breathing became ragged, and I saw the hurt. I could sense the disapproval rolling off him in waves. I took a breath, setting aside my own irritation, and said, "Easy, nephew. There is an explanation."

"Is that why you sent me off? While I am spying and collecting spoils to bring back, you are pledging loyalty to a murderer?"

"We need him as an ally."

Joab said nothing.

"We are grieving, and Abner is partly responsible, but—"

"Partly? Is that how you see it?"

"Yes, partly. His sword killed Asahel, but Asahel should not have continued pursuit. Do not interrupt me again." I glared at Joab, daring him to defy me. When he stayed silent, I continued, "Abner came to me. I did not go to him. He came and offered his allegiance, already leading discussions with tribal elders on becoming one kingdom again. Can you not see how much we need Abner to make this come to pass? And he has fulfilled his word thus far. The elders have agreed to talk, and he went and retrieved Michal for me."

"Well, as long as you have another wife here, then it makes all things better." Joab's words were heavy with sarcasm.

"Careful, nephew," I warned, my irritation rekindling. Knowing I had to put an end to any thoughts of vengeance Joab may still foster, I added, "I order you to not lay a hand on Abner or on any Hebrew soldier who joins ranks with us from Israel. Is that understood?"

Joab's jaw clenched.

"Is that understood?" I repeated.

Joab gave a stiff nod.

"You may go and rest. On the morrow, help sort the spoil. We will discuss your findings when the both of us are not so volatile."

Joab left without another word.

"He is displeased with you," Eleazar said.

"I have a long line of those not happy with me." I wiped my face, suddenly feeling the exhaustion from the previous sleepless night.

"His brother is dead by Abner's hand. You cannot blame him for seeking closure and for despising his brother's killer."

"I do not judge him for those emotions, but Abner told Asahel to stop pursuing him. Abner is only partially to blame, and I am surprised that so many do not see this simple truth."

"Would you have stopped pursuit? If the opposing side's commander was in your sights, would a young David have stopped pursuing him?"

"What do you suggest? Not make peace? Maybe I should go and kill Abner in his sleep. That would surely go over well with the tribal elders."

"I am not saying that. What is best for the kingdom is not what is best for Joab or Abishai. Just please do not forget their pain in your pursuit of Israel."

I turned to my friend and saw the sincerity of his plea. "I will not forget their pain. I only hope they will listen to orders long enough so that I may continue peace talks."

Eleazar grimaced, indicating his uncertainty about my nephews' willpower. "We can hope, but we should also devise a plan of action should they not obey orders."

"If they defy orders, it could turn into an all-out war. No one wins at war." I thought of my relationship with Michal. I thought of the civil war started by Saul that ripped me away from my wife. And I had been at war ever since. "No one wins," I repeated. "Saul made sure of that."

"Then let us watch Joab and Abishai closely and deter them from the temptation to avenge Asahel's death should an opportunity arise."

I agreed. "Station more detail outside Abner's doors, and no one is to obey any order that does not come from my lips."

Eleazar went to leave, then paused. "We are going to survey borders. You should come. Your men's morale is higher when their king is present."

I opened my mouth to protest, thinking of my desire to spend time with Michal.

"David, I am sincerely glad Michal has arrived, and you have your queen under your roof, but do not forget that you are king.

Decisions need to be made for the good of your people, which means that your relationship with Saul's daughter cannot distract your mind or your emotions."

"Fine," I said. "I will go. Let us wait for the celebration feasts to be over, and we will head out."

16

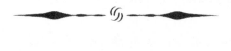

Michal

Hebron

1011 B.C.

I slammed the door behind me and slumped to the floor. My insides boiled from fury, anguish, and a host of other emotions. My David. He had stood in front of me after all this time. Why did I not run into his arms? For years I longed for him, barely able to live without him, yet at first sight, I pushed him away.

I stayed on the floor, my knees drawn into my chest, my heart aching so deeply, I could hardly breathe. The day turned to evening, and the setting sun cast fading light through the balcony and into the chamber. Dinah knocked at the door periodically, but I turned her away. "Leave me be."

The celebratory feast for Abner and his men was tonight. I could hear the merriment, music, and loud conversation echo from the main courtyard. And David planned another feast on the morrow. One for me. But what was there to celebrate?

The setting sun eventually gave way to nightfall. No lanterns were lit in the room, but I welcomed the darkness.

A soft knocking startled me awake. I sat up, realizing I must have fallen asleep still on the floor by the door.

Another soft knock. "Michal?"

I heard him quietly call for me. My heart began to pound.

"Michal, please let me in." His words were barely above a whisper.

No words came out. I moved away from the door but couldn't bring myself to open it. My mind became a litany of arguments. Back and forth.

It is David. Finally. Let him in.

No, he must suffer as you do.

This is the moment you have desired for years.

He does not deserve your love. He turned to other women for comfort.

"Michal. Please." His words softly soothed me. I heard the longing.

Before I could talk myself out of it, I cracked open the door but stayed silent. I just wanted to see him. I peered out through the small opening that I allowed myself and took in the sight of my long, lost love. He had been a man before, but now even more so. He seemed taller and leaner with a strength that radiated off of him. His eyes, those beautiful blue-green eyes, appeared to have been crying.

He reached through the opening and trailed his hand down my face. "I had to see you again."

Every fiber within me awoke at his touch. I tried to keep my guard in place, but when he dropped his hand back to his side, my skin felt cold without his hand on me. I reached for him and placed his hand back against my cheek. It felt warm and safe. And I couldn't keep the wall up. It crumbled at my feet.

"May I please enter? Just to be with you. Please?"

My brain was a muddled mess, and I found myself nodding.

He slipped inside, quietly shut the door, then wrapped his arms around me.

I leaned into him, not wanting to admit how much his presence undid me.

His shoulders shook, as he openly wept. "Michal." He repeated my name over and over.

I gave myself that moment. Not to overthink, but instead, to allow me to be comforted.

Time passed, but it mattered little. I finally felt back where I belonged. In my husband's arms. Eventually, David's sobs subsided, and he relaxed his arms around me. We stayed quiet, not quite letting go. David whispered in my ear, "Go for a walk with me."

"Now? It is still hours before dawn."

"That never stopped us before."

Even in the dark, the moon illuminated David's features, and his eyes twinkled in mischief. There was no helping myself. I whispered, "Yes."

He led me out of the chamber and down a set of hallways and stairs. I felt disoriented. Without him guiding us, it would have been difficult to find my way back to my chambers.

Neither of us spoke. I followed him through the compound and out onto an expansive veranda. He kept walking, pulling me with him, down more stairs, and through paths outside of the lit walkways. Eventually, we made our way to his stables. He paused and pointed at one. "This one is yours."

"What do you mean? Is my horse in there?"

"The entire stable is yours. Most of the stalls are empty, waiting to be filled. I did not want to make any decision about a horse for you without your consent, but…" He hesitated briefly. "Well, in this one instance. Come with me."

His hand still in mine, we walked into the stable and up to a stall. A gorgeous black horse poked its nose out of the opening and started nuzzling David.

"Hello there, Princess. I brought my wife to meet you." He glanced over at me. "This is Princess. She is beautiful and regal and gentle, and I knew you two would love each other."

I felt overwhelmed by so many things, but it all melted away when I placed my hand on her mane. "Hello," I said breathlessly.

She watched me curiously, but when David handed me a carrot, and I fed it to her, she nuzzled me sweetly. "We should get along fine," I said, running my hand down her neck. "I am a princess too."

"You are not just a princess." David placed his hand on mine. "You are my queen."

I stopped and stared at his hand over mine. His touch still created butterflies in my stomach. It was hard to think straight with him so close. Not knowing what to do or say, I slipped my hand from under his and let it rest at my side.

"Do you like her?" he asked.

"Of course. I cannot wait to ride her. I do have two other horses. At Paltiel's."

And there it was. Both of us stood facing each other, neither moving. Just his name affected the atmosphere.

"Michal—"

"It is best we head back to my chambers. I am suddenly exhausted."

He reached for me. "I have something to say. Please, just listen. I need you to hear this."

"There is nothing to say." All the hurt began to bubble up to the surface. I pressed my hand to my heart as if that would stop its ache.

"Yes, there is. There is so much to say."

"You have always been the one in love with words, not me."

"Then simply listen."

"Not now. I need to get back."

David turned me to face him completely. "I am sorry. Please forgive me, Michal. For everything."

I swallowed hard. It was once again becoming difficult to hide my anguish. Tears trickled down my face, and I silently cursed them.

"I let you down in the worst possible way. I was not there for you. I can give you all of my excuses. I kept waiting for something to happen. For Yahweh to bring us together. I told myself I was protecting you, but none of that matters. I let you down. I cannot even begin to imagine how horrible it must have been for you to hear news of me..." David paused and dropped his gaze.

My insides shook as I thought of the other women. "Please, release me. I cannot bear to talk of this right now."

"I only desired to apologize. Without anyone else around. With you, I am still simply David."

The question repeated itself over and over, and I simply blurted, "Why?"

David kept his gaze at my feet.

I continued, "I have asked myself that question for over eight years. Why has he not come for me? Why am I still here at another man's house? Why did he get married again? Why did he forget about me? Why was I not enough?"

He leveled his gaze at me. "Let me answer these questions. I did not come for you at first because Saul had men surrounding Gallim. My men did not want to jeopardize lives when we foolishly thought that Saul's anger would eventually fizzle out. But the days turned to weeks turned to years, and Saul continually pushed us further and further away from Israel's border. Tribesmen were confused as to where and to who their loyalty should lie. We were often betrayed by our own Hebrew brethren and would get word that Saul was in pursuit and right at our heels. Remember the deaths of the priests because Doeg saw me there?"

"Yes, I remember. They were innocent."

"They died because they helped me. I ran away from all my men too. I went and hid amongst the Philistines. I was so scared. I did not want anyone else to die because of me. If Saul could touch God's holy men, what of those close to me?"

I imagined David in Gath, hiding among our enemies. All alone. And I began to understand the torture my father put him through. "It sounds horrible," I admitted.

"I cannot explain how unsettling all of that was."

"Who found you?"

"My men searched for me in numerous locations. Jashobeam

and Eleazar are the two who found me and rescued me from Gath."

"It is good that the Philistines did not find you there. You would not be standing here today."

"They did find me. Thank Yahweh, I survived."

"How did you survive by yourself?"

"I killed the innkeeper. He knew who I was almost immediately. I hid him, hoping to buy time. I ended up being found out by his comrades, and I had to act like a delusional crazy man. They threw me out of their city's walls to die among the diseased. It was the lowest point of my life. Well, that and when Jonathan told me that Saul had given my wife to another man. Those were low moments indeed."

I contemplated the new information. David alone in Gath? David alone among the diseased? And had he felt betrayed when he heard I was with Paltiel? "You must have been lonely and hurt."

"Yes. I do not like to think about it. It brings back those feelings of isolation and pain."

"Is that why you married another woman?" My words sounded bitter even to my ears, but I had to know the answer.

"The further away we became, the more I lost hope that I would soon be reunited with you. But no, I had no thoughts of marrying again. I already had a wife."

"So, what happened?" I tried not to raise my voice, but I was unsuccessful. "Something must have happened that pushed you into betraying me and our marriage bed."

David studied me, a deep frown on his face.

"I am trying to understand. I upheld our vows, so I do not understand how my husband could step over our vows to do such a thing."

"The answer is not so simple."

"Is it not?"

"My men were starving. Our rations were meager. My men were relentless in securing resources for us. The easiest way to do that was to secure unions with prosperous families who supported the giant slayer. Both marriages to Ahinoam and Abigail came about out of necessity. We gained resources from the unions, and those resources helped us live to fight another day."

"The only answer that I could come up with is that you chose to live life without me."

"Running for all those years was not a choice." David now closed his eyes and grimaced as if the memory itself caused pain. "I even had to resort to working with King Achish and the Philistines. We became their mercenaries. We did horrible things."

"I heard. I could not believe it."

"We had nowhere else to run." David opened his eyes and stepped closer. "The only thing that kept me going was Yahweh's promise to me that I would one day become king...and you. And that is the truth. I tried so hard to be kingly. I tried to protect my men. I tried to make sure they had food and basic provisions. Thoughts of being reunited with you kept me alive in so many ways, but it was also torture because I did not know if it would ever happen."

"I want to believe you," I said. "But I cannot escape the hurt. When I saw you at Samuel's funeral, I—"

"I remember the hurt on your countenance. It broke me."

"You ripped my heart out, David."

"I sent you a message. I tried to explain."

"I know. That is why I came to you in the forest. I would have gone with you then."

"If I could go back to that moment, I would have picked you up off that horse and taken you. I have thought about it many times."

"Why didn't you?" I cried.

"Too much was happening. Saul was on the move. And suddenly you were there, like an aberration from the past. I was frozen. All I could think about was whether I could protect you and my men at the same time."

Now I closed my eyes and envisioned the memory. Jonathan helped me sneak out during the night to see David. But our meeting was short-lived because my father had decided to use Samuel's death as a means to kill David. "He ruined everything."

"We cannot let anything else come between us."

"But so much already has!" I opened my eyes to see David's crestfallen expression. "I believe you, David. I do not think you fell out of love with me, and I cannot imagine how difficult it was being on the run from my lunatic father. But you made decisions that have impacted us. There are women in the compound right now who are married to *my* husband. I cannot simply forget about that."

"I do not want them! I want you."

"And how do they feel about being nothing more than business transactions?"

"I treat them with kindness. They do not love me either. It is the custom of our people. Kings need to protect their legacies through large families."

"That does not make it right."

David took a breath. "Then let us start fresh from here. I am king of Judah, and I have even more responsibilities now. That does not change how I feel toward you. I am yours, Michal. If you want time, then I will give you time. Just please, please forgive me. I acknowledge that my actions have hurt you."

I wanted to be angry. Everything seemed so complicated, but how could I blame David for the entire mess? He had been as much a pawn in my father's mad game as any of us. Yet, I still had so much hurt. "I have a lot going through my head," I admitted.

David placed his hand on my face, and like a reflex, I leaned into it.

I could no longer fight back the longing within myself to be with him. I had waited years, and now, if only for these precious moments, I made a decision right then to stop fighting the desire. I turned my face slightly and kissed his hand. We held each other's gaze briefly before David brought me to him and kissed me.

For the first time in over eight years, my drowning heart felt like it had finally come up for air.

17

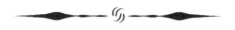

David

Hebron

1011 B.C.

When I opened my eyes and saw Michal sleeping beside me, I nearly wept again. For years, I wondered if being with my wife would ever happen. But here she was. My true love beside me.

Even on the hard stable ground, I had slept well with Michal here. I leaned over and kissed her shoulder, then paused as I heard footsteps approach. Joab's voice was muffled, but it was his. Of course, my men would find me. I moved my cloak to cover her more fully and quickly dressed. Thankfully, the morning air was cool but not cold.

I walked outside the stable doors, hoping not to disturb Michal while she slept. Even though she was as beautiful as I remembered, I also noticed the dark circles under her eyes and the weight loss. She needed to heal, both physically and in matters of the heart, and I was determined to see it happen.

Joab and Abishai were nearing the stable's entrance when I stepped outside. Both of my nephews still held downtrodden features, not just in their countenances, but also in their sagging shoulders. Yet, when they saw me approach, both expressions and stances changed. Their backs straightened, and their countenance turned guarded. "Nephews," I said. "It appears you are still troubled."

"Our brother was murdered. My apologies that we still grieve." Joab's words lashed out, then he pressed his lips together.

"Yes, Asahel was my nephew, as are you. I worry about *you* now."

Abishai defended his brother. "Abner falsely labeled Ishbosheth as king of Israel! We fought for you, as we have always done, as we always will do!"

"I did not ask you to fight that battle. And it was nothing more than a war game between two prideful commanders. If Asahel would have stepped back and followed the command of ending the pursuit, he would still be here. If you would have used some sense and never agreed to participate in such a match, your brother would still be alive! Alas, headstrong brothers made poor decisions."

"So, you do not blame Abner for our brother's death?" Abishai asked in shock. "Someone must pay for his spilled blood."

"As I stated before, I wash my hands of this entire situation. And I order you both to stand down. Hebron is a city of refuge, so if for no other reason, we need to honor our people's sacred traditions. Besides, Abner is a better ally than foe. He is an essential playing piece in bringing all of Israel together under my throne. Now is that why you came out here this morning? Or is there something more pertinent?"

"He requests a meeting." Joab all but spat out the words. "His men found us while we were sorting through the spoils from our attack on a Jebusite band of soldiers. I thought it best I find you before my sword meets his heart. Or theirs. At the moment, I am not feeling too picky."

I reached for my nephew and rested my hand on his shoulder. "Joab," I said. "My heart hurts too for my sister's youngest son. Asahel was special, and I know how difficult his loss is."

"Then let us avenge him. His murderer stands in your chambers.

With one word, I can cut him down."

"No. Vengeance is not the answer, and how will our people react when they discover we killed Abner when he sought refuge? And with Abner on our side, the future of the Hebrew people can once again be unified."

"I did not want to believe it to be true, but I sense that it is." Abishai deepened his frown and turned to Joab. "He met with him already?"

"Yes."

Abishai turned back to me. "And you prepared a meal for him and his men?"

"That is our tradition. Abner has gone to the tribes and spoken highly of me and our kingdom. It is working. To show my appreciation for his efforts, a feast was prepared for him."

"A feast that we were not invited to?" Abishai glanced over at Joab, and they communicated silently between them.

"It is not as it sounds," I explained. "You had just arrived with the troops, laden with spoils from another victory. This simply happened in your absence." When neither answered, I continued, "We need him. And have I not planned a feast for your return from victory?"

Joab shook his head, refusing to listen. "If it was your brother who was killed by that murderer's hand, you would think differently."

"He *was* my brother-in-arms. And I mourn him, but we have to look at what is best for the greater good of the kingdom. Please, trust me, nephew. All of Israel's troops will soon be yours to command, but I need to know that you are of sound mind." I glanced behind me to where Michal still slept. I did not want to leave her alone or unescorted, but I needed to see Abner. "Abishai, stay here and see that the queen is escorted to her chambers. Do not disturb her."

Abishai looked from Joab to me then nodded. He was not one to hold a grudge, so his anger at me would not last long. Joab, however, would stew for a while. Abishai went and stood at the stable doors.

To Joab, I said, "Let us go and greet Abner." I took one last glance at the stable before walking in the direction of the compound.

———◆— ⟨⟩ —◆———

"Abner."

Saul's former commander stood in the center of the compound's entrance, his hand moving to his sword at the sight of Joab. I heard Joab give a low growl.

"We will not have any of that," I warned both of them. "Abner, you are welcome here. Hebron is a city of refuge for our people, and we honor that tradition."

Joab said nothing, but his displeasure rolled off him like dark fog off unsettled waters.

"I brought the princess to you, as you requested. The tribal elders are also impressed with you and feel safer with you than with Ishbosheth." Abner still eyed Joab warily.

"Yes, thank you. And what of Ishbosheth? Is he willing to talk with me?"

"No. Since he removed me from my position, he has several friends as his advisors now. I am not privy to their discussions. However, word from his men is that he refuses to surrender."

"I understand his desire to continue Saul's throne, but I weary of his refusal to talk with me."

"He is fearful. The fear torments him almost as much as it did Saul."

"Of course, he is fearful," Joab interjected with a scoff. "David and his mighty men can and will snap him in half."

"I do not want war, nephew." I gave him a slide glance. "We already know that war takes lives. And no more games with Israel's men from any tribe."

"Yes, and how many of your men were lost in our little skirmish?" Joab was not directing the question at me. "Last number I heard was around 360. We lost barely twenty."

Abner frowned. "And if you would not have followed me and simply accepted my decision to end it, your brother would have listened to you and would still be alive."

Joab stepped closer to Abner until they were almost nose to nose. "You do not speak of my brother, or I will slice your tongue out of your mouth."

"I do not want to quarrel with you."

"Then maybe you should have thought twice before killing Asahel."

"I did think twice. I told him to stand down."

"He does not take orders from you."

"Yes, and that is why he is dead. I had no choice but to defend myself."

Both men stared each other down, both with hands on their swords. I felt the same foreboding from earlier that Joab's unfinished business would eat away at him like a slow-acting poison. Yet, I could not have any part of vengeance. Even though I understood Joab's displeasure, Abner was a needed ally to bring the tribes back under one kingdom. The only solution I could muster was to keep them separated.

"Abner, please continue your talks with the tribal elders. See if some agreement can be reached that does not involve killing Ishbosheth. Report back to me at the next new moon. I will travel with Joab and the troops to assess the cities of Zion and Jerusalem."

"Jerusalem?" Abner's interest seemed piqued. "Saul was always too busy trying to squash the Amalekites and the Philistines to pay them any attention."

"We will keep you updated on the situation, but first, I need to see for myself what it will take to possess it."

Cush approached me, reminding me of my next appointment. "The prophet and priest have arrived at your table, per your orders."

"Thank you." I released Abner, then asked Joab, "Are you going to be all right? You at least see why we need him?"

Joab kept his attention on the floor. "What have you done? He enters into your presence like old friends, and you send him away with a pat on the back."

"That is not what is happening, but even if that is the way of things, then trust me as king to make the best decisions for the good of the kingdom."

"This is perfect for him. Now he can see your plans. He will know when you come and when you go. You have already told him about Jerusalem. Do not put it past him to deceive you."

"I have chosen to make peace with Abner. You should know by now that everything I do is through prayer and through seeking Godly counsel."

Joab lifted his gaze to mine before looking back down. "What I know is that you are king, and you have made a decision. I am sure this will not be the only time we do not see eye-to-eye."

I walked to my nephew and rested my hand on his shoulder. "Then please trust me. Uniting the kingdoms is best for all of us, and Abner is a key player in making that happen."

Joab did not look up, nor did he say a word.

"I am breaking my fast with Abiathar and Nathan. Make sure to stop in to provide a report to them of your findings from your most recent excursion." I left him because there was no more left to say. We disagreed, and ultimately, he needed to follow orders. But the foreboding was still there, and I could not shake it.

Nathan, the prophet, sat across from me with Abiathar, the priest from Nob, beside him. Neither of them touched their food.

"Is the lamb not to your liking?" I asked them. I made eye contact with Abiathar and raised my eyebrows. He and I had a close relationship due to the years of suffering while on the run. Abiathar was the only survivor after Doeg's massacre of the priests and their families. I took him in, and he in turn often interceded on my behalf and on behalf of my men. It was he who helped pacify the men when they wanted to kill me after the Amalekites took our families hostage.

"I will break bread when our guest of honor breaks bread." Abiathar indicated Nathan.

Nathan sat with his arms crossed and his eyes closed. He had been in that same position since first entering the room and taking his seat. Since he arrived on my doorstep last moon cycle, he had kept to himself, either staying in the small dwelling I provided him on the outskirts of the property or praying on his roof. I had tried engaging him in conversation and requested meals with him, but he had politely declined every opportunity, telling me that when God had something to say, then would I hear from him. It was a surprise that he accepted this morning's request for a shared meal.

"Nathan, surely you are hungry. Please, let us thank Yahweh and eat." My stomach grumbled as if affirming my statement.

He opened his eyes and looked from me to Abiathar. "Yes, let us break bread." He said a prayer of thanksgiving and took a bite of the lamb stew. He nodded in approval. "Delicious. To God be praised."

Abiathar and I agreed and then began to eat. The three of us ate the meal, mostly in silence. Nathan had a quiet confidence that was a bit unnerving. He would take a bite, then close his eyes and slowly chew, as if desiring to focus on each morsel.

"I hope you find your accommodations comfortable," I said to them, needing to break the silence. "I am blessed that the elders of Judah have bestowed this property on me."

Nathan opened his eyes to address me. "Yes, thank you. God's provision upon you has blessed me indeed. Though you will not stay here long."

I glanced at Abiathar to see him nodding in agreement. "Let Yahweh order my steps, and I will follow."

Joab entered my chamber, then stood outside of our small circle, waiting to approach. I waved him to me, noting that he still did not meet my gaze.

"Nephew. Share with Nathan and Abiathar the reports of the Jebusite settlement."

"They have refused to meet with us and have insulted our king."

"Let them insult me to my face." To Abiathar, I asked, "Should I go up with my troops? The Jebusite settlement has much to offer."

"You are referring to Jerusalem?" Nathan asked before Abiathar could answer.

"Yes," Abiathar answered for me. "Through prayer, it was revealed to me for David to pursue Jerusalem."

Nathan and Abiathar seemed to measure each other, then Nathan nodded and said, "That is why I am here." To me, he said, "Go with your men to Jerusalem. It is not yours yet, but it will be."

Something within me stirred like burned embers rekindling. "Joab, go and refresh yourself. We will leave at first light following the queen's celebratory feast."

Nathan asked for another helping of stew. "This really is delicious."

Abiathar did the same, and once each of us had another serving of lamb stew, we continued eating and discussing my next steps toward Jerusalem.

18

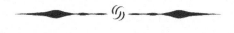

Michal

Hebron

1011 B.C.

I woke to the sun's warmth on my face. I stretched still in a sleepy daze. An insect buzzed at my ear, and I shooed it away. Realization hit me as I remembered the night's events.

David. My husband.

Someone stirred and coughed outside the stable's opened door. It sounded like a man!

I doubted it was David, for why would he be outside the stable doors and not with me, so I hastily assembled myself. Stepping outside into the sunlight, I saw one of David's men standing watch.

He was young with similar eye color to David's. Coughing again, he bowed. "Queen Michal, I am to escort you to your chambers."

"You know who I am, but I do not know who you are."

"I am Abishai, King David's nephew."

"Ah, yes, I see the family resemblance. Are you the eldest nephew who commands his troops?"

"That would be my older brother, Joab. He is with the king as we speak." He motioned for me to begin walking. "After you, my queen."

Hearing him refer to me as queen felt strange, especially after being so far removed from palace life for nearly ten years. "Please, call me Michal."

The young man blushed. "The king will not allow it. You are second to no one here, other than the king himself."

Now I found myself blushing.

We hurried along, but the grounds were expansive. "I did not realize we walked so far last night."

"I'm sure the king made a better companion than I."

We stepped into a small orchard with a direct path to the compound. "This looks vaguely familiar."

"We can continue on this path, or if you would prefer, we can shorten the distance by cutting through these fruit trees."

"I will follow your lead."

Abishai grinned, and I could see the boyishness in him yet. He led me through one set of trees, and then another. We turned onto a closer path when I nearly plowed into a young woman.

"Queen!" Abishai called just as I nearly collided with her.

"Watch yourself!" the young lady demanded, stepping away from me and brushing off her garments.

I was so struck by her beauty and her entourage that I had yet to process her rebuke.

"Do not address the queen in such a way," Abishai said, although his voice was more of a plea than a demand.

The girl eyed me suspiciously. I became very aware of my tousled appearance. Still, I lifted my head high and looked down my nose at her.

"The queen?" She turned to the young women around her, and they shared a look among themselves. "I must admit, you are not at all what I had pictured in my head."

I wanted to say something withering, but her beauty and elegance seemed to hold my tongue down with a heavy rock.

"I am Maacah, daughter of Talmai, and King David's newest bride." She smirked in my direction. "Is that straw in your hair?"

I reached up and touched my head, pulling the straw out. Embarrassment heated my cheeks. *Say something. Do not let her have the upper hand.* "Yes, it is straw," I said, finding my voice. "Forgive my appearance. I was with the king last night. Now, if you will excuse me, my servant is waiting for me."

Without so much as a backward glance, I walked the path toward the compound with my shoulders back and my head high. Thankfully, she could not see the war within me.

———————

Dinah was in my chambers, helping other servants arrange my furniture.

"Dinah!" I rushed in and hugged her neck. "You have arrived!"

"It was merely a day."

"A day is too long to be apart."

Dinah smiled and blushed at the kind words. Then, she studied me with a twinkle in her eye. "So, I take it you are well? I heard that you left in the middle of the night with the king."

Now it was I who blushed. "It is as well as it could be given the circumstances." Changing the subject, I asked, "How is my mother? And Rizpah? And others?"

"There were high emotions through the evening and into the night. I was busy assembling your belongings, but I do know that your mother left for the palace before I left to come here."

"And Rizpah?"

Dinah whispered, "Other servants told me that she comforted Paltiel last night."

My eyes widened in surprise.

"She is an opportunist, so this makes sense. With Laia gone, and Paltiel mourning his loss with you, Rizpah must have seen it as a perfect opportunity."

I shook my head. "If Ishbosheth hears of this, it will not go well for her. Then again, she is trying to make a home for herself. She has been discarded, so if she and Paltiel can find comfort in each other, then I see no need to tell anyone."

"Agreed."

"Since you are here, I need to clean up."

"I will prepare the bath water." Dinah reached up and pulled a long stem of grass from my hair.

"Yes, yes," I shooed her hand away. "It was an interesting night. I will tell you about it once we have some privacy." I saw Raja, from Paltiel's house, with a stack of linens. "Raja? What is she doing here?"

"She was taken from Paltiel's, along with a few others."

"We must send her back. I do not wish to cause more disturbance to him and his household."

"He permitted it. He knows she has a good rapport with the children."

"She does."

"Have you asked David yet to bring them here?"

"We did not get a chance to discuss them. I will bring it up this evening. They need somewhere to go."

"Paltiel sent them to Adriel, informing him to await word from David."

I frowned. Adriel preferred distance when it came to his sons.

While bathing, I told Dinah about the princess I ran into on the way to my chambers.

"Do not give that girl one more thought." Dinah massaged the oil onto my upper arm. With my bath complete, Dinah took extended time on my beauty ritual. And I let her.

"She is my competition. Of course, I must think about her. If for no other reason than to make sure she is nothing more to David than a business transaction." I paused, thinking about the encounter. "She is beautiful, Dinah, with plumpness in all the right places. Look at me. I am skin and bones. Nothing more than a walking skeleton."

"You are the one that the king loves. You are his queen, and the daughter of the late king."

"So, you do not refute my words about my appearance."

"No, I do not. You have been grieving, which has affected your appearance somewhat, but you are already pushing past the pain. Continue eating and find things to do that bring you happiness. Your appearance already has more of a glow since you began your daily rides with Eglah."

"Yes, I do miss her. Has she been delivered yet?"

"Not that I have heard, but I will continue to inquire."

"David gifted me a majestic black horse. He named her, Princess."

"Hopefully she gets along with Eglah." The two of us shared a smile. Eglah had the sweetest disposition, and she was loyal, but she could also be a bit jealous if she ever caught me doting on another beast.

"David is to dine with me tonight."

"Good, and you look lovely." Dinah stepped back and scrutinized me. "Just make sure to eat something."

"Yes, yes." I rolled my eyes and threw a small pillow at her.

Someone knocked at the door. A deep voice called out, "King David requests to visit the queen."

"It is only afternoon. Should I tell him you are still in preparations to see him?"

"No, it is fine. With your help, I am ready now. Please, allow him inside."

Dinah opened the door without making eye contact. Instead, she bowed low.

David entered, looking freshly bathed. I fully took in the sight of him. With his height, stature, and the evident confidence that emanated from him, he looked every bit a king. And my insides turned to a thousand butterflies, my breath catching. His gaze locked with mine momentarily before grabbing Dinah and embracing her. "Dinah! It is good to see you, old friend."

Dinah froze, her eyes widening. I laughed. "It has been too long, David. No one, not even I, has greeted her in such a fashion. You have surely seized her heart."

"There, there," he said, setting her down and patting her shoulder. "My apologies for startling you, but it has been too long." He kissed her cheek before heading to me. She stared after him, bringing her hand to where he just kissed. To me, he said, "My queen," and then leaning down, he kissed me slowly.

"Let me know if you need anything," Dinah said. I heard the door shut behind her.

David paused long enough to say, "I came to tell you something, but now I am quite distracted."

I smiled. "Well, let me distract you further."

19

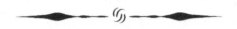

David

Hebron

1011 B.C.

"How did she take the news?" Eleazar waited for me outside the grounds where he and Joab had called the men to meet.

"It did not come up."

"So, you are leaving after her celebration feast, but she does not know?"

"I will find a way to tell her beforehand."

"Did you not just come from her chambers?" Abishai asked, overhearing the conversation. He looked from me to Eleazar, then nodded in understanding. "Oh."

Uriah slapped Abishai's back. "You are young, but not that young."

The men laughed.

"Where is Joab? I would like to begin."

"He is detained with the elders of Judah. They requested a meeting with the commander of the troops."

"He did not tell me this," I said. "What do they require of him?"

Abishai stumbled over his words before simply saying, "I am not entirely sure, uncle, because he told me after ordering me to meet with you and the troops here. He said he will return as soon as the meeting is over."

I glanced around at the men. Those around me seemed to look anywhere but at me. "If there is something that needs to be said, say it already."

It was uncomfortably quiet. Before I could open my mouth to demand answers, Joab approached us. "My apologies, uncle, for my late arrival. I had to deliver a message to the Judean elders about a meeting. I sent word that I will come to them once we are finished here."

"Why did you not bring this up earlier in conversation?"

"I received the invitation this afternoon. You were otherwise engaged."

A few of the men snickered.

I needed to tread carefully. *You do not require Joab to tell you of his goings. Do not require it now. He will be insulted.* But I did not want these men to question my authority or to make a joke of my decisions, even if those decisions involved the women in my life. Instead of saying anything directly to them, I stepped up onto the wooden platform and greeted the men in the name of the Lord. Over a hundred stood around me, waiting to hear their orders. These men oversaw thousands upon thousands of troops who pledged their loyalty to me and my kingdom. "We are grateful to our elders and brothers in Judah for offering a place of refuge and a central location to our kingdom."

"Long live the king!" The men shouted.

"In merely a year, we have outnumbered what this compound can successfully sustain."

The men cheered. Bigger numbers meant more power.

Motioning for them to quiet down, I continued, "We continue to investigate other areas as a refuge for our kingdom."

Someone started chanting, but I could not make out what it was. I leaned over to Jashobeam. "Do you catch what is being chanted?"

He shook his head, but the chant caught, and soon the men

chanted together, "A city for David! A city for David!"

Jashobeam answered, "Are they saying 'City of David,' or 'City for David?'"

I quieted them down again. "We will not stop until we find *our* city!" I indicated all of us, and the men answered favorably.

After assigning posts and rations for those to begin traveling, I stepped down and, to my inner circle, said, "The City of David. I like it."

Uriah cheered and slapped everyone's back, including mine. "Let us go and find this city."

I turned to Joab and raised my eyebrows. "Go ahead and tell them, Joab." When the men turned their attentions to him, I continued, "Tell them about Jerusalem."

Cush waited for me at the compound and followed me as I continued in the direction of my chambers. Michal's feast began this evening, and I already looked forward to the three-day event. So much so that I missed what Cush was saying. "Repeat that."

"The princess requests a meeting. She says it is of utmost importance."

"You mean the queen? Please refer to her as Queen Michal from henceforth."

"Yes, your grace. I mean, no, your grace. I do not refer to the queen. I refer to the princess...Maacah. She has ordered all servants to not use her name, but to refer to her as princess."

I stopped. "She did what?" Cush opened his mouth to answer, but I put up my hand. "Never mind. I will deal with her later. Today and tomorrow and the day after that are for Queen Michal."

"Yes, my king. I will relay the message."

"Is there anything else?"

"Your brother has returned from Bethlehem."

"Shammah! Yes, and where is he?"

"He is resting with his family, but he plans to be at the feast. He has also brought with him another brother, Eliab."

I remembered when my relationship with my oldest brother, Eliab, was strained. But time changes things and heals wounds. "This is good news indeed. Make sure to extend the invitation to him and his family as well."

"Consider it done."

"Make sure to assemble the household in rank and order. I will escort the queen myself to greet each member." We stopped in front of my chambers. "Thank you, Cush, for your loyalty and hard work. I am blessed to have you."

Cush bowed low, but I could see him suppress a smile. "The honor is mine. Long live King David."

I hurriedly prepared myself, even allowing the maidservants to help assemble my attire. With all of the meetings and details of the day completed, it was now time to focus on the one person who meant the most to me. I felt nervous with anticipation at showing my queen off to my world. Many of the people she would meet tonight she had yet to meet. The only introductions that worried me were with my other wives. I did not worry about Ahinoam and Abigail, but the new one was not used to being second to anyone else. Still, she would have to grow accustomed to Michal being my queen. As I made my way to Michal's chambers, I silently prayed that God would bless the evening.

Dinah opened the door and bowed low again.

"Stop that. It is only I, the same David from before."

She still did not look at me.

"She is not used to seeing you, is all." Michal opened the door wider. I saw several servants moving about the room, but my attention quickly focused on Michal. The deep purple of her gown with gold stars embroidered throughout brought out the copper of her skin. She was heavily adorned with gold and silver bangles up both arms and stars in her ears, but her neck held one necklace. The one I had given her many moons ago. She saw me looking at it, and said, "I promised I would never it off, and I never have."

"I now have one more gift for you." I delicately took the dainty crown we had been gifted from the Moabites and placed it atop her dark hair, now twisted in intricate braids at the base of her neck. "We discussed having an official ceremony crowning you queen, but I wanted this moment to be special. Between you and me."

"I prefer private moments with you. If I had my way, I would not step anywhere near this celebratory feast."

"You know more than anyone here that it shows your value to the king. You are second to no one else." I kissed her, praying she believed my words. Even though we had spent time together, there was something different between us. There was a sadness in her that had not been there before. *You caused it.* The nagging thought came from out of nowhere. I shook it off. "Are you ready, my queen?" I offered my arm and began walking Michal to the central courtyard.

20

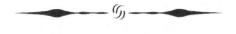

Michal

Hebron

1011 B.C.

I swallowed hard, placing my available hand on my chest to calm the pounding of my anxious heart. I desired to be with David, but that did not stop the thoughts of running far from this celebration and hiding until it was over.

Part of it came from nerves, but the other part of my displeasure came from the dark thoughts that would not leave me alone. They whispered my deepest fears and were relentless.

I was raised in a palace. I was the king's daughter. More importantly, I was the queen's daughter. Not the daughter of a lesser wife or concubine. I had been at numerous feasts in honor of the queen. On one particular occasion, father had thrown a lavish celebration for mother after a victory over the Amalekites. Father boasted loudly at the dinner how he watched in horror at how they treated their women and children. With pride, he showcased Mother and then each of us. Everyone cheered, but when the night was over, he left us in Mother's care while he visited Rizpah. I remembered her tears vividly and my confusion at how Father could say such words of respect, only to seek the arms of someone else.

157

"Michal?"

My thoughts paused long enough to see David had stopped us and now watched me with an arched eyebrow. "Yes?"

"Are you all right? I have asked you about your horses three times, and you have failed to answer."

"The horses? Which ones?" I felt discombobulated. I glanced around these foreign walls and suddenly missed Paltiel's home and vineyards it nearly took my breath away.

David took both my hands and turned me to face him. "Michal, breathe. You are with me now. You will never be taken from me again."

I closed my eyes as the thoughts tore through me.

Lies! He lies!

Leave him before it is too late.

The same thing that happened to Mother will happen to you.

What are you waiting for? Demand to leave at once!

David squeezed my hands, and I felt his lips brush the backs of them. "Talk to me. We could always talk to each other."

"I am not as ready for this as I thought I was," I said feebly. "Being alone with you is one thing. I do not desire the pomp and circumstance that comes with this title."

"You do not wish to be celebrated?"

"What have I accomplished that deserves to be celebrated? Let your subjects celebrate you."

David blinked in surprise. "But you are a part of me. We are one. The world needs to know who reigns by my side. And that starts first with our kingdom. Come, I promise I will be at your side, and I will not leave it."

David ushered me down a long hall. "This compound does not have a banquet hall per se. But the courtyard will be perfect. It is a clear night. I thought after the celebration, we could explore the rooftop. I sleep up there many nights."

I pushed away the anxiety long enough to smile at him. "You have always preferred open skies to enclosed chambers."

"Always. Many refer to me as the *shepherd king*. They may mean it as an insult, but I like the coinage. It is who I am."

We stepped into the central courtyard, and every inhabitant of the House of David, along with first commanders, and upper-tiered servants lined the walls in rows. But my attention immediately zoned in on the line of women. It was a small line. There were only three of prominence that I noticed. Two of them had children. The third in line was the princess I plowed into earlier. "I cannot...I am not ready..." I tried to pull my arm away from David, but he held it in place. His strength overpowered my weak attempt.

"Michal, please. Do this for me. I need my kingdom to see you as a strong and capable queen."

"I do not feel strong nor capable."

David paused briefly and whispered in my ear. "You are the daughter of Saul and Ahinoam, sister of Jonathan, Abinadab, Melchishua, Ishbosheth, and Merab. You are married to and preferred by the giant-slayer. Lift your chin and show them who you are."

I thought of my family. I could see Merab entering the room, her head high and making each person lower their gaze in submission. I could see her looking down on the other women, scorn and contempt upon her countenance. Oh yes, Merab would make an entrance.

Do not do this for David, the voice hissed. *Do this for yourself. Do this for the House of Saul.*

As we greeted the men, my confidence built. Many I remembered, and they were all pleased to have me reunited with David.

"He was a lost puppy without you," Uriah teased.

Benaiah agreed. "Too true. Maybe now that you have arrived, he will stop the melancholy writings and choose more light-hearted themes."

"Never," David jested. To me, he said, "You can be sure I will be writing more melodies of love and beauty. Now that my muse has returned."

By the time we reached the women and children, the smile had returned to my face. David must have missed me for his men to tell me tales of my forlorn husband. Until we reached the young princess.

"Maacah, this is Queen Michal of Judah and soon of Israel. Please greet your queen."

Maacah lowered her gaze but did not bow. "We met earlier, but it is an honor. Forgive me for not bowing, I find my knees are weak with this bout of sickness that has come upon me recently."

It was a challenge to my power, but David and she waited for my response. "I am glad to see that your recent sickness has not hurt your coloring, which looks fresh and healthy."

The princess said nothing, and David acted uncomfortable. "My king," she finally said, directing her statement to David, "I requested a meeting with you earlier because I have happy news to share with you." She rested her one hand upon her lower abdomen.

"Now is *not* the time," David said sharply, stepping to his next wife.

With David moving on, the princess risked eye contact with me. A smile played on her lips. I looked down to where her hand still rested on a slightly protruding belly, and I could not move.

This girl...this insolent girl...is carrying David's seed.

"Pay her no mind," David whispered. "I will handle it. I promise."

"I think you have already done enough with her. Would you not agree?" I gave him my coldest glare. "Now excuse me while I meet the other women who bore your seed."

The next woman bowed low; her eyes downcast. A pale, little boy beside her followed his mother's directive and did the same. "It is an honor to meet the queen," she said. "I am Abigail, and this is my son, Daniel."

Daniel had already tired of bowing and now hugged David's leg. "Can I ride your back?"

I watched David smile at the boy and pat him on the head. "Another time, my son."

My son? My son?

I wanted to run. Far. But David had placed his hand on my elbow. He must have sensed my change of demeanor because his grip was iron. "Almost done with the most difficult part," he said, as we approached the last woman and her son.

She too bowed low and stated her reverence. The boy, however, did not. He stared at me and then gave a curious look to David. He resembled David so much that all I could do was stare. "Papa, why are we bowing?"

"Amnon," the young lady admonished. "Hold your tongue."

"It is all right," David said to both of them. "We have never had a true royal procession. We will work on getting it right next time." He winked at the boy and ruffled his hair.

By the time we finished greeting the servants and found our way to the front of the courtyard, I could barely see. David led me, or I would have collapsed right there.

He held up his goblet and everyone did the same. "Long live the queen!"

"Long live the queen!" everyone shouted in return.

But I was not desiring long life. What I desired was for the floor to open up and swallow me whole. Enduring that would be better than this torture.

I could not get out of the celebration fast enough. David finally released me when they brought out the dancers. The girls sashayed in front of us, several of them eyeing the men seductively.

He was too busy enjoying himself to realize the celebration was about me, and he waved me away after I requested a reprieve. "Have a good night." He barely glanced in my direction.

Now in my chambers, I allowed Dinah to wash my face. "Please do not say a word."

Thankfully, she obliged. Once finished, I stepped out onto the balcony. I was thankful this compound at least had a small balcony with my chambers. I waited for Dinah to leave for the night before I gave in to the high emotions that burst from inside of me like water breaking free from a dam. I slid to the floor, clung to the railing, and let the dark thoughts of anger and betrayal overtake me.

21

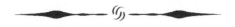

David

Hebron

1011 B.C.

What was I thinking? I took another gulp of the warm wine. I needed to stop, but the evening's celebration had turned into an absolute nightmare. And I reasoned that becoming inebriated would take away the horrible guilt I felt.

"She did not stay long." Benaiah came and stood beside me. My only response was to take another swig of wine. "Does this post need help?" He indicated the pillar I leaned upon.

"No, but I do." I offered him wine, but when he refused, I poured more for myself.

"A good night's rest will help."

"This was a disaster," I slurred the words. "Whose idea was it? I am going to slice through their hearts."

"It was yours. You pushed for a celebration honoring Michal as queen."

"It was not," I said. "I would have never wanted Michal to meet the other women."

"It had to be done. Michal must come to terms with you being king. It will take some getting used to. Give it—"

"Ah, ah." I stopped him by putting my finger on his lips. "If you are going to say, *Give it time,* let me stop you right there. Those words are now forbidden in my kingdom." I lost my balance and fell into him.

"I suggest we discuss this when you have slept off the wine. Come now. I will retrieve servants to get you to bed."

I pushed off of him and moved back to my place in the front of the room. The dancers had worked themselves in a frenzy. Now that the women and children had left the courtyard, the dancers moved with less inhibition. One caught my attention. The same one from the other evening. But too much wine mixed with too much irritation. "She announced her pregnancy. She has gumption, a true princess, but she chose the wrong time and place. She will not bow to her!" I turned to see if Benaiah still listened. "She blamed it on weak knees."

"I am confused as to whom you are referring. Since you did not say queen, I am assuming this is about the princess, Maacah."

"Yes," I seethed. "She ruined tonight. It is her fault that Michal is angry with me."

"She does have an arrogancy about her, but the alliance with her father complicates such matters."

"I know, but she knew what she was doing."

"Of course, she knew. Meeting your two children would have triggered Michal though. This was a difficult evening for her. Your other wives have children, and now, it seems the new wife will have one. Until Michal bares a child, the situation will continue to breed contempt and will widen the gulf of your relationship."

"The gulf? You see it too?"

"Yes. You would be blind not to see how uncomfortable Michal is here."

"Why is she uncomfortable? I am her husband! We are finally together again. But it is as if there is this stone wall protecting her heart, and it will not crack."

"Having your fourth wife pregnant with your child does not help the situation."

I glared at him. "I never wanted to marry another woman! And what was I supposed to do all these years without a wife by my side?"

"I am not blaming you for your decisions. They needed to be made, but your perspective and Michal's perspective differ."

I went to pour more wine, but Benaiah stopped me. I snapped, "Do not do that again. Let me drink away my sorrows."

Eleazar approached. "Why are you yelling at Benaiah?"

"You." I jabbed my finger at Eleazar's shoulder. "You forced me to marry again. It is your fault Michal hates me."

Eleazar and Benaiah exchanged a knowing look between them.

"Do not look at each other like that, like I am not here before you."

"You have had too much to drink," Eleazar said, "and you are making a scene. Come, let the night be over. Sleep will make things right, and then I will hear how I am at fault."

I stumbled again. "I want to see Michal. I need to explain things to her. She needs to understand."

Eleazar walked with me, leaving Benaiah in the courtyard. "Are you sure I cannot change your mind? Michal is probably sleeping. Let her rest. I have found that women need time to calm down."

I swayed in the hall, and he helped me balance. I paused, feeling the room spin in circles. "My head hurts."

"Come, rest is needed. I will have Cush schedule a meeting with Michal first thing in the morning."

"Take me to the roof."

Eleazar must have found help because two servants materialized on either side of me, wrapping my arms around each of their shoulders. "Good night, my king."

"She hates me," I said, as the servants led me to the stairs. "She hates me."

"Excuse me, my king?"

The servants stopped at the sound of Cush's voice.

"Cush?" I asked. "Why are you still awake? You should be resting. Everyone should be resting. I need to be resting."

"There is a young woman, one of the dancers, that informed me of a meeting you requested with her." He handed me my leather bracelet. "She said to give this to you to remind you."

I fuzzily remembered giving the young, tantalizing dancer my bracelet. When did I do that? Why did I do that? I handed the leather bracelet back to Cush. "I am going to bed."

The servants helped me up the stairs. If the servants said anything, I did not hear it. They had my dinner attire off and my night tunic on before I figured out that we were already on the roof. I shooed them away, but they still helped me down onto my mat. I stared at the stars above, the familiar feeling of loneliness descending upon me. I called a remaining servant over to me. Before I could talk myself out of the decision, I said, "Bring me the dancer."

My pounding head and sick stomach woke me long before the early light. I leaned against the roof's ledge, taking in deep breaths, hoping that I rid myself of the last of the sickness. Resting my head in my arms, I prayed, "Forgive me. I know better than to lose myself to the goblet." I paused as if He would respond. I turned to the sound of quiet breathing. The young dancer still slept.

I closed my eyes and looked away. What did I do?

Sometime in the night, I promised her marriage. Why did I promise that?

Because you desired what was not yours.

Through the pounding between my ears, I heard the shuffling of feet from the ground below. I peered down and saw someone walking with a lantern. Nathan!

I moved quickly, then stopped, the queasiness coming back. I forced myself to keep going, my need for a conversation with the prophet superseding any discomfort. I bounded down the steps and ran down the great hall, cold sweat forming. I could feel the sickness rising. *No, no, no, no, no! Not now.*

Several of my men at their posts requested if I needed help, but I waved them away while I kept running. As soon as I was outside, I found the path Nathan had been on and followed it. I called his name, no longer seeing him.

Nausea caught up with me, and I stopped next to a patch of garden to empty the sickness still within me.

"It is not wise to give one's senses over to drunkenness," the voice said beside me.

"Yes," I croaked before giving in to another wave of my stomach's purging. I wiped at my face, took in a shaky breath, and turned to face Nathan. "I saw you out here walking in this early morning, and I hoped to reach you."

"I heard my name being called and turned back around. Are you better now? Are you able to walk with me as I continue my morning prayers?"

I nodded, guilt heating my face. Here was the prophet using the early morning hours to strengthen his relationship with Yahweh, while I was sick with the spirits of the previous evening's festivities. As we walked, Nathan began chanting his prayers in the form of a melody. I listened, allowing my mind to clear and focus on the words.

My Adonai.
High and lifted up.
I bow before you.
Lead me in the steps I should take.
My Adonai.
Holy is your name. Honor is your crown.
Let your glory rest among your people.
Fill us with the spoils of your love and compassion.
My Adonai.

At some point, I followed his cadence and chanted with him, *My*

Adonai.

Around the paths, through the orchards and gardens, beyond the stables, we walked and prayed. Eventually, we stopped at the top of a rolling hill. From this view, we could see the entire compound and surrounding villages. My men's tents littered the landscape, many of whom erected their tents at the base of the Judean mountains.

"Are you not celebrating the queen for the next few days?" Nathan asked.

"It ends tomorrow at sundown. I have a feeling though that it ended last night. I doubt Michal will agree to any more festivities."

"You choose to walk with me than to be with her? Interesting."

"Life has become far more complicated now that I am king. I thought that once I attained the throne life would become simpler and follow a routine. It is not so. At least not yet."

"The path we follow is never over until we are dead. I do not expect you to ever live a simple life." Nathan took in the view, then asked, "What do you see?"

"We have already outgrown this compound."

"Yes. This will not be your home. Soon, the tide will change. But really look. What do you see?"

I scanned the area, the early morning sun now stretching her arms across the landscape. Many were already beginning morning chores, and I could hear the animals near the stables already out to pasture. But this was not to what Nathan referred, so I said the first thought that came to mind, "Blessings."

"Go on."

"I came from nothing. While on the run, we had nothing. We lived in caves. We would have to pack and leave with little warning, sometimes in the night. Here, all I can see are Yahweh's blessings."

"Past. Present. Future. That is what you see. You see your past and the pain and uncertainty that came from never quite having or being enough."

I swallowed the emotion back as his words rang true. "I have often questioned God about my struggle. I do not understand why I had to journey through such trials."

"You have questions about your past. You have questions about your future. Yet, you are distracted here. In your present."

I felt the conviction and nodded in response.

"Your future depends upon this moment. Right now. Yet, you distract yourself with women and wine. Be careful. If you do not control your passions now, you will fall into temptation."

"I do not know what to do," I lamented. "Everything is different. How can I be king and be a husband? How can I be good and kind to my family and stay loyal to my queen?"

"Did you ask Yahweh to pursue any of your wives?"

"Yes. No. I am not sure."

"You did not," he said simply. "And it shows. There will be contention in your house because of it. Innocence will be taken. The sword will rise up. Conflict now resides in your home."

"What of Michal? I earned her. Was that not God's design?"

"Did you earn her or Merab?"

I opened my mouth to defend myself but closed it because I could not. "I was supposed to marry Merab, but I asked Jonathan to talk to the king. Michal was given to me instead. We loved each other. I could see no one else but her. I could not marry Merab and destroy Michal."

"Did you ask Yahweh for guidance? Or did you follow your passions?"

"So, I should not have married the woman I love?"

"Our hearts are fickle. God's heart is not."

"Men's hearts may be fickle, but my heart is not."

"That is interesting. You love her, yet you marry other women."

Anger stirred within me. "I did not have a choice. How else was I to feed my men?"

"Did you ask Yahweh for guidance?"

"Yes! On that, I did. Abiathar and I often prayed together and sought the Lord for direction."

"Rumor is that you offered marriage to Abigail as soon as you heard of Nabal's death. Is that inaccurate?"

"I sought the Lord on what to do with the land and resources that should have been ours. Nabal refused to honor Hebrew tradition. Is that not why God took his life? Marrying Abigail provided the land and all that came with it to us."

"Yes, by threatening Nabal's kinsmen. You used his death to overthrow the region."

"That is not what happened." I shook my head, getting worked up. "We had no choice."

"What did Abiathar say to that?"

"I am not sure. The events happened quickly."

"And Ahinoam. How did you end up marrying her? She came before Abigail, did she not?"

"My men thought I needed a wife. Not only for resources but to begin my lineage. They pushed me into the marriage contract."

"Did you not already have a wife?"

"Yes, but we were estranged. Michal was already with another man."

"Ah yes, by protecting you, she faced her father's wrath."

"Enough!" I erupted. "I did not come out here so that my sins may be laid out before me! I am aware of my transgressions."

"So then, for what reasons did you pursue me?"

"I wanted to know what to do about..." I paused, embarrassment burning my face.

Nathan rested his hand on my arm. "Past. Present. Future. My king, do not become distracted. Stay focused on your future. The hand of the Almighty is still on your life, but let this be a lesson that every decision, no matter how small, will reap a harvest of consequences."

I thought of my rash decision last night, and the ramifications to come from that decision. What would Michal do when she found out that after she left the celebration, I became drunk and promised marriage to a dancer? I tried to even remember the name of the young woman. I covered my face in shame. "It is my fault," I confessed. "My past decisions have affected my present and my future. I am guilty."

"My Adonai is faithful and forgiving. Now, go and focus on the path set before you by the Almighty Himself."

"Yes," I said. "You are right." Then I thought of my most recent past decision and sighed. "But first I must clean up the mess I just made."

22

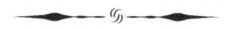

Michal

Ashtoreth Temple

1011 B.C.

I stepped into the Ashtoreth temple and took in the incense that fragranced the small shrine. I hoped the messenger had been successful in giving my request to Mother. I needed to see her, and due to the volatileness of the two kingdoms, I could not risk going back to my father's palace without an invitation.

Approaching the Ashtoreth pole erected at the center of the room, I stared at the face of the goddess for some time. I sank to the floor, the exhaustion from my night of travels catching up to me. I dreamt of vineyards and horses, of Merab and my brothers. I ran after them, desiring to wrap my arms around each one. "Merab! Jonathan!"

Merab turned to me, cocking her head peculiarly to the side. The closer I became, the more she shifted into a creature that resembled more snake than human.

"Michal."

I awoke with a start. Mother knelt beside me. "Mother," I said in relief, hugging her desperately.

"What is this about? Are you in danger?"

But I could not speak. Instead, I clung to her. She wrapped her arms around me, and for some time, we did not speak.

"Talk to me," she finally said, wiping my sweaty hair from my face. "You have seen better days."

"Yes, I have." I swallowed the lump in my throat.

"Are you in danger?" she repeated.

I shook my head. "No, I sought you out because I need advice."

"Why meet here?"

"Because now that I am at the House of David, I must receive an invitation to enter the House of Saul."

"As long as I am alive, you have a standing invitation."

"Can you make that decision? Ishbosheth is not happy with me."

Mother waved her hand like shooing a fly. "I will handle my son. Besides, that was several moons ago, and he is too busy figuring out how to rule Israel without Abner by his side." She stood and gave me her arm to assist me. "Come. The gardens here are beautiful. Follow me."

I took her arm and let her help me stand. I pushed back my hair and tried to tame it, realizing I still wore the same attire from last night's feast. "I left in a hurry late last night."

"How did you leave without getting noticed?"

"The festivities went well into the night. I made it to the stables before anyone noticed me. Then, I waited for the stable manager to be occupied elsewhere before mounting Princess and leaving. I took a risk because I had yet to ride Princess, but she is magnificent, and we have already bonded. Oh, do not tell Eglah. She can be jealous."

"Who? What are you talking about?"

"My horses. Princess and Eglah. Although, Eglah has yet to arrive at the compound."

"Why would I ever talk to a beast? You must be deliriously tired because you are making no sense. Come, it could be the incense too. It is often laced with mind-altering herbs."

I followed Mother to the back of the temple. Several priestesses, who I did not notice before, knelt in a circle, incense burning in the midst of them, while they murmured a chant. Goose bumps shot up my arms as I thought of my dream.

Once outside, the fresh air awakened my senses. I took in a breath, realizing the sun already set to the west. "How long did I wait?"

"As soon as I received the message, I left, but it is nearly a full day's travel to get here."

I wondered if David was looking for me. For a moment, I questioned my decision to not tell anyone. But the worry did not last long. *Let him worry for once about you,* the voice whispered in my head.

"Mother, do you ever...hear voices? In your mind?"

Mother stopped walking and searched my face. "Why? Is that happening to you?" When I did not answer immediately, she said, "Your father heard voices. You know that."

"But have you?"

"There have been times when I am in my trances that I open myself up to the voices that try to take over. But that is rare. I do not prefer it." She gave me a peculiar look. "But I control what comes into my mind. Your father seemed to lack that control. They seemed to possess him at times. Especially when...well, never mind about that."

"Tell me," I pleaded.

"Especially when it came to David. Once the jealousy and rage took over, it was as if he had no control over the madness."

I covered my mouth, trying to mask the fright. "I am not mad though. I have not lost all my senses."

"What makes you hear them? Is there some type of warning?"

"I hear them when I am angry or upset."

"Can you try to prevent becoming angry?"

"Sometimes, I cannot help it. Mother, you were right. Marrying David is not what I thought it would be. He has other wives, and now, I have met them. They have already born children to him! Even the newest bride carries his seed within her. And when I think about it, it is like the anger and betrayal and hurt…it has a mind of its own!"

Mother's expression softened. "Oh Michal, I did not want this for you."

"Does it get any better?" I whispered as the tears threatened.

"No. Not unless you stop caring. I had a difficult time because I never stopped loving your father. Some women learn to let go of earlier romantic feelings and live comfortably raising the man's child."

"And if I have no children?"

Mother reached out and touched the vile that still hung around my neck. "Drink this right before you lie with him."

"I do not know if I will ever do that again." I closed my eyes and thought of that princess and the child growing in her womb. "It is unbearable to share him with anyone else. I want to punish him for it!"

"Which only pushes him into the arms of another woman. I tried punishing your father, and in turn, I lost him to Rizpah. If David cannot have you, he will have another, and if sharing him is difficult, try living in a home where your husband *prefers* someone else."

I shook my head. "Then why would he not leave me at Paltiel's? Why not leave me where I have some semblance of a life?"

"Power. Pride. Oh, he probably has some affection for you still. And he made a promise to come back, did he not? That is one thing about the glorified shepherd, he tries to choose the honorable path."

"I do not see what is honorable with multiple wives."

"Pray nothing happens to Ishbosheth. If he dies, David will take everything, and that includes the concubines, of which your father had many."

"Then I wish he would let me go. I wish he would have never come for me. I had made my decision, and now, I realize what a blessing Paltiel and his vineyard were. Oh, I have been so foolish."

"You had years to choose him! For years, we hoped you would

come to your senses and see that comfort and ease may not make your heart beat with wild passion and abandonment, but there is beauty to life if you find contentment in the quiet."

"It is easy to say I desired passion over comfort, but that is not entirely true. It was like a part of me was severed. I did not know what to do with the pain. And David promised to come for me. What was I to do but take him at his word?"

"At the very end, you finally surrendered to the idea of building a life there, but your heart has always belonged to David. Now that you have David, you are realizing that it is not what you wished for."

"I want what we had! Before father ripped us apart!"

Mother took my hands in hers. "Michal, you are living in a dream if you think that staying with David all these years would have prevented him from marrying again. He is a powerful man with lofty ambitions."

"You do not understand the love we shared. We would have built a life together."

"Your father and I loved each other for a time. We were not separated as you and David were, yet your father's love for me waned. Most men are motivated by their lusts. They may tame their urges for a time, but not for long."

"Well, we will never know, will we?" I asked sarcastically. "Because we were never given that chance."

"Your life with David filled with wedded bliss and romance is in the past. You now have a new life with him that will fill your future days. How you spend it is up to you. But Michal, he is not going to discard the other women. If for no other reason than Hebrew tradition forbids it. Those women are in his life, and knowing David, he will do the honorable thing and provide for them, which includes providing each of them heirs."

I grimaced.

Mother and I walked the gardens, and I relived many of our past conversations. "I thought you were so harsh," I murmured,

ꯇꯦꯛꯁ-

recalling her words on the day of my wedding.

"I can be harsh, but it was only out of the need to protect you from this cruel world. You and Merab never seemed to understand that."

"You desired to protect your reputation too," I said. "You and father both conspired against me and David. I have not forgotten that."

"I do not deny it. David was beneath you. It was only a matter of time before he would succumb to his base desires, which in turn would hurt my daughter. Yes, Paltiel initially blackmailed me, but when I viewed his land and saw all that he promised, I thought a quiet life of wealth would lead to some peace." She paused, then continued, "I do admit that locking you in your chambers was too much. If anything, your anger toward me pushed you even more toward David."

"What a cruel twist of fate. My mother was right, and I was wrong."

"Maybe you will listen to me now. My fertility aided in our relationship for years." Mother reached out and touched my stomach. "Give him an heir. A queen who provides heirs can truly control the kingdom."

"How do I get past the fury and betrayal?"

"You just do. You cannot change this, Michal. You either do what you can to preserve the romance in your marriage for as long as possible, or you stay angry and be miserable and alone."

"And if I would rather die?"

"Think of Merab's sons. They need you as their mother. Think of me. I cannot lose another child. Let me die first."

I sighed. "I do miss them. They are still with Adriel."

"So, David has approved?"

"I have yet to ask. I keep forgetting I need his approval for everything."

"Does he know you are here?"

"No. I do not need to tell him everything. You traveled all the time without informing father."

"When he was away at war, yes, but when he was home, I was required to notify Enos. Some find the queen a valuable commodity. How did you get here?"

"By horse."

"By yourself?" Mother did not hide her surprise.

I lifted my head. "Yes, and I will do it again. I am tired of being a player in another person's story."

"Of course. You bow to no one, but I would at least inform someone at the palace so that you are not left for dead in the forest where no one will find you, and you are nothing but food for the vultures."

Mother acted so seriously that I found myself smiling. "Do not become vulture food. Duly-noted."

"Come. Since I have you here, let us break bread, and offer our goddess a sacrifice. If anyone can help you, the lovely Ashtoreth can."

No one can help you, the voice whispered. *You are alone now, and you will die alone.*

I tried to ignore it. If Mother could control the dark thoughts and voices, then so could I. As we walked back to the small, Ashtoreth temple, I focused on Mother's conversation and the beauty of the gardens. But no matter how hard I tried, I couldn't shake the dark thoughts for long.

23

David

Hebron

1011 B.C.

My head throbbed throughout the rest of the day. I ate an early afternoon meal with my brothers and their families, truly grateful to see them and to hear good reports from Bethlehem. But between my ears was a beating drum, and it took much effort to focus on the conversation or anything else for that matter.

I needed to go see Michal, but more than that, I needed to lie down. Cush approached me as I entered my private chambers. "Make sure I am not disturbed."

He nodded quickly and bowed. "There is the, uh, matter of the girl, sir. The dancer? She has been waiting in the familial courtyard, waiting for you."

"Why would you put her there?"

"Because she is your betrothed?" Cush acted unsure. "No? Does she lie? Some servants overheard—"

"Thank you," I interrupted him. "I remember, and yes, I suppose she is. Do the other women know?" I cringed just thinking about Michal hearing the news. Then again, she was on the opposite side of the compound for the express purpose of not sharing the same courtyard with the other women.

"Those in the courtyard have heard the news. She has engaged all who will listen on her rendezvous with the king." Cush still kept his eyes lowered.

I gave a humorless laugh. "Do you know what is sad? I do not even remember her name."

"Haggith, sir."

"Haggith. Well, there you have it." I rested my head against the door post to my chamber. "What is a man if he does not honor his promises?" Without waiting for an answer, I continued, "Locate her family, arrange the marriage contract, and do so discreetly. I do not want any celebration with the household. Say that it is to keep the nuptials intimate."

"Consider it done. Should I arrange for her to…go home?"

I thought of the previous night and my indiscretions. Nathan had it right. Every decision had a consequence. "This is her home now. We will sign the marriage contract as soon as her father is notified and accepts."

I entered my chambers, stripped the previous evening's attire off my body, and fell onto the bed and into a deep sleep.

"Uncle?"

I opened my eyes to Joab standing over me. "Leave me be."

"You wanted me to notify you when we found an entrance into Jerusalem."

I rolled over onto my back, stretched, and rubbed my face. "Fine. I am awake now. Give me a moment to dress."

Joab handed me a clean tunic and turned around. "You decided to forego last night's dinner? It seems odd to have a three-day celebration for the queen, only to have the king and queen miss the event."

I noticed the morning light casting shadows in the room. "What day and time is it?"

"It is the morning of the last day of the queen's celebration. About the third hour of the day."

"I slept that long!" I stood up quickly, throwing on my tunic and slipping into my sandals. I rushed to the door, opened it, and called out, "Cush!" To a bustling servant, I ordered, "Get Cush. Now."

"So then, you did not mean to miss the evening's dinner?" Joab approached me.

"Michal will think I abandoned her," I said, sighing loudly.

"Do we need to talk about Zion later? It seems you continue to have personal matters to address."

I stopped at Joab's words. "Careful, nephew. Speak carefully."

"Forgive me for seeking clarification. I was told to spy on Jerusalem. I was told to find a home for our king since we have already outgrown this one. We have found that place, but time is of the essence. I need to know if this is still a high priority or if you still need time with your wives."

"What news do you have?"

"The troops are ready to descend upon Zion. It is the outpost of Jerusalem upon a glorious hill. It is said that one can see enemies' land from all directions."

Cush entered the chamber and bowed repeatedly. "My king, you are awake. You said not to disturb you."

"Yes, I did say that, but I did not plan to sleep through the afternoon and into the evening and all through the night. I missed Michal's celebration."

"I have the full report of the celebration."

"I do not want the report. I wanted to not miss the celebration."

"My apologies, my lord."

"Joab and I will break our fast together. Bring in the morning's meal. Also, notify Michal that I desire to visit her today."

"I do have news of the dancer's family," Cush said. "They have agreed to the marriage contract. They will arrive by nightfall."

Joab raised his eyebrows, and I scowled. "Set up a private chamber for them. I will deal with that situation when they arrive."

"There are no more private chambers, my lord."

"What do you mean?"

"We are filled to capacity. With the queen's celebration not completed until this evening, we still have Judah's elders here, as well as other officials."

"We have to offer them a room, Cush. Find out who may be leaving early. See if you can convince anyone to do so. Make it happen."

Cush bowed low before exiting.

To Joab, I said, "We might as well eat while we discuss Zion. We are going to need to secure a larger place as soon as possible."

"Who is the dancer?"

I raised my hand to silence him. "I do not want to talk about it. As you already stated, my personal matters will need to be set aside for the time being. And I, for one, will be glad for it."

Joab acted like he had more to say, but thankfully, he chose to keep his mouth closed.

By the end of the hour, our morning meal was prepared, and other commanders began to arrive after receiving my rushed order.

"Where were you?" Jashobeam asked.

"No doubt with his wife," Benaiah said with a smirk. "You both were noticeably absent. It was fairly obvious the reason."

"I did not call you here to discuss my whereabouts yesterday. We are here to discuss our next steps toward Jerusalem. According to Joab, that starts with Zion."

"Does it not make sense to wait for all of Israel to come together?" Shammah arrived and greeted me with a kiss.

"Abner is making that happen as we speak," I said, noticing Joab stiffen and exchange silent communication with Abishai. "Once we have all tribes swearing allegiance to me, we will try to negotiate with Ishbosheth."

"Will he abdicate the throne?" Shammah asked.

"I will not harm him," I said. "However, I hope to strongly persuade him to abdicate willingly. He does not have the mental and physical fortitude of his father or brothers."

Cush entered again quickly. His brown eyes widened in an apparent upset, and his breathing was labored as if he had run a long way.

"Cush?" I interrupted Shammah's questions to approach my manservant. "Do you need to sit? You seem unwell."

Cush's gaze landed on someone past me, so I turned to see who had his attention. Joab stared back at him, his countenance cold and hard. "The elders of Benjamin demand to see you," Cush rushed the words out.

By now, all of the men in the room turned from Cush to Joab then back to Cush.

"What is wrong?" I asked. "I demand you tell me. Why do they need to see me?"

"I have the answer," Joab interrupted, stood up, and set his goblet down. "They are probably upset that the commander of Israel's army was killed."

No one spoke or moved. All of us stared at Joab as if waiting for him to tell us he jested. After some time, I found the words. "What are you saying, nephew? Tell me it is not what I think."

"Abner is dead. My brother's death has been avenged." He took his goblet, raised it, then swallowed the liquid in one gulp. I saw Abishai raise his goblet and follow suit. Several others did the same thing.

"What did you do?" When he did not answer, I stormed to him, grabbed him by his shoulder straps, and dragged him from the men. I slammed him against the wall. "*What did you do?*" I bellowed with spittle landing on his face.

"I did what you could not do. I handled a threat to your kingdom and killed the one responsible for our brother's death."

Rage filled every part of me. I balled my hand into a fist and hit his face with all my power. I heard a bone snap, but I did not stop.

I threw another punch, but this time, Joab blocked my blow. He did not move, nor did he fight in return. He took my beating, blocking as many blows as he could.

Men came around us and pulled me away from my nephew. Somehow Eleazar had entered the room, and he now stood in front of me, his arms wrapped around me, literally holding me back. "Breathe, David. Breathe."

"Get out!" I screamed at Joab. "Get out of my sight, you wretched dog!"

Joab's face was unrecognizable with so much blood. But somehow, he managed to straighten himself, bow quickly, and leave.

"Out!" I screamed at Abishai. "I want no part of this! Get out of my sight!"

Abishai kept his gaze lowered, bowed, and moved toward the door.

"Anyone who knew, get out! Anyone who knew and went against my orders, *get out*!"

The rest of the men stayed where they were. "None of us knew," Eleazar said. "Come now. Take a breath. We need to deal with this."

I shoved Eleazar aside and rent my tunic in half. "No. First, we deal with this tremendous loss. My men disobeyed me, and now Abner is dead."

"What do I tell the elders from the tribe of Benjamin? They are here, and they are angry." Cush's words brought my emotions back down.

But I still fell to my knees and wept. Everything was finally looking good for the kingdom. With Abner on my side, all the tribes were listening to the many reasons why there should be one kingdom under God's true, anointed king. And now? Now, it looked like I conspired to murder Israel's top commander.

After the initial grief and rage passed, I got up and turned to Cush and the men still in the room. "All available commanding officers and officials are to meet in the large courtyard. The throne room is not large enough to hold all the men that need to be there. They are to come immediately. Bring the elders of Benjamin there." I left the room and moved through the halls and outside. Suddenly, I ran down the path that led to Nathan's dwelling. Once there, I pounded on the door. "Open the door, Nathan!"

The door opened slowly, and Nathan peered at me from behind his servant. "What is this? Is all well in the kingdom?"

I pushed past the servant and entered.

"I take it from your rent clothes that someone has died."

"Do not play coy with me as if you do not know. I tire of those who play games with me. Even my own men play games, and now? Now my kingdom is ruined. Everything I worked for has been in vain."

"Pull yourself together," Nathan said. "With Yahweh, nothing is impossible, nor is His plan derailed by our stupid decisions. We have to face consequences for decisions made, but He will work through our mistakes to fulfill His will."

"Abner is dead."

Nathan's eyebrows raised. "Oh."

"Joab murdered him in retaliation for the death of Asahel. He went against my order to stand down. Now the elders of Benjamin are demanding to meet with me. They are angry and no doubt see this as what it is. Cold-blooded murder."

"You did not decide to kill Abner. Someone else did. The consequences of that decision rest upon his shoulders, not yours."

"The elders of Benjamin will not see it that way."

"They will if you make them see it that way. The tribes are underwhelmed with Ishbosheth. They were easily persuaded by Abner to consider you as their king. So, remind them of who you are and why you are still kingly. Mourn with them, punish those who need punishing." Nathan stepped to me and grabbed my thick arms. "Remind them of who you are. You are David, the anointed heir of the throne of Israel."

I desired to stay longer and to be encouraged by the prophet, but I needed to address those who have assembled in the courtyard. "I must go. Thank you. I know what to do and what to say."

"Good. And David? Remember my words from earlier. It is time to set aside distractions and be king. Your Hebrew brothers and sisters and even those of foreign blood within Israel need their king. Yahweh will use this situation to bring about His will."

I left him and headed back to the compound. My heart overflowed with anguish. I thought of my nephews, thought of my love for them, thought of how hurt and betrayed I felt. But did I not bring this on myself? Had I not been so focused on Michal and the other women who now clutter my life, would I not have been a better mentor and king to Joab, Abishai, and even Asahel?

Stopping in the path, I tried to catch my breath. Once again, I felt alone. No one truly understood my journey. I rubbed my face and whispered the words of a melody I had written while still on the run. I found myself reciting it often.

My God, my God, why hast thou forsaken me?
why art thou so far from helping me,
and from the words of my roaring?
O my God, I cry in the daytime,
but thou hearest not; and in the night season, and am not silent.
But thou art holy, O thou that inhabitest the praises of Israel.
Our fathers trusted in thee: they trusted, and thou didst deliver
them.
They cried unto thee, and were delivered: they trusted in thee,
and were not confounded.
But I am a worm, and no man;
a reproach of men, and despised of the people.
All they that see me laugh me to scorn: they shoot out the lip,
they
shake the head, saying,
He trusted on the Lord that he would deliver him: let him deliver
him, seeing he delighted in him…Be not far from me; for trouble

is near; for there is none to help. *

My hands caught my attention. Still bloodied from my vicious attack on my nephew. The men would side with Joab. Blood for blood, they would say. Even Eleazar warned me about isolating Joab in his grief. But I had been distracted. Nathan's words replayed in my head: *It is time to set aside distractions and be king.*

As I continued walking back to the compound and the courtyard, I held my head high. I was king, and I would handle this situation in a way that showed my power and authority. The courtyard was full of my commanders surrounding the elders of Benjamin. They argued amongst each other while elders wailed with ash upon their foreheads and their outer robes ripped showcasing their grief over the loss of their leader. I noticed Joab standing before the crowd. He had cleaned up, but his nose was swollen at least double in size and had turned black and blue, along with his left eye.

I moved past him, avoiding eye contact. I stood upon the makeshift platform and raised both of my arms. The crowd hushed immediately. The elders quieted their weeping.

"As we all know at this point, Abner, the mightiest of Israel's commanders is dead. I mourn with Israel today. I stand with my Hebrew brothers and sisters of the tribe of Benjamin. I and my kingdom are guiltless before the LORD forever from the blood of Abner." Turning to my nephew, my voice as steel, I continued, "Let it rest on the head of Joab, and on all his father's house, and let there not fail from the house of Joab to be severe punishment and affliction for this senseless act."

No one spoke. No one seemed to move.

"Rend your clothes, gird yourself with sackcloth, and mourn before Abner. He is the mightiest of commanders, and he is dead." I stepped off the platform, knelt beside the elders of Benjamin, and lowered my head. One poured ash over me, and then I wept with them. And I prayed that this would be enough.

24

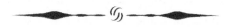

Michal

Paltiel's Vineyard, Gallim

1011 B.C.

The Ashtoreth shrine was close to Paltiel's land. I knew this. It was one of the reasons I requested to meet Mother there. Now I sat upon Princess and observed the surrounding valley and its vast vineyards. So many emotions ran through me, but it was regret I felt most deeply.

Oh, what a foolish woman I was. And so many people were hurt because of my foolishness. I desired to visit, but would he receive me? I wondered about Laia and her children. Had they returned from their visit to her mother's? Did she know about my leaving?

The sun had already begun to set. I stayed with Mother longer than I intended, and I needed to return to Hebron before any more time had passed. Yet, I could not seem to move from this spot. I watched as lanterns were lit and dispersed among the servants. The lanterns seemed to bob along the paths of the vineyard with mere shadows carrying them. But I remembered the names of most of them.

Traveling at night was not a smart decision. With no lantern, I had nothing to light my path. Mother's words also echoed in my mind, reminding me of vagabonds that would have no qualms over kidnapping the queen of Judah and requiring a ransom. A part of me wondered if David would even pay it.

I released Princess's reins, and she happily galloped down the meadow's hill toward Paltiel's east-facing vineyard. If I could find a servant before nightfall, I could talk them into letting me stay in one of the upper rooms in one of the storehouses. I decided to leave Paltiel alone. He needed his peace. He needed to be free of me.

By the time dusk descended, I had arrived at the storehouse. Now that I was here, no one had yet to see me, and I wondered if it would be best to sneak into one of the upper rooms and not notify anyone of my being here. Then I thought of Princess and how hungry and thirsty she must be. "Hiding you in the upper room would be impossible," I whispered to her, patting her frame.

"Who goes there?" Malak, one of the head laborers jumped out from around the corner, holding a pitchfork in one hand and a lantern in the other. Princess spooked, but I easily calmed her.

"Tis I, Michal." I dropped my hood and presented myself.

"Queen Michal." He dropped to the ground and bowed seven times. "Forgive me. I did not know it was you."

"It is only me, Malak. There is no need for ceremony among friends."

"It is an honor to see you again, my queen."

"So, you have heard of my reunion with David? News has spread to these parts?" I was unsure how much Paltiel would have told the field laborers.

"All of Israel knows. Talk of the giant slayer reigning over all of Israel is on everyone's lips. Can you tell me? Is it so?"

"My reunion with David has not yet seen the new moon. I am not privy to all of the information."

"What brings you here? Did you lose your way? Is the royal procession close by that I may escort you?"

"I traveled by myself to visit my mother, and we lost track of time. I do not wish to inconvenience the master of the house, so if I could rest in one of the upper rooms here, I would be most appreciative. I will leave at morning's first light."

Malak took a moment to scrutinize my predicament. "It is not favorable for me to hide information from the master."

"I understand that. Paltiel had a difficult time letting me go, and I am trying to save him the pain of seeing me again. I would continue to travel, but it is already night. I merely need shelter for a few hours."

Malak nodded, then said, "Of course, you are more than welcome here, but please know that if the master asks anything directly, I cannot lie to him."

"Then let us hope he does not ask any questions."

<hr />

I slept fitfully, not accustomed to hard floors and buzzing insects. It reminded me of my night with David in the stable. Only then, I had no problem sleeping with David's strong arms and rhythmic breathing. He was all I needed. But those thoughts led to the dark thoughts of the other women he had held in his arms. Eventually, I dozed but was awakened by something crawling in my ear.

I sat up and screamed, leaning to the side and smacking my ear until the culprit—an ugly beetle—fell onto the floor and scuttled away.

Fully awake, I stood and stretched before cleaning myself up as best I could. Without Dinah here to comb and braid my hair, I patted it down as best I could. A water pitcher and bowl had been placed in the room at some point during the night. Grateful, I washed as best I could while still remaining covered.

I heard movement up the steps and quickly pressed myself up against the wall. Rizpah entered carrying a basket. "Michal?"

"Here." I stepped to her and hugged her neck, kissing her cheeks. "It is good to see you. I hoped it was not a man coming up the steps."

"The servant you spoke with last night ran into me and confided that the queen requested shelter for the night. He said you were insistent on not informing Paltiel, and he sought advice as to what to do. I knew immediately it was not your mother, for she would never stay in a storehouse. I told him I would watch you and provide you food and drink."

"You brought me the water pitcher? Thank you."

"You did not appear to be sleeping restfully when I approached, but I still did not wish to wake you. But now, here you are." She smiled and presented the basket. "It is full of loaves of bread and goat cheese and enough grapes to eat for the entire day. You will not go hungry."

I took the basket and the wineskin. I drank heartily from the wineskin. "I did not realize how thirsty I was."

"How are things?" Rizpah asked. "Is it everything you desired?"

I frowned and looked away. "It is as everyone said. He has wives. One is carrying his seed as we speak. It is not as it once was. I am a foolish woman."

"We are all foolish women when it comes to matters of the heart. And really, what choice did you have? David was going to claim his property at some point. It is divine providence Abner came when he did before you could truly give yourself to Paltiel."

"You pushed me to him. You must have known it would not have ended well if David heard the news of my consummation."

Now it was Rizpah who looked away. "I admit I was motivated by selfishness. Forgive me. I was afraid and alone. I thought if you stayed with Paltiel then I would at least have a place here."

"You have a place here now, and I am glad for it."

Rizpah smiled sadly. "Abner never came for me. He has joined forces with David, so he must be busy securing allies for him."

"Yes, that is true. Many elders from the different tribes have been at the Hebron compound. These are men I saw at my father's palace. Men who swore allegiance to the House of Saul."

"Paltiel's heartache worked to my advantage." She, once again, did not meet my gaze.

"Has Laia returned from her mother's?"

"Not yet. Her mother is still gravely ill."

"I wish I could have seen her and said hello. Please give her my best."

"I will."

"And Paltiel too. I am grateful for his provisions through the years, and I realize—too late at this point—what a blessing it was to live here with him."

"I will. He knows you are here. He saw me assembling your basket and inquired. I decided on honesty. It would not bode well for me if he caught me in a lie."

"Oh, is he coming? I look a mess."

"He is not coming." Rizpah paused. "He allowed me to continue packing the basket and even handed me the filled wineskins, but he said it would be best for him not to see you."

"I understand." I masked the disappointment, knowing how much I hurt him.

"Has Adriel sent you the children? How did you convince David to let you raise Merab's children?"

"It has yet to come up. I have not heard from Adriel, so I have some time. I do miss them though. They will bring some normalcy back to my life."

"When is palace life ever normal?" Rizpah teased. "Speaking of which, how did you travel by yourself? Where is your entourage? How would you know where to go?"

"I know this entire area by memory. Nearly every day, I would ride Eglah throughout the surrounding area. And Judah is not hard to find. I studied my father's maps whenever I could sneak into the library."

"I am impressed, but I am also nervous. A woman should not travel on her own."

"I travel during the day, and I keep to the familiar paths. And with that, I should get going. I do not want too much light to escape.

I will need every moment of it to illuminate my journey."

"I suppose you will be taking your horses? At least Eglah. She has been miserable without you."

"That is a great idea. If Paltiel will allow it." I thought about Eglah's temperament. "I do not think Eglah will respond well to Princess. She is loyal and protective to a fault."

"Paltiel asked if you were going to take the horses, so it should be fine. They are yours. My suggestion is to ride Eglah. She will not act out as much."

"I could ride her and leash Princess to us. Princess is calm and trained well. I think I could do it. I will leave the other horse for Laia and her children. She enjoys riding."

Rizpah pulled me to her. We embraced for several moments. "Stop fighting what you cannot change," she whispered in my ear. She kissed my cheek and released me.

Of

Decisions

And

Destinies

25

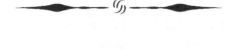

David

Hebron

1011 B.C.

My stomach grumbled. I had followed the bier to a location in Hebron offered as Abner's resting place. All twelve tribes were represented, and I made sure that I grieved loudly. What others did not observe was my masked worry over my nephews.

Despite my fury and indignation, they were my blood. I was not stupid. I knew that I gave them an order that they would not be able to follow. They mourned the tragic loss of their brother. I hoped they would see the greater need for Abner to align and merge the two kingdoms, but how can one clearly see through grief?

The worry reached beyond my nephews. I had a mess waiting for me back at the compound. The dancer's family had arrived and seemed honored that I sought an immediate marriage contract, but the elders refused a delay in burial. That meant that the girl, whose name I kept forgetting, and her family waited for me at the compound. The princess, Maacah, sought my attention due to her delicate state, and it had been three days since I saw Michal. And what would I tell her? She already knew since the dancer took it upon herself to notify all the women in the courtyard. Word travels fast. Deep down, I knew that Michal had purposefully kept away from me. The hurt was deep.

So, who first? Who took precedence over the others? My heart instinctively lurched, desiring to see Michal foremost. But responsibilities needed to be addressed first, and I did not relish the sight of hurt and betrayal upon her countenance.

No distractions, David, my mind warned. *You have a kingdom near the brink of shambles. Everything else needs to wait.*

I arrived at my compound and hurried to my chambers. Cush would have my evening meal waiting for me.

"Brother?"

"Zeruiah," I said in surprise. "Why do you stand outside my doors?"

She took my hands and kissed me. "This is not official business, my king. I hoped you would allow me a few minutes as your sister and not as your subject."

"Of course," I said. "Please come in and dine with me. I am breaking my fast."

She followed me inside the large room that was designated as my living quarters. It did not escape my notice that her eyes were red-rimmed. She lost one of her sons, and now her other two sons faced punishment from their king. The anguish was nearly palpable. "I am not hungry, but thank you for offering."

Maidservants were in position to serve us. Immediately, goblets of wine were poured and handed to us. I sipped the liquid, reminding myself that drunkenness did not lead to good decisions. I set the goblet down and washed my hands in the bowl of water. I situated myself among the cushions, prayed a blessing on the food, and began to eat. With my mouth already full, I indicated for Zeruiah to follow suit. "It is good to see you, although I am sure you are not pleased with me."

"You are king, brother. Who am I to judge what is best in ruling a kingdom?"

"I am your brother first. Talk to me. I am not unreasonable." I broke bread and dipped it into my stew before bringing it to my mouth.

"Will you forgive them?" The words caught on her tongue.

I set the bread down. "I love my nephews. You know that. I would not have elevated them to such ranks if I did not know beyond a shadow of a doubt that they are loyal to me and my kingdom."

She dabbed at her eyes and nodded.

"But they did violate a direct order. Is not punishment a reasonable expectation?"

"It is, but trust me, your displeasure already brings them such dishonor. And they were stuck between two people they love. You...and me."

I raised my eyebrows. "Did you do something, sister?"

Zeruiah kept her gaze lowered. "I too desired vengeance." She quickly added, "Abner killed my son! My Asahel! I was desperate for retaliation. I needed him dead. It was I who encouraged Joab and Abishai to remember their brother above all else. Even though I did not specifically ask them to disobey their king, they knew of my desires. David, punish me, but please be merciful to my sons."

"I do understand, but as king, I have to show the other tribes that I mourn the loss of Israel's commander. If not, there will be an all-out war. I am tired of fighting my Hebrew brethren. Abner was working with me to restore Israel as one kingdom."

"But Asahel! What of him? Does his death mean nothing? You weep and mourn for Abner, yet were there tears for Asahel, your own blood?" She quickly pressed her lips shut as if realizing she said too much. Tears flowed down her cheeks. "Forgive me. I am not myself."

Even in my exhaustion, my heart moved with compassion. I wiped my hands and made my way to her. I wrapped my arms around her and let her cry on my shoulder. "I wept," I said to her. "I wept for my nephew, and I wept for you and Joab and Abishai.

The loss we feel is great. If I seemed callous to that, it was never my intent." I released her and met her gaze. "But being king means making decisions for the good of the kingdom, for the good of all Hebrew brethren, even if it means setting aside my pain."

"I do understand that, and I am sorry to have compelled my sons to pursue vengeance at the expense of the kingdom. But, please, place the punishment on my shoulders."

"I will do no such thing."

"What of Joab and Abishai? I could not bear to see them demoted or cast aside or flogged or worse!"

"Dear sister, do not worry. Even though I am angered over their disobedience, it is partly because of how it will look to the other tribes. I cannot have them see us as murderers. I need them to see that I am angry and that Joab's decision to kill Abner was made outside of my will or desire. Give this time. Once the grieving period is over, I am hopeful that bad blood between tribes will extinguish."

"Oh."

I smiled gently and kissed her forehead. "Trust me when I say I love my nephews. I will deal with them, but I think their pride has already taken quite a beating. Let them fester in my anger for a while longer. Then I will reevaluate the situation."

Zeruiah exhaled in apparent relief. "Thank you for seeing me. Our family is so proud of you. And it is such an honor for my sons to hold such high rank."

I walked back to my late dinner and sat down again. I did not want to talk about certain members of my family. The estrangement from my father still hurt deeply. The tension between us, even with my help and provision, had never dissipated. "I am still hungry. Now that you have expressed your message, do you wish to join me?"

"David," she said gently, situating herself beside me and taking my hand. "Father is very proud of you. As was Mother before her death. I know they cannot take back how they treated you, but you are held in great esteem among our people, including Father."

I paused before taking another bite and glanced over at her. "Thank you for the kind words. Having my family at my side is such a blessing. Now, no more talk of the past." And with that, I finished the meal with my sister beside me.

———————

The next morning began with a ceremony, which annoyed me. It had been several days since I saw Michal, and I missed her. I desired to be with her even if it meant dealing with her displeasure. But upon waking, Cush presented me with a list of priorities to be completed. At the top of the list was the marriage ceremony and celebration with the dancer.

"What is her name again?" I grumbled.

"Haggith, and she and her family can barely contain their excitement at this marriage contract." Cush grimaced slightly before becoming expressionless.

"Promises are promises," I said with a sigh. "Do not ever let me become drunk again."

"I will endeavor to do my best in that regard. Of that, you can be sure."

Even in my grumpiness, I laughed. "She is not that bad, is she? I seem to remember her being lively and entertaining."

Cush gave a tight smile. "Who am I to comment on your decisions or on those with which you choose to keep company? But I will say that making sure you do not overdo the wine is going to be a priority."

"Speak openly, Cush. I need to know what I am getting into."

"Haggith is lively, sir, and she has told any person in this compound who will listen of how she turned the king's heart toward her. Her family is loud. They are not true followers of the Hebrew tradition because they break many rules. What is the word? Uncouth. Yes, they are uncouth."

"Once the wedding feast is over, you are to inform them that the rooms are needed. I do not want them to stay any longer than what our traditions dictate. Also, the wedding feast is to be small. No announcement."

"They will not be happy about it. Their plans for the feast are quite extensive."

"I will tell them. Have them meet me in the throne room before the ninth hour."

Cush bowed and scurried out.

"Send in my morning meal," I called out.

"Eleazar to see you," Cush popped his head into the room.

"I do not need to be announced," Eleazar said as he entered. "Busy morning?"

"Ugh."

The maidservants brought in trays of steaming fish and loaves of bread, bowls of fruits, and lentils. I sat down and began eating, and Eleazar joined me. We ate in silence for a few moments.

"Who is the dancer?"

"Her name is Haggith." The name sounded foreign to my tongue. "I need to do a better job remembering it as I am going to meet the family today."

"How is she?"

"I do not know her very well," I said in embarrassment. "It was not a good decision, but I made a promise in my drunkenness, and here we are."

Eleazar grinned and shook his head. "And this happened the night of Michal's celebration?" My grimace must have answered his question. "And Michal? I assume she was overjoyed at you taking on another wife."

"She does not know. I have yet to broach the topic with her."

"Trust me. Haggith has told everyone about how she seduced the king. Michal knows."

"Which explains why I have not seen nor heard from her since that night. And now, I have no time to see her. From the funeral and mourning period to Haggith's family demanding a wedding feast and contract, I can barely think straight."

"Then there is the matter of Joab."

"Yes, that too."

"And the matter of Jerusalem. We need to find another place than this compound."

I shook my head, feeling overwhelmed. "I have decided that I am better off out on assignment with my men. Personal matters have a way of becoming complicated."

"That is why I have one wife. One is all I need."

I scowled at him. "This coming from the one who pushed Ahinoam at me!" I threw a fig at his head.

"I am not king. You needed a woman while out on the run. It is what it is, but I do suggest giving it a rest for a while. If for no other reason, we are running out of room." Eleazar's eyes danced with mischief.

"As soon as the marriage contract is sealed and the wedding feast is over, I will be gone. I do desire to visit Michal. She probably feels I have abandoned her."

"I think she has realized that your marriage now is nothing like what it was in its early years."

I closed my eyes and dwelt in sadness for a moment. Those early married years were the best in my life. I had never felt such love and devotion than during those intimate moments with Michal. Not knowing what else to say, I quipped, "What is done is done. Let us move forward."

That did not stop my mind from wandering. It wandered as I met with my commanders, excluding Joab and Abishai. It wandered as I washed and assembled the formal attire for the marriage feast and contract. Later that afternoon, as we headed to formally greet Haggith and her family, I asked Cush, "Have you spoken with the queen? Is she well?"

"She has kept to her chambers. I have not seen her since the first night of her celebration."

I stopped walking. "At all? What about passing in the hall? Or walking in the gardens? She enjoys exercise."

Cush thought for a moment. "No, my lord. I can recall no such passing. I will call upon her now and inquire."

Something did not sit right. "Eleazar? Have you seen Michal these last few days?"

Eleazar had stayed with me most of the day, leaving only to wash and change into his own formal attire. "We have been busy with Abner's funeral. I have not been within the compound besides today."

I changed direction and headed toward Michal's chambers. "This will take a moment."

"Haggith and her family are already assembled."

"Yes, I am aware." I reached Michal's chambers and knocked on the door. After a moment, I knocked again. I heard hurried movement, and then the door opened. Dinah bowed low.

"My king," she said in her soft voice.

"I am here to see Michal. May I enter?"

"She is not here." Dinah had yet to look up. "She is visiting her mother."

Cush made a small noise but quickly coughed in an attempt to cover it.

"She is visiting her mother? Where? At Ishbosheth's?"

"My apologies, my lord, but she did not explain."

"Who is her escort?" My voice slightly raised, as I poorly hid my panic and annoyance. I glanced at Cush, but he seemed just as shocked and unaware as I was. "And why are you still here? Would her maidservant not go with her?"

Dinah began wringing her hands. "I do not have the answers. She left and said she was going to visit Queen Ahinoam. That is all I know, my lord."

"How long?" My voice was near a shout. "How long has my wife been gone?"

Dinah was near tears. "I—I am not sure…a few days…"

"*A few days!*" I yelled. Dinah jumped. I spun around to face Cush. "How did my queen leave this compound with no one aware? Who is traveling with her? *What happened to Michal?*"

Cush too acted near tears. He darted his eyes as if an answer would miraculously appear in the air. "Sir, I do not know…but I will ask every breathing soul who has been in this fortress…I will find out…I will not stop investigating."

"David," Eleazar said calmly.

"What?" I snapped.

"Send someone to the stable. See if her horse is gone. If it is, and I suspect it is, she probably fled to her mother purposefully avoiding discovery."

"I will go and find her myself." I attempted to walk away, but Eleazar stopped me.

"We will do everything we can to find the queen, but you are needed here."

"The queen is off by herself, and you want me to stay here?"

"We will send patrols and scour this entire area. We will not stop until we find her."

"She is my wife."

"But you have another waiting for you. You cannot break the contract."

I turned back to Cush. "Inform Haggith and her family of my sincerest apologies, but there is an unforeseen situation that has presented itself. I will fulfill my promise, but first, I have to find my queen."

"May I suggest you tell them yourself?" Eleazar would not leave me alone. "Greet them warmly. Show them the signed contract. Seal it with a kiss. Explain to Haggith of this immediate situation. While you are doing that, I will secure troops and supplies for us to leave before the sun even sets."

Even in my frustration, Eleazar's words made sense. It would take time to assemble a search party. Without saying anything more, I marched down the hall and toward Haggith and her family.

Another complicated mess of my own doing. Most of my anger was directed at myself. How could I be so busy to not know that Michal had left?

Before entering the throne room, I took a deep breath, prayed for Michal's protection and strength to get through this mess, and entered.

Haggith's eyes brightened immediately, and she made a move toward me. Her father—or the stocky man with graying hair that stood beside her that I presumed was her father—grabbed her elbow and held her back. "He must invite you to him first," he whispered loud enough that most of the room heard him.

Haggith's face reddened, as she stayed in place. Her thick, dark hair cascaded down her back and shoulders in soft curls, and the memory of our night together and the promises made brought heat to my face. Was this the man I had become? Was this the king I would be?

I mentally shook myself. If I was to leave before sunset to find Michal, I did not have much time. "Greetings," I said formally, sitting on my throne. "What a joyous occasion that brings us together."

The family, which consisted of her father and mother and several sisters, fell on their knees and bowed repeatedly before me. "We bow before our king in humble submission and patronage. Please accept our humble wedding gifts."

I noticed the chicken and livestock in cages at the far end of the room. "Enough of this. Please stand and face me." To one of the guards, I ordered, "Take the animals out and find a place in our stables. And who let them in?" Turning my attention back to Haggith and her family, I said, "The marriage contract is signed and a small celebratory dinner is planned. This will not be a large affair due to pressing concerns along our borders. I must leave almost immediately." I walked to Haggith, took her hands, and kissed each cheek. "Forgive me that an urgent matter dictates immediate attention, but I will return and celebrate our union as soon as I can."

Haggith bowed, bringing her forehead to our hands. "I look forward to our continued time together."

I gently pulled my hands away from her grip and smiled tightly as the family who all seemed very eager to be in my presence watched me as if to see what might happen next. I could not get out of the room fast enough.

Just as I was leaving, Cush rushed in. "The queen has been located," he said, slightly out of breath.

I fled the room without so much as a backward glance.

26

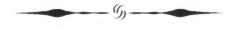

Michal

Hebron

1011 B.C.

Any doubt of David knowing about my disappearance left when I saw his men approaching me on their horses. They surrounded me, blocking me from moving any further.

"Queen Michal," one said, bowing his head briefly. "Are you harmed?"

"No, although your approach startled me and my horses."

"Were you followed?"

"No, not that I saw."

He motioned to two of the men. "Verify a secure perimeter." As they left, he said to me, "We will escort you home."

One of the men took the rope I held, pulling Princess to him. She was such a gentle beast, and she easily followed him. I was thankful that I chose to ride Eglah. She was more territorial. For the rest of the journey to the stable, we rode silently. My thoughts were everywhere: longing to be anywhere but here, glad that David knew I had left, worried as to his reaction, knowing I had to keep the peace if I were to raise Merab's sons, and angry at *so* much.

At the stables, two stable hands helped me off the horse. And I came face-to-face with David. "Michal!" He threw his arms around me. "Are you all right?"

His tenderness made me feel guilty. He must have been genuinely worried. But the thought of why I left resurfaced, and I pulled away. "I am fine. There is no need to worry. I can handle a horse. You know this."

David watched me for a moment, then called for the stable manager. Still leveling his gaze on me, he ordered the stable manager, "These horses are to be guarded night and day. Do not let them leave the stable without my man's knowledge. Is this understood?"

The stable manager fumbled with his words but eventually found them. "Yes, yes, sir. I mean, yes, my king. These horses will not leave our sight."

"Cush?" he called to his manservant but still held eye contact with me.

"I am right here, my lord."

"The queen is to be guarded at all times. There must be an entourage of protection always."

"Am I to have no privacy?" I asked. "You know I enjoy riding."

"I am not keeping you from riding, but you will have someone with you always. You were raised in a palace, Michal. You know the level of danger that surrounds us. You should not have left without an escort."

"I needed to get away."

"Where did you go?"

"To visit my mother."

David's eyes widened. "You went to Israel's king? Without an invitation?"

"No, I went to visit my mother, not Ishbosheth, but he is my brother, and I am sure he would have gladly received me." I chose not to tell him how Ishbosheth had kicked me out and how I had not visited since.

"Not as the *Queen of Judah!*" David looked at me like I had grown two heads. "He could have kept you hostage! Demanded a ransom! Or killed you!"

"Need I remind you that the King of Israel is my brother? He and I share the same parents, which means if I am to see my mother, I will have to visit his palace."

"Never. I forbid it."

"You forbid it?"

"Yes, and I forbid you to ever travel anywhere unattended. This is not to happen again."

"You forbid me to see my family? The only family I have left?" My voice raised unintentionally.

"I am your family now. And your mother can visit here. Your brother too. If they come in peace, they will be welcomed."

I rubbed my forehead, knowing this was a fight I could not win. But I could not stop the bitter words. "Are you going to lock in my chambers too? Just like my parents? You are becoming more like them with each passing day, especially my father."

No one spoke. No one moved. Even David stood as if frozen. I refused to look away. I kept eye contact. David's mouth moved. "Everyone out. Now." When everyone left, he said, "Do not talk to me like that again in front of my subjects. If we need to have words, we will do so privately."

"I used to be able to speak freely to you. Has that changed too?"

"Michal, those days are in the past. The quicker you realize that I am king, and you are queen, and with these titles are roles and responsibilities that must be followed, the better off you will be."

"I do not need to be reminded of our days long past. I think of them often. You are different. You are not the same David."

"And you are not the same Michal. When did you become a bitter, angry woman? Since you arrived, I have not known how to act or what to say around you because anything upsets you anymore."

213

His words hurt deeply. "If I am bitter and angry it is because I was abandoned. By *you*! And all of your excuses mean nothing when I see your other wives. *You* made me this way."

"For eight years I did not have a place to call home. My people turned against me. My king stopped at nothing to kill me. But I did not become bitter, Michal. This bitterness you are fostering is a choice. Here, you are loved and have provision."

But I do not have you. The words came, but I held my tongue.

We stayed quiet for some time. Neither of us moved toward the other as if an invisible wall separated us. David broke the silence with a question. "Why do you have cuts on your arms? Did someone injure you?"

"You already know the answer." David was well aware of my mother's worship of Ashtoreth. He knew of the rituals in which she involved herself.

"You traveled with your mother to the pagan temple?" David set his jaw like stone.

"She met me there. I did not go to the palace as you assumed. We met there. In Gallim."

"Gallim? Where Paltiel lives?"

"Yes. Gallim. Where I lived for eight years. The home I was recently taken from."

David closed his eyes and breathed in through his nose. "You went to see him?"

"No. I went to see my mother. At the Ashtoreth shrine. I had to pass through Gallim."

"You are not to step foot in Gallim again. At either place. Worship of pagans is forbidden under my roof. When I become king over all of Israel, I will tear down every pagan shrine. And your days with that man are over."

Stubbornness rose within me, but I needed to tread carefully. My five nephews required my care. Antagonizing David anymore would not help my cause. With great self-control, I said, "You are right. I only desired to rest during the night. I thought it would be safer. I did not speak with him. I merely slept in an available storehouse."

David seemed pacified. "I do not wish to keep you from your mother. I do not want to order you to *do* or *not do* anything. But I do *request* that you please stay away from pagan worship and that you leave Gallim behind. I think it is best for our relationship as we move forward." David took a step closer to me. "I do not wish to quarrel. It was disconcerting to find you gone."

"The celebration was too much. Meeting…the others…was more than I could handle. I tried to tell you that, but you insisted."

"I am still learning how to be king." David held up his hands and then dropped them. "I was so determined to showcase the queen and establish your power over the household, and yes, it became clear to me that I rushed it. Forgive me?"

He gazed at me with those blue-green eyes, and my angry resolve melted under the heat of it. "I will try. I have a lot to process."

"About the other women," David paused and glanced at his hands. "I seek your forgiveness because I made a poor decision, and there is one more."

"One more?" I did not understand what he was trying to express.

"One more woman."

"Oh." I swallowed back the negative emotions. *Do not give in to the dark thoughts*, I ordered myself. *Remember what Rizpah and Mother said! If he does not feel wanted by you, he will go to others.*

"I became drunk and made a foolish promise to a dancer. She is holding me to that promise."

"The dancer from my celebration?" I shook my head at the irony of it.

"I did not handle the situation well and becoming inebriated did not help my judgment. I have no other excuse, but I desire to be honest with you."

"And you will not break a promise," I said bitterly. "Other than the promise to come back for me."

"I did not break that promise. It only took longer than either of us anticipated."

I did not say anything. It took all my willpower to keep my emotions under control.

He lies, the voices whispered. *All he has ever done is lie to you.*

"Michal." David took another step, coming closer to me. "It is not, nor was it ever, my will to upset our relationship. Yet, it is not the same, and I recognize a lot of the changes are due to my decisions. I have my reasons for the other women, but I can only imagine the pain you are enduring. I do not know what to do with your pain. There are other women, and they are here, and they have my children. It would be reprehensible to turn them away. They are mine now. I must offer provision and care. It is my obligation."

I did not desire to hear anymore. I looked away, not wanting to be lost in his gaze. "Decisions were made, and we cannot change them. Let us not dwell on this."

"Because I need to share these thoughts with you." David closed the gap between us and took my hands. I tried to pull away, but he gently held on. "You are who I desire above all. I understand that is hard to believe because of decisions made, but it is the truth."

I took a deep breath. *Why do I struggle with letting this go?* Here David stood, in all honesty and tenderness, and I had to contain the bitterness and anger not to lash out. But Rizpah had it right. I could not change the circumstances. If I desired a better, happier life, I needed to move past these negative feelings. I needed to take control of the situation. I needed to be queen. "Will you escort me to my chambers? I would like to clean up."

David gave me a small smile, and with my hand in his, he led me out of the stables and to our home. With my other hand, I fingered the vial that still hung around my neck, already contemplating when to use it.

27

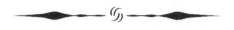

Michal

Hebron

1010 B.C.

I held the empty vial in my hand, praying it worked. Living in this compound would at least be tolerable if I birthed a child. Several moons passed since my return from visiting Mother. David's attention, when not focused on politics or alliances, stayed focused on me. When he was home, which had not been often.

Dinah reported at my insistence every time David visited the other women. Which had not been often. Most of his visits were to the princess who paraded around the entire compound with her large belly protruding. "It will be a son." I overheard her speaking to David's newest wife. The young dancer also bragged about signs of pregnancy. The two of them together were awful. Each trying to out-boast the other. "Twins run in my family," the dancer said. "We are praying for two sons to bless David's kingdom." Just his name on their lips set my mouth in a frown, but I pushed past it.

The other wives were quiet and kept to themselves. I did not need any of them.

For I had a plan, and I would see it to fruition.

Before David left to pursue Jerusalem, he spent the day and night with me. Gathering the courage, I followed Mother's instructions and drank the entire herbal concoction before David and my time together. That had been many days ago. I tried not to worry, but if the vial did not work, I was not sure when I would next see my husband.

"You have added weight to your frame," Dinah said as she brushed and braided my frame. "Your face is full, as are your hips. These are good signs that your body is ready to grow a child."

I smiled at the compliment. "No more walking skeleton."

"I am glad for it. You worried me."

I took Dinah's hand and kissed it. "A true friend indeed." I went back to fiddling with the vial.

"Fretting about it is not going to make it happen." Dinah finished braiding my hair and began wrapping it in a knot at my neck.

"I know, but I cannot help myself. This must work, especially since he is already gone! His campaign in Jerusalem could last several moons."

"The servants talk of Jerusalem. Some of them were indentured servants there with the Jebusites. They talk of a vibrant land close to the sea."

"I know one thing." I stood up and examined myself in the looking glass. "If David wants Jerusalem, he is going to get it. Now come, let us walk the gardens before I exercise the horses. I am determined to keep up my health."

As we walked out of the room and toward the gardens, Dinah looked over her shoulder at the two guards following us. "You will not know privacy. No more sneaking around and hiding in corners."

"That was a long time ago when we were children. I do not hide in corners anymore. And David is still learning how to be king. It seems that my decision to leave without notifying anyone has led to my every move being watched."

Dinah gave me a sideways glance. "You seem changed. You do not seem nearly as angry or irritated as you did before you left."

We had entered the gardens, and though they were not as lush or extravagant as my father's palace, they were fine enough and provided some semblance of privacy. I saw the guards still stayed within eyesight but had given more space between me and them. "There are things I need from David, so it does me no good to irritate him."

"You are merely playing the part of dutiful wife?" Dinah seemed surprised.

"No...yes...maybe." The question bothered me more than I cared to admit. "I desire David the way it used to be, but that is not ever going to happen. He made decisions that have hurt me deeply, and it has affected our relationship and will continue to do so. But if I stay cross and holed up in my chambers, then I will fade from his memories. That means that my plan must work."

"What is the plan exactly? Other than bearing his child."

"I miss the boys terribly. Over a year has passed, and I have yet to be brave enough to ask David for my sister's sons. We are so full here at the compound. Plus, he travels more days than he is present. At some point, Adriel is going to send them to me. I cannot be at odds with David and request that my sister's children live under our roof."

"True, and I was hoping to see them soon. I had grown quite attached."

We followed the winding path and nearly stumbled upon the princess, Maacah, and her gaggle of servants. Two of them fanned her while she lay across a stone garden bench. She appeared flushed and miserable. But my attention did not stay upon her features. It landed upon her very round, protruding belly.

"This idea was stupid." She shot angry glances at her girls. "I am still hot and miserable."

Memories of Merab flooded my brain. She, too, was miserable during all her pregnancies. I always envied her pregnant belly, and I found myself pushing back the jealousy now. If the goddess, Ashtoreth, granted me a pregnancy, I vowed to never complain about the condition. David vowed to pray to his Yahweh to bless my womb, but I prayed only to the goddess. For all my youth, I prayed to Israel's deity, and all it did for me was to rip me from my family and my husband. My misery lay at His feet, so I would pray to the goddess and hope she was kinder in her answers.

Maacah noticed my approach. With a sneer, she said, "Oh, look who it is. The queen of Judah. Everyone, bow in her presence."

"Now, now, dear princess," I said in mock sweetness. "Be careful. Your ugliness is showing."

"So? What of it? It is not as if our husband is here, and even when he is, he ignores me."

I could not mask the grin. "That is because his queen satisfies his needs."

"Not all of them," she said cruelly, rubbing her round belly.

"Enjoy that child," I said through gritted teeth. "Because it will be your last."

Maacah actually laughed. "Oh Michal, be careful. Your *jealousy* is showing."

"Do not refer to me by name. I am queen." My blood boiled.

Maacah laughed again. "Thank you for the amusement. Now ladies, help me to my chambers. Absalom is moving." She turned to me, her nose in the air. "My son's name is Absalom. When he arrives, David will be all mine."

"Keep lying to yourself." I took Dinah's arm, and we turned our backs on them. "I hate her," I whispered to Dinah.

"You are not the only one. All of the king's servants despise her."

"I am going to ask the gods to give the child two heads and five eyes."

Dinah and I laughed on our way to the stables. We discussed how ugly the baby would be. And it helped. The jealousy subsided, as did the dark voices.

"Are you sure about this?" Dinah asked, petting Princess.

"Yes. There is nothing to fear. Princess is gentle and patient.

You will ride her, and I will ride Eglah." I kissed Eglah's nose.

Dinah eyed the horse nervously. For years, I tried to teach her how to ride, but she was always busy with the children or her other duties. But last night, I convinced her to give it a try.

The stable hand helped her up and showed her how to situate herself. I expertly lifted myself up and onto Eglah. "Come. The world awaits us."

Dinah looked unconvinced. "Start slow, please."

For the rest of the afternoon, Dinah and I rode the horses. I helped her handle the reins until eventually, she picked it up herself. By evening, I barely gave Maacah or her baby any more thought.

———— ✵ ————

"You learned quickly."

"That is because Princess was patient." Dinah opened the door to my chambers and waited for me to enter before she followed. "May I have permission to sit for a spell? My legs are burning."

I grinned. "Oh yes, I should have warned you. Riding horses may affect your legs, arms, and everywhere. You will get used to it though, I promise."

Dinah shot me a withering glance. "That sounds like useful information before a person jumps on a horse for the first time."

"Go. I give you the evening off. Soak in warm water. It will help tremendously."

Dinah did not reject the offer. She nodded and thanked me. "I will send your evening meal through Raja."

I tried not to laugh as she slowly walked out of my chambers.

After the evening meal, boredom settled on me, and I decided to walk the rooftop. Rooftops reminded me of happier times when David was truly mine and mine alone. He loved rooftops because he was under the open sky. For years, whenever I studied the stars, I would somehow feel close to him. Since the other women seemed to avoid the rooftop, it was also free from their chatter and annoying drama.

I leaned against the edge of the roof and gazed at the stars for some time. The wind blew gently against my face, and I could see the flames from fire pits throughout the landscape. "Please," I whispered before I could stop myself. "Please let this work. Grant me a child." I stared up into the heavens unsure to whom I was praying.

My prayers were interrupted by the sound of someone crying. I could not see who it was, but it was far enough away, that I turned back to the stars. None of my business, and honestly, I did not care.

But the crying did not abate. If anything, it increased to sobs. Annoyed that my quiet star-gazing was interrupted by obnoxious emotions, I moved toward the person, determined to use my station to order them off the rooftop. Unless it was David himself, whoever it was would have to obey my order.

I followed the sound to the private area David used for sleeping. Who dared go to his private spot? I opened my mouth to say something until I saw who it was. "Haggith?" I stumbled at her name, surprised to find her here. "What are you doing? This is the king's rooftop arrangement."

The young dancer immediately jumped up, for she had been lying down across his bedding, and wiped at her face while bowing repeatedly. "My qu-queen. My apologies. I did not know you were here."

"That matters little when you steal into the king's private area. How dare you!"

Her face crumpled, and tears formed again. "He said that when he was away I could visit our spot where we promised our love and devotion to each other. When I come here, I feel close to him. I miss him so."

This was *their* spot? He had a special place with another woman? Anger turned to fury, and without thinking, I slapped her with all of my strength. She yelped in pain and brought her hand to her face. "You do not have his love. It belongs to me. Do you understand? And if you dare come up here again, you will answer to me, and trust me when I say that my wrath will be far worse than his."

She stared at me with big, round eyes before running away from me, weeping all the more.

I shook with anger. With jealousy. Because even though I knew about this special place of his, he had yet to take me here.

28

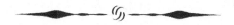

David

Outer Walls of Jerusalem

1010 B.C.

We road through the morning light, breaking at high sun, and then continuing through the evening. It felt comfortable being with my men again. This was my first journey of length since arriving in Hebron and setting up my base. But as I chatted with Uriah and Eleazar over an open fire, I realized I missed the camaraderie of my brothers-in-arms. And they were much less complicated than women.

Jashobeam approached us. "The fortress of Zion will work as our first capture."

"Joab? Do you agree?" I turned to my nephew who had kept quiet throughout the first day's travel. We had yet to truly have a private conversation. I owed him that. Until then, I desired for him to know I still saw him as commander of all troops.

Joab briefly acted surprised, but just as quickly, he agreed. "I have the map that shows the weaknesses of the area."

"Walk us through it." I indicated he open the map.

He glanced at the men around him as if waiting to hear any

protests. When none came, he nodded and opened up the map of Jerusalem, and pointed out Zion.

"If diplomacy does not work, then we will consider using these weaknesses to our advantage," I said. "But let no one say of me that I did not choose diplomacy first."

"How many messengers should go before you?"

"You already sent messengers. We will march this time. They can speak to me directly. It can be a peaceful discussion or not. We will leave that decision to them." As the men dispersed, I reached out to Joab. "Stay a moment longer. I need to speak with you." Once everyone left earshot, I said, "I do not enjoy being at odds with family. I endured years of silence and isolation when I was a boy, and I do not desire any of my family to feel that same isolation."

"I was surprised at your invitation to join this expedition. I did not know if I had lost my place at your table and among your men." Joab paused, then said, "But I do not regret my actions, uncle. If that means I must leave your presence, then I will suffer the consequences."

"I know you do not regret your actions, and I understand why you do not. I also have a kingdom to appease. You took what was a precarious relationship with the other tribes and nearly crushed it with the weight of your vengeance."

Joab leveled his gaze. "That was not my intent. My only intent was to take the life of the one who killed my beloved brother."

"I know," I said again. "But can I trust you to follow orders? Can I trust you to lead my troops and be loyal even if it means going against your own desires?"

"You can trust me, uncle. I will not let you down. I have always been and will always be loyal to you and your kingdom."

I nodded content with the answer. "I will have to continue to publicly decry your actions. Do you understand?"

"Yes, sir."

"I will not strip you of your title or responsibilities. Do not make me regret this decision."

Joab bowed then left quickly.

On the third morning of travel, we arrived outside the mighty walls of Jerusalem. The entire Jebusite settlement was a marvel. The city sat upon a high hill with a clear view from every angle.

"How many walls are there?" Eleazar asked.

"Walls surround Jerusalem at the top, but there are also walls surrounding their outlying cities," Joab explained. "Nothing is exposed. If they do not agree to an alliance, we will be the ones at a disadvantage. They will see us from any direction."

"That would not be the first time we were at a disadvantage," Uriah said with a shrug. "I welcome the challenge."

I questioned myself. The walls seemed impenetrable. Fighting up a hill where they could see us, but we would not be able to see them sounded like a losing battle. Surely, there was another place to serve the Hebrew people? Yet, both Abiathar and Nathan agreed that Yahweh's hand was upon the move and that the city was mine. "Diplomacy first," I eventually said. "Let us pray that they respond well."

Uriah arched an eyebrow. "We want their land. I do not think we will reach an amicable arrangement."

Joab and the other men murmured assent.

"That is up to them." I chose a hundred commanders to ride with me while soldiers took formation along the forest line. Our arrow shooters and javelin throwers had already left to take their places in trees and other secure locations should there be a surprise attack.

Days later, as we approached the city's gate, I took only a handful of my mighty men with me. I felt the eyes of the Jebusite guards upon us and counted many in position from their vantage point above us. A line of their soldiers was on the other side of the thick iron gate. I held up my hands to signify a desire for peaceful conversation.

Their commander sneered in my direction. "Turn around, Hebrews. You are not wanted here."

"I am King David of Judah, and I desire a conversation with your king. We seek peace and an alliance."

"We know who you are, and our king scoffs at an alliance with the likes of you. Now turn around before you and all those with you die with your heads severed and your bodies hanging outside our walls." The soldiers with him leveled their bows and arrows in our direction. Even with the iron bars between us, they easily had clear shots.

I kept my gaze locked on the Jebusite's commander. The commander even cocked an eyebrow and smirked at me. Taking a deep breath, I tried one more time. "I am King David of Judah, and I request a conversation with your king. This will be the last time I ask for it. But, mark my words, I will have a conversation with him, one way or another."

The Jebusite commander turned to the other soldiers before throwing his head back and laughing. "Are you threatening us? This is comical. Look around. We are fortified, and you are exposed. Even our blind and lame could defeat you. Now, mark *my* words. This is the last conversation I will have with you. Turn around or die."

Everything in me desired to fight, but the outcome would be catastrophic. The thought of turning around with our backs to these soldiers did not sit well with me, yet what other choice did I have? "Men," I called out, steel in my voice. "Retreat."

I turned first and moved out of the line of vision from those who congregated at the gate. My men followed me creating a formation of protection around me. If arrows or javelins flew, they would be the first hit. It still humbled me to think of these men willing to sacrifice their lives for my kingdom. So, I moved with purpose, finding the quickest route to the forest.

We rode hard, pushing through the trees and underbrush. I allowed the frustration to stew while I rode. Their insults fueled me, giving me a renewed purpose in Jerusalem as my capital. "Somehow, Lord," I prayed. "Make this right. Establish my kingdom as you see fit, but do not allow these heathens to make a mockery of your anointed."

By dusk, we made it to our camp. I slid off the horse, and handed the reins to a young servant who came running to greet me. Shammah approached also already on foot. "Is there enough distance between us and the Jebusites?" I asked him, glad that he was with me on this journey.

"Let us hope so. We are more vulnerable traveling at night. Staying here is our best bet. Those at our outposts will notify us if there is movement."

"No need to worry about them following us," Joab approached, still on his horse. "They do not have our numbers, nor do they match our skill. They are arrogant only when those walls surround them."

"Therein lies the challenge. How do we scale those walls without exposure?" Shammah asked the question to both me and Joab.

"I have an idea," Joab said. "I have yet to mention it because it is farfetched."

"Right now, I am open to all ideas," I said. "We will clean up then meet at the fire. Tell the others."

Joab nodded and left me with my brother.

"Our sister, Zeruiah, will be pleased that you have chosen forgiveness."

"She came to see me, desiring all punishment to fall upon her. She said she persuaded her sons to go against my wishes and kill Abner."

"Will you punish her?" Shammah acted surprised. "She is but a woman."

"Of course not," I reassured him. "She is not just any woman. She is our sister. I do worry about Joab's hothead."

"He is what we need as commander. He will not hesitate to defend you or anyone else to whom he is loyal."

"I do not disagree. I only hope I have done enough to appease the tribe of Benjamin. They may not be as forgiving." I took a deep breath and stretched. "I will clean up and meet you by the firepit. We shall hear together of Joab's farfetched scheme."

After washing and changing from war gear to tunic, most men had returned and were congregating around several blazes. Although many troops stayed with their units, my close circle of commanders and those on duty to protect me gathered to report out. The young servant assigned to me during travels handed me a bowl of lentils and broth. I prayed a blessing, then the group began eating. The men chatted as they ate, but my thoughts were undeterred. There had to be a way to capture the city. But however I imagined it, the outcome was the same. The slaughter of my men.

"You are quiet." Eleazar approached me. "I have sat by your side for years, and you have not changed. You stare into the flames as if the weight of the whole world is on your shoulders."

"When I was younger, I was often alone, watching the shepherds and their families enjoy their meal and conversation."

"You always had me."

"I know, but it was not the same. You would go sleep in the tents of your father, and I would sleep in a tent with men assigned to me."

"Is that what you are contemplating? Now that you are king, you have several choices of who will sleep beside you."

I shot him an annoyed glance. "No, that is not what I am contemplating. You were the one who brought it up."

Eleazar laughed. "Guilty as charged. I was only mentioning that you are often pensive around the fire. That has not changed."

"I am frustrated that there is no clear path to Jerusalem. Not one that does not get my men killed."

"We will find a way. We always do."

"This is different. It feels different. It is as if Yahweh has brought me to this place for a reason. Like a puzzle to be solved, only I cannot solve it."

"If the Most High brought us here, which I believe He did, He will make a way. In that, I am most confident."

"I am too, but I cannot help feeling perplexed." My eye caught Joab talking quietly with Abishai. The two had grown even closer after Asahel's death. "Joab said that he has a farfetched idea. No doubt it is most likely highly convoluted."

"Sometimes the most convoluted plans are the grand design. Is that not how you escaped the Philistines? By acting as a madman? Or, is that not how we survived for over eight years while on the run? The convoluted plans may be unorthodox, but they often work." Eleazar rested his hand on my shoulder. "Let us hear what it is, and then we will determine how farfetched and convoluted it truly is."

I called out to Joab. The men quieted and turned their attention to me. "Joab has an idea. Lay it out before us." I motioned for him to speak.

Joab stepped forward and addressed us. "Jerusalem is fortified on every side. It has a steep cliff and the sea on one side and sloping hills descending on the other side. We cannot orchestrate a direct attack." The men murmured in agreement. I waited for him to continue. "So, we do not execute a direct attack. We sneak in."

"How do we sneak in without knowing how many men they have, or where they are fortifying the city?" Shammah asked.

"How do we sneak in enough men to handle the conflict?" That question came from Uriah.

"I have walked the streets of Jerusalem," Benaiah added to the conversation. "This was during the times of Saul seeking peace with the Jebusites. I was a part of Abner's company. This is probably why they would not even let us in to speak face-to-face. The conversation between Saul and their king was not productive, nor did it end well."

"What can you tell us about their infrastructure?" Uriah asked.

"That it is tight and locked down." Benaiah turned to Joab. "I am sorry it is not better news, but I was standing in a similar position under Saul. We tried to find a weakness in their walls, but there is none. We tried to find any way to get us inside without going in through the gates, and we could not find one. Saul gave up on the idea."

"But there is a way in," Joab said with a gleam in his eye. "Jerusalem has tunnels underneath it that water the land."

"We swim up a mountain?" Eleazar acted unsure.

"I need to catch up on my swimming," Uriah added. "It has been a little bit."

Benaiah shook his head. "It is impossible. The tunnels were not built for men to be in them, just to transport water."

"One of them can," Joab said with a shrug.

"How do you know this?" Benaiah asked. "Have they built a new one?"

"I know this because I found a location outside the city walls during my reconnaissance where one of the older tunnels ends."

"That does not mean a man can fit through it, let alone an army."

"This one can." Joab gave us a mischievous grin.

"And you know this how?" I asked, sensing where he was going with this. He was, after all, my nephew.

"I climbed a portion." Joab had our attention. "When I found it, it was guarded. I was able to travel by night with the use of a lantern. I went until the shaft shifted into a completely vertical tunnel. I could not hold my lantern and climb it, but I saw enough to know it could be done."

Uriah laughed and pointed a finger at Joab. "You are crazy, and I love it."

Benaiah held up a hand to quiet those who agreed with Uriah. "How did you get a lantern there? In the dark? How did you light the lantern? In the dark? And how will an army climb up a vertical shaft?"

"Good questions," I said to Benaiah, then looked over at Joab. "I was thinking the same thing."

"This event took several nights of planning, uncle. Those with me could not guard me closely, or else, we would be seen even in the dark. Abishai was my right-hand man. He hid in the closest tree that would be the clearest shot should anything go amiss. Others hid in various locations in case the trouble followed me. It took a few attempts to hide a lantern in the shaft that was not water-logged. We devised a tightly-bound wicker container covered in tar that somewhat worked. I hid it on a rock ledge that jutted out above the water line. I did the same thing for the lantern oil, and then waited some more until the guards were distracted enough for me to pass through into the shaft undetected."

"This took several attempts," Abishai said. "But my brother was undeterred. He was determined to find a way to secure this city for our people." Turning to me, he added, "And for you."

"Benaiah's question was not answered," I said, turning the conversation back to Joab. "This worked for you. Traveling alone with minimal help. How do we all into that shaft and travel it up the mountain before anyone finds out?"

"And the water tunnel is heavily protected once inside the city," Benaiah said. "Maybe one could sneak in through the protection of night, but a group? Highly doubtful."

"Benaiah's right," Abishai said. "They have a set of alerts. All soldiers we observed had trumpets ready to sound the alarm if there is any perceived threat. And they are positioned at various posts to make it difficult to get to all of them before the trumpet alerts the city."

"I am not saying my plan is perfect," Joab said to Benaiah. "But it is worth exploring. We made sure to go undetected. We knew that if we needed to hurt any of the Jebusite guards that our chances to sneak an attack would decrease substantially. The last thing we desired was for them to fortify the Gihon Springs. Right now, they are not suspecting a sneak attack through the tunnel, which is why it could work."

"The question bears repeating, *how do we get an army through a vertical tunnel?*" I made eye contact with all the men. "This is the best idea to capture the city as of yet. So, how do we accomplish it?"

"The tunnel is not for the army," Uriah suggested. "It is for a select group who will infiltrate the city from the inside. If they can sneak in undetected, they could walk right to the gates and throw them open where the rest of us will be waiting."

"If an army gathers at their gates, will that not alert them that something is amiss?" Benaiah asked.

"We travel the tunnel in increments," Joab said. "Only a few will travel together."

"That will take a long time," I said. "But what if we line the city walls among their sick? Disguise ourselves. When the gates open, we drop our disguises and enter. And not the entire army at first. Just enough to get us in and overwhelm their defenses."

"Timing is crucial," Benaiah said. "If we get in the city and open the gates before they can put together what is happening, then we could increase in numbers through the open gate. We could then have our troops in the forest. Out of eyesight but just on the edge. When we are inside, we send them our message with our trumpets. We attack from the inside, keeping the Jebusites distracted. While they are fighting us, the army moves forward and marches right inside."

I contemplated the plan, and the others followed suit. For several moments, all that could be heard was the crackling of the logs in the fire, and distant conversation and laughter from other groups. "I have fought for so long, and one thing for which I am certain. The battle is not mine. It is never mine. It is the Lord's. I was told that this Jebusite settlement would be the City of David. It is where all of Israel will be unified. That is why I know that this will work."

"What are our next steps?" Joab asked.

"Making any move right now would not be prudent. They have already notified their men to be on the lookout. They insulted a king to his face. They are not stupid. They know I will retaliate. We will order our troops to return to Hebron's border. Select a small group of spies to stay here with you. Watch the Jebusite's every movement. When they start to relax their patrols, send the messenger. Next time, when we return, we will not bring pomp or circumstance. We will come quietly with half the men. From there, we will make our move."

"Are the rest of us to head back to Hebron?"

"Troops will occupy select stations until they hear word about next steps. Those with me will travel to surrounding tribes. We need to assuage any trepidation about aligning under me as king."

29

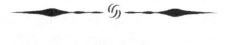

Michal

Hebron

1010 B.C.

D o not complain," I ordered myself as my head rested against my sick pot. Dinah gently took it and handed me another one.

"I will clean this and return soon."

I nodded as another bout of nausea hit me. "You said this only happened in the mornings."

Dinah had opened the door but paused before leaving. "I said that it often happens in the mornings. But this is good, Michal. It strongly suggests a healthy pregnancy."

As she left, I smiled at the thought. Until my stomach rolled.

When I was not sick, I still pushed toward staying healthy, which included daily walks through the garden paths. And I made sure to order that my paths were clear of all women. I never wanted to lay eyes on them again. I was surprised when it worked.

For my entire royal life, I was not heard, and I had little power. But as queen, the entire household listened to me. As long as it did not contradict any of David's edicts, they completed my requests. One of which was that the rooftop must be cleared before I approached it. Even still, I avoided David's private rooftop arrangement. It brought back all the negative and dark emotions of that night, and I must stay strong for my plan to work.

Providing David an heir would bind him to me wholly and completely. I thought of my own father and how much he preferred his legitimate children through his queen than any of his children through lesser wives. With our own child, we would not need any of the other women and their lesser seed.

I rested my hands on my belly, wondering when I would show the signs. Other than nausea and lack of monthly cycles, I had no other symptoms, and my monthly cycles were sporadic anyway. I pushed doubt out of my mind. The dark thoughts were there too, but I refused to listen to them. If Mother could keep the darkness at bay, then I would do the same. I did not have to suffer the same fate as my father.

When Dinah returned, she scowled and hurriedly went about tidying the chamber. "What is it?" I asked. "Did one of the servant boys poke fun? Do not worry yourself over such trivial experiences."

Dinah stopped fluffing pillows, and without meeting my gaze, answered, "The princess has begun the birthing process. They set up the birthing tent and assisted her there. The birthing pains are already magnified. I heard her screams from the communal courtyard."

I frowned. "Of course, she will have the baby now. David will be returning soon, and she will demand his attention."

"She will be even more insufferable once she becomes a mother," Dinah admitted. "She is cruel to us servants. Anytime she sees me, she orders me to do her bidding. I avoid the communal courtyard as much as I can, but sometimes, it cannot be helped."

My nausea forgotten, I stewed in jealousy and irritation.

"Do not fret." Dinah placed a cool, damp cloth on my forehead. "Once you have a child, all of those women will be forgotten. You must not be in distress. It makes your body suffer terribly."

"Find David's man, Cush. Tell him of the queen's request to

visit with the king immediately upon his return. And send Raja in. She can prepare my bath while you complete my errand."

Dinah left, and moments later, Raja rushed in. "My queen," she bowed low then began to prep for my bath. "Water is already warming over the fire in the courtyard. I have others who will fetch it here as soon as it is ready."

"Did you hear about Maacah's imminent birth?" I moved toward her, desiring to hear more gossip even if it would bring distress upon me, as Dinah mentioned.

"The entire compound has heard it," Raja said. "Even if a person did not hear her lengthy moans and yowls, she sent a formal message to the king's man, demanding notification be delivered to the king."

"That conniving woman," I hissed, more annoyed than ever. "She is determined to lure David to herself."

"She does not have to lure the king. He visits her often when he is here."

"You are mistaken. He spends his free moments with me, not her."

Raja's face turned red. "Yes, of course. I spoke out of turn."

Just then several servants entered with buckets of warm water. I waited for them to pour the water and watched as Raja busied herself with a tray of ointments and cloths. *She's hiding something.* I waited for the servants to leave before responding, "What do you know? And measure your words carefully. Do not lie to your queen."

Raja's brows bunched together and she bit her lip. She wrung her hands and still would not provide eye contact. "I do not desire to lie, but what if I have orders from someone else?"

"I care not of anyone else's orders. I am queen, and I demand you tell me whatever it is you are hiding!"

Her eyes filled with tears. "The orders are from the king. I dare not disobey him."

The dark thoughts slipped from the corners of my mind, fanning

Janice Broyles

the flames of my anger, but I was rational enough to know Raja was fearful of David. And rightfully so. If a servant defied a direct order, they would die. "Take a deep breath." I made sure my tone was soothing. "You are not in trouble. I am not angry with you." I took her hands while she tried to manage her emotional outburst.

"I do not like keeping things from you, my queen, but Dinah said we must."

My blood turned from fire to ice. "What did you say?" I squeaked out as if my voice box was crushed.

"I expressed concern about keeping secrets from you, but Dinah agreed with the king that it was best due to your...episodes."

Do not lash out at her, Michal, I ordered myself. *Keep your own emotions in check until you find out the answers.*

"I assure you that you will not endure any punishment by being truthful to me. As far as Dinah and the king are concerned, if they are keeping secrets, then maybe they do not have my best interests at heart." I smiled kindly at her while my insides screamed.

She still acted unsure, but eventually, she murmured, "Cush told all the servants of the household that no one was to speak of the king's whereabouts, especially around the queen. He said it was not to disturb your tender disposition. All gossip about the king and his activities is not allowed. I mentioned it to Dinah, and she said that the king is right in protecting you, and we must ensure that you are protected at all costs."

"So, David went behind my back and ordered all servants and staff not to even gossip about his whereabouts or activities. Is this correct?"

Raja swallowed and acted unsure again. "I- I think so."

"And Dinah not only knew about the lies, but she also encouraged them. Is this correct?"

Just then, the chamber door opened, and Dinah entered. She looked from me to Raja then back to me. "I thought you would be enjoying the warm waters of your bath. That is all, Raja. I can complete the bathing ritual."

240

"Oh no, Raja will complete it. It seems she is the only one to be trusted." To Dinah, I added with steel in my voice, "If I were you, I would leave before I change my mind and have you thrown in the dungeon for lying to the queen."

"What do you speak of now?" Dinah pinched her nose between her fingers.

"How often does David visit his other wives?" I asked, approaching her. "And think twice before answering incorrectly."

Dinah turned to Raja. "What did you say to her?"

Raja would not look at either of us. She opened her mouth to speak, only to close it. Tears welled in her eyes again.

"I asked you a question," I said to Dinah. "How often does David visit his other wives?"

"I do not know." Dinah raised her arms and then dropped them. "I spend nearly every waking moment with you."

"Stop playing games with me!" I yelled. "I know of your secrets with my husband! I know about the lies to protect me from what apparently are *episodes*!"

"He ordered the household to not speak or gossip about his whereabouts. Your father had similar orders when he was in power. And of course, I agreed. David is, after all, *king*." Dinah acted annoyed with me just as she did with Merab's sons as if I too was a child. And it only made the anger burn hotter.

"Do not address me as if you are my equal." I watched Dinah's lips press together, and she reluctantly bowed her head. "You went behind my back, and you lied to me. There are consequences when you lie to the queen."

"How did I lie to you, *my queen*?" Her tone had not changed. If I was not so furious, I would be shocked at her lack of decorum.

"You informed me…repeatedly…that he had not visited the other women!"

"I was following direct orders from the king. Direct your hostility at him."

My mouth fell open. Dinah never spoke to me like this before.

She still acted perturbed at me. My body shook from the hurt, as well as her absolute defiance. "Guards!" I called out. Two entered the room immediately. "Take this defiant servant and throw her in the shackles."

Dinah's head snapped up, and she stared at me in shock. "What are you doing?"

"I am teaching you a lesson. I thought you were on my side, that you were loyal to me. And after *your* secrets that I kept! I could have turned you in when my father's men searched for you, but I kept the truth hidden. Yet, you dare to keep secrets from me? Maybe it is time for you to remember that you are my servant, Dinah."

Dinah shook her head then walked to the guards, her back to me. My stomach flipped as they led her out. For a moment, I questioned my decision and my sanity. This was Dinah, my friend. But the thought of David seeing other women while everyone knew but me only rekindled my anger. Dinah betrayed me just like everyone else.

Raja had begun to sob again. She muttered something unintelligible.

"Oh, shut up," I snapped. "The last thing I want to hear is you crying when you are just as guilty as everyone else. Get out. Leave me alone before I send you to the shackles too."

Once alone, the dark thoughts raged.

They all betray you.

You are alone.

End it all. It is the only way to retaliate.

"No!" I shouted, bringing my palms to my eyes. I imagined stuffing the darkness down again into the crevices of my mind. "Leave me!"

Feeling some relief, I stepped into the water to bathe myself. Sighing, I pulled my foot out. The water was already cold.

30

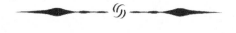

David

Hebron

1010 B.C.

News reached me of my son's birth, so my men and I traveled from the furthermost tribe to Hebron. It took longer than anticipated.

Each village and town heard of my passing through. The crowds were just as large as the days when I was hailed as the giant killer. They poured into the streets, and women danced before us. Even in my haste, their favor filled my heart. Israel's tribes desired me as king. I would need to discuss with Nathan and Abiathar how to deal with Ishbosheth. I refused to kill Saul's only surviving legitimate son. But still, I felt the tide changing in my favor.

Nearly a full moon later, I arrived at the stables. I handed the reins to the stable manager and made my way to the cleansing chamber. Cush rushed to me. "My king." He bowed low several times.

"Cush, I must bathe and fast before entering the household. Send me Abiathar."

"He is already on his way. There is much to tell about the goings on—"

I interrupted him. "It can wait. I will call for you when I am

243

ready."

He nodded, bowed, then left me.

I took the time for quiet reflection and prayer. Abiathar arrived and chanted over me, adding to my prayers and thanksgiving for a successful journey.

As the third day ended, I itched to see my new son, to bless him and his mother, and to see my other children. I desired Michal's embrace, but duties and fatherhood needed to come first. When I entered the compound, I address Cush, "I will visit my families and then I will spend time with the queen."

"As you wish, my king."

"She does not know I have arrived?"

"No, I have told no one other than the priest."

"Good. Anything pressing that cannot wait?"

"All is calm here, sir. There has been some trouble with the queen, but she is still being guarded, and her health is well enough."

I stopped walking and turning to him, raised my eyebrow. "Explain."

"The queen has dismissed all servants. She allows one to bring her sustenance and to take her cleansing and excrement pots, but that is it."

"She often relies on Dinah. This is nothing new."

"It is not Dinah."

"Is Dinah unwell?" My heart immediately became concerned for my wife's closest friend and servant.

"The queen cast her out. Placed her in shackles."

I stared at him for a moment in disbelief, only to chuckle. "Cush, you have heard incorrectly. Michal loves her servant nearly as much as she loves me, maybe even more at times."

"I send someone out to Dinah daily, feeding her and providing her fresh water. It is true, my king. According to Dinah, the queen learned of your order to household servants to keep your activities from their lips."

I felt the color drain from my face. "Who?" My breathing

became ragged as I forced myself to contain the irritation of someone's disobedience.

"Dinah will not say, only that it was not her. Yet, the queen accused her of deception and betrayal, casting her out."

I sighed and rubbed my face. "Oh Michal, why must it be this way?" To Cush, I said, "I will see my families, but first, take me to Dinah. I need to find out who disobeyed and then punish them. Severely."

The Hebron compound did not have a dungeon, per se. Instead, it had tiny underground chambers made of packed dirt. I barely used them, for I had not retained many prisoners of war as of late. Still, when one of my men lifted the heavy door, and I took in the stench of filth and excrement, I nearly cried out. "Pull her out," I ordered.

A rope was dropped into the darkness that was knotted at the end. At first, nothing happened. There was no sound, no movement. "Dinah? It is I, David. Just wrap your arm around the knot," I said into the darkness. "The guard will do the work."

A moment later, the rope tightened and pulled.

"Are you ready?" I gently asked. "I do not want to hurt you if you do not have a good grip."

No answer.

"Pull her up," I said, my stomach rolling at this poor woman suffering in darkness for however long. "Gently." The guard did the best he could, but I ended up helping him. Dinah's matted head appeared, and my eyes welled at just the sight of her disheveled appearance. I reached down and pulled her up the rest of the way. She covered her eyes and stayed slumped on the floor, not moving. To Cush, who stayed pressed against a wall by the door, I ordered, "Get her a warm bath and clean garments. Bring a maidservant to wash her. And a meal. I demand food and water."

Cush moved quickly and left the chamber.

"Dinah, speak to me. What happened?"

She pushed herself up and blinked, still adjusting to the light illuminating from the lanterns. "She found out." Her voice sounded scratchy. She coughed heartily in her hand.

"Food and water will be here momentarily."

"I was fed well," she said, not looking at me. "Michal's guilt brought much food and drink."

"So, she visited you? I have a hard time understanding how she could keep you in here."

"She tried to get me out not even an hour after sending me here. When she called upon me and saw where they had placed me, she wept and ordered for me to be removed from the shackles and underground chamber. That was three days ago."

"I do not understand. Why were you still down there?"

"I was waiting for you." She turned to me then. I had knelt beside her, and her eyes, bloodshot and swollen, bore into me.

"You chose to stay in here?" I shook my head. "How would you know when I returned? I could have been gone for many more moons. Had it not been for the message of my son's birth, I would not be here."

"I knew you would be here as soon as you heard word of the birth. You are a nobleman in some ways. Cush did provide me the information too." She paused, "I desired a conversation. As a servant, I cannot simply approach you. I must be called upon. I took this opportunity and hoped that your kindness toward me would bring you here."

I stood up and stepped away from her, breathing through my mouth. The stench was strong, but I also needed a moment to figure out what in the world was happening. "I am confused, Dinah, and I have much to do. It sounds as if you are playing with me and with Michal. My time is precious. So, speak."

"May I speak freely? May I have your word that no punishment will befall me or anyone else?"

"You may speak freely, and you have my word that no punishment will befall you if you are not the one who disobeyed direct orders. I will not promise anything else."

She stood up and faced me, keeping her gaze on me. It was not often a servant made eye contact, but Dinah did, and she kept it there. "Please do not ask me to deceive the queen again."

"I did not ask you to deceive the queen. I ordered you and every other servant to never speak of my activities within the compound. Do not bring it up. It is that simple. I would think for the good of my marriage that this would be an easy action."

"It is neither simple nor easy. She would ask me if I had seen you or observed you from afar and who you were with. I had to lie many times."

"Dinah, I realize we have history, and we both love Michal, but I do not have to explain myself to you or even to her. This conversation is out of line."

"I will not lie to her again." Her gaze turned cold and her jaw set. "She is not only my queen, but she is my friend and sister. I have broken her trust, and it is because of you."

My mouth opened to reprimand her, but no words came out.

She continued, "I have been with her since the beginning. I was there to keep your secrets quiet. I was there to watch the two of you navigate your marriage, and I did whatever I could to protect her from her father. I did whatever I could to protect her from herself. And now, I will do whatever I can to protect her from you."

"I am not the enemy, Dinah. I am her husband, and I will protect her just as I will protect my other families."

"You have *not* protected her for years. The moment you climbed out the window so many moons ago, you left her and never came back."

"Be careful," I said, the irritation turning to anger. "I am king, no longer a shepherd. And I may not punish you at this moment, but I will also not be disrespected by a lowly servant."

"Lowly servant? I know where you came from. You were a

servant, just as I am. You might not have cooked and cleaned, but you were at the beck and call of the king. So, I will not be careful, even if it means my life. Do what you must to me, but I will not ever again deceive the queen."

I could not decide if I was angry or shocked by Dinah's unapologetic words. More than anything, I felt an overwhelming desire to defend myself. "I am not being deceptive, and I do not appreciate being accused. I am merely keeping troublesome information from Michal. We both know that she does not respond favorably if anything is mentioned about the other women and my children. But they are mine, and I cannot forsake them. They deserve my companionship too. If Michal could see that, this entire situation would be easier, but she has changed. She is not the bride of my youth."

Dinah coughed violently then shook her head. "You judge her?"

"I am not perfect, Dinah, but I am trying to have a relationship with her despite the constant struggle she makes it."

Dinah watched me for a moment in what seemed disgust. Here she stood, soiled and reeking of stench, yet I was the one who felt dirty. "You never came back," she eventually said. "For years, she waited for you. For years, she mourned the death of your child. For years, she stayed faithful to your marriage covenant. In one way, she has not changed, and that is she loves you fiercely. And it guts her to see you share intimacy and relationships with other women. So, do not say that she is not the same because it is you, King David, who is not the same."

I could not help but get defensive. "And what of you? You still keep secrets from her. Does she know who your father is?"

Dinah coughed. "That matters little. I swore to Saul to never reveal myself."

"It matters little? You are half-sister to the queen, Dinah. Everyone in Saul's palace knew it. Even Merab knew it. Yet, you choose to serve her? How is that any different from me keeping things from her?"

"It is vastly different. What good would it do to tell her of her father's actions? Or to inform her that I became her servant because Saul felt guilty when my mother died? No, it is better this way."

"And what good would it do for her to know of my visits with the other women?"

"The difference is I have not asked you to lie."

"Then I may tell her your secret?"

"If it means me never lying to her again, then yes, tell her." Dinah turned and coughed forcefully.

I opened my mouth to say more, but I could see the moist, cold air of the underground chamber had been too much for her. "We both love her and are protective of her," I said. "We are more alike than you realize."

Maidservants came pouring in, each carrying buckets of water, rags, and meal trays. I said nothing more, only walked out without so much of a background glance. A part of me desired to punish her. How dare she say such things to me? Another part of me was impressed. She stayed in shackles, even though Michal desired to pull her out, simply so she could have an audience with the king.

I noticed Cush had not entered the chamber but waited in the connecting hall that led to the stairs. "You knew about her plan to speak with me?"

Cush stumbled over words. "N-No, my king. She asked if you had received word of the newborn, and she asked if you could be notified of Michal's mistreatment of her. I thought you would want to know. I did not perceive any trickery."

"I do better when I am at war," I said to myself. "I have always had conflict in my personal life. From my father's abuse and brothers' rejection to Saul ripping my wife from me and pursuing me for years. Now I still have no peace. Will there ever be peace in my household? Will I ever desire to come home more than I desire to be out on conquests?"

Cush seemed unsure how to respond. "Would you like to meet your newborn son?"

"Yes," I said and moved in the direction of the stairs. "I desire to see the goodness of God in the face of my newborn son."

———

"He acts as if he is angry with me," I said, marveling at the alertness of the newborn.

Maacah approached, moving slowly. I requested her presence, even if she was still bleeding. Right now, I desired companionship. And here, with this child we made together, I felt the strong response of protection. Here, in my arms, lay my third son. How could I turn him or his mother away? Yet, I could not escape the harsh truths of Dinah's words. They replayed in my head as I counted the baby's fingers and toes. *You have not protected her for years. The moment you climbed out the window so many moons ago, you left her and never came back*

"Is he not beautiful?" Maacah sat beside me, moving slowly and trying to hide her grimace.

"You are still in pain?" I adjusted the cushions for her.

"Yes. Absalom left unresolved pain in his wake." She gave a tired smile.

"Absalom," I said, turning back to the child. "That is a strong name. I am glad we came up with it."

Maacah shook her head. "We came up with it? That is not how I remember it."

We shared a smile, but I could see that she was uncomfortable and could not find a suitable position. "Please, go and rest. I am glad to see you and to see that you are well, but you need to regain your strength."

"Will I see you again soon?" she asked.

I kissed Absalom on the forehead, whispered a blessing, and handed him to the wet nurse. Then I stood and helped Maacah up as tenderly as I could. "Yes, of course. I will visit my son daily while I am here. If you are available, I will visit you too."

"Yes, I am available. Even if I am resting, I desire to see you." She rested her head against my shoulder.

I gently wrapped my arms around her as she leaned into me. "We have a son together. A growing family. You will see me. I promise." I kissed the top of her head, then led her to her bed. When she was laying down and more comfortable, I took my leave.

Even though a visit with Michal was in order, I did not want to see her just yet. I was surprised at my feelings, but after holding Absalom in my arms, I desired to see my other children. I told myself it had nothing to do with Dinah being thrown underground in shackles. I told myself it had nothing to do with the angry words from the maidservant.

What I did tell myself was that my family came first, specifically my children. It grieved me that I did not have any children yet with Michal, but I did have children through other women. So, Michal would have to wait.

31

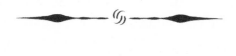

Michal

Hebron

1010 B.C.

I t had been three long days and excruciating nights of torture.
The guilt and shame suffocated me. Dinah would not speak to
me.

The cold bath from three days earlier had shocked the sense
back into me. Dinah, my friend and confidante, in a dungeon? I had
thrown on some semblance of attire and asked the guards to bring
Dinah to me, that I had made a mistake. When they came back to
report that she refused, I went to see for myself.

One look at the dark, underground chamber, and I was begging
Dinah to take the rope and climb out. "Please, forgive me. I acted
in jealousy, and I am despicable."

Nothing. No words exchanged. No movement.

I ordered a guard to climb down and bring her out. When he
climbed back out, he said that she refused and had clung to the
chains in the wall.

"What should I do, my queen?"

I stared into the dark pit, wishing I dared to go down there myself. But I lacked the courage. Fear took over, which sent the dark thoughts into a flurry.

Leave her down there.

If she refuses to come out, then you are relieved of the burden of guilt.

Leave her. Leave her. Leave her.

I visited every day, begging Dinah to talk to me, to forgive me, to come back. I questioned if anyone was down in the darkness, but there would be the occasional cough as a reminder of my horrible decision.

My stress over Dinah's predicament temporarily paused my concern about the pregnancy. I still felt the painful cramps on occasion, but I did not dwell on them.

On this day, the fourth morning of Dinah's and my separation, I woke up to intense cramping in my lower abdomen. I pulled up my legs and wrapped my arms around them as I often did when my monthly cycle came. "No," I whispered, begging my body not to reject the baby inside me. Another cramp twisted, and I cried out. Then as quickly as the cramping came, it dissipated. I lay still for some time, but my heart rate calmed.

The door to my chamber opened, and I heard David's voice call out, "Michal? Are you here?"

David was back? Of course, he was. Another woman birthed his child. I almost did not answer, but I had to stick to the plan. Placing a hand on my lower abdomen, I hoped all was well. "I am here." I pushed myself up and stepped out of the bedchamber to my sitting area.

"What happened with Dinah?" He stayed where he was and did not approach me. He crossed his arms across his chest as if to close me off.

"I caught her in a lie, and I sent her away. I did not realize that this compound did not have a proper dungeon. My thought was to release her immediately, especially when I discovered where the guards dumped her."

"A proper dungeon? If there had been a proper dungeon, you're your actions for dumping her there would be justified?"

"No, that is not what I am saying. And my actions were the result of finding out that my servants lied. You know deliberate disobedience without punishment could lead to rebellion and potential mutiny."

"We are talking about Dinah, not foreign slaves who we do not know." David's words carried an angry clip in them, and it irritated me. "You truly felt justified that your loyal maidservant was deserving of being shackled?"

"Yes. If you lie to the queen or king, there is severe punishment, is there not? Once, when I was young, a servant disobeyed my mother's direct orders, and she received twenty lashes. I did not want to hurt my friend, but I needed her to understand that lying to the queen has consequences." I suddenly felt defensive about my actions. Did he not see his culpability in these events?

David stared at me in seeming disbelief. "She was following *my* orders."

"Yes, from what I understand, every person in this compound has been ordered to deceive me about your whereabouts." I purposefully added a bite to my own words.

"Because my whereabouts are not your concern." His tone turned to ice. David had never looked upon me with this type of coldness. "I have tried to be reasonable with you because I understand that these last several years have been painful. For *both* of us. I also understand that you place the blame solely at my feet for decisions made. Be that as it may, decisions *were* made, and they affect a lot of people, including the women and the children who are a part of *my* family unit."

"And you thought that deceiving me would do what? I already know about the other women and children. Why would you ever jeopardize the servants to any form of punishment, especially when I did not know about such orders?"

"To keep the peace," he said rigidly. "When you are *not* volatile,

I can still see glimpses of my wife and first love. But I have other wives and children now. I cannot neglect them."

My first instinct was to lash out, but I kept my mouth shut. The cramping had returned, even though it was not as intense as earlier. David's anger toward me was not helping. I considered telling him, but what was there to say? I was not even sure I was pregnant. I had morning sickness, which was a good sign, but my monthly cycles had always been irregular. The cramps were not a good sign.

The outer chamber door opened, and Raja stepped in. She took one look at David and turned and walked out.

"You realize I after punish her," he said to me. "Her name was given as the one to defy orders."

"You cannot be serious," I said. "She is a young girl still. Then again, you are not the same man you once were. The David of my early years is long gone. I suppose neither of us is the same."

He glared at me. "If I allow anyone to defy an order, as you just pointed out, it makes me look weak. You know this. You just enacted punishment on your closest friend for this very reason!"

"Dinah suffered the punishment. Let it be on her head. No need for two maidservants to suffer when your orders were faulty."

"Faulty? Oh, pray, do explain to me how my desire to have a content queen is faulty."

"Because it is based upon a faulty pretense with deceit as the foundation. Keeping servants quiet while you visit your women only benefits you. It does not benefit them or me."

Another maidservant entered, greeted us, and addressed me, "My queen, your maidservant, Dinah, was released yesterday, but she cannot attend to you today. She is unwell."

"She was released?"

"I released her," David said. "She had a terrible cough. I encouraged her to get some rest."

"Her condition has progressively worsened through the night."

"Where is she?" I asked the maidservant, ignoring David. My irritation at my husband became secondary at the news Dinah was unwell.

"She is isolated in the sick tent."

I moved past the maidservant and left the room, heading outside. As panic set in, my steps turned into a run. The sick tent was at the far end of the compound. Whether or not David followed me, I cared little. Dinah was sick, and the guilt was so strong in my chest, I could barely breathe. The cramping from earlier had lessened considerably, but that too mattered little at the thought of Dinah's discomfort.

The guards outside the tent door stopped me. "You cannot enter, queen. This tent is unclean."

"I care not. Let me pass."

They looked past me, then stepped aside. I glanced back to see David approaching, but he paused at the entrance. Of course, he would. He would not want to contaminate himself with the unclean.

The tent was dark with dim lanterns only sporadically placed. Even with the cleansing incense lit, it still smelled of sickness and death, and I brought my hand to my nose.

There would be no physician or healer in this tent. If the sick were determined to be unclean, this is where they were brought. They either became better and presented themselves to Abiathar, David's priest, to be determined clean, or they died. The poor guards assigned to the tent would search the tent daily to carefully take out any of the deceased, making sure to not touch them or become unclean themselves.

And this is where they placed Dinah? Flies buzzed, and I waved them away as I searched for my maidservant. Other than the buzzing and the shuffling of my own feet, there were no other sounds. I swallowed down the scream of grief and listened. I heard distant coughing and moved in that direction. I lifted the flap that opened to the back corner of the tent and immediately zeroed in on Dinah laying on a filthy mat on the floor, flies landing on her. She violently coughed, and the flies flew overhead, only to land once again upon her.

"Dinah," I whispered, waving the flies away again. I touched her forehead and moved my hand quickly. "Your skin is as fire."

She coughed again. I heard the rattle within her. I was no physician, but I knew enough to realize it was not a good sound. She grabbed my hand and closed her eyes. "Unclean," she said, rasping for air.

"Stop it. I am here for you. I am going to demand that you come back to the compound under my care and supervision. I will not leave you here to…" I stopped myself before saying the rest. I could not think of my best friend dying. "Whoever left you here will be punished."

"Shh," she said, her eyes still closed.

"You need a cool cloth. I did not think to bring anything." I was torn. Should I leave and get the supplies? But I would not be allowed in the compound without a cleansing ritual now that I was contaminated.

"Thirsty…"

I jumped up and searched for a drink, but there was no bucket to be found. "I will return momentarily." I left the back of the tent and marched to the outside flap at the front. Without stepping outside, I called for the guards.

"You cannot step outside," the guard said. "You will need to cleanse yourself for three days and nights and receive a blessing from Abiathar."

"Yes, I know that," I snapped. "I need one of you to provide a bucket of water, a wineskin filled with wine, some morsel of bread and broth, clean rags, and a change of clothes for my maidservant." When I heard neither move, my irritation bubbled out. "Now! That is an order!"

"We cannot leave our post," one said.

"Is David still here?"

"No, there was an urgent message that sent him back into the compound."

I groaned. "I need these supplies, and I am unable to leave the tent. Please, I beg you. What about water? There must be something close, or you two must have supplies of your own."

"One of us will retrieve water, but that is all we can do. As soon as our commander makes his rounds, we will notify him of your orders. He should be visiting us soon."

I waited for the water bucket to be brought. They left it outside the tent flap. I reached out and grabbed it, making sure not to drop any of the contents. Unfortunately, I was not skilled at menial labor, and the bucket was heavy. By the time I reached the back of the tent, I was sweating heavily, and the cramping from earlier had begun again. I paused and gathered my breath.

Dinah's coughing brought me back to the situation at hand. I lifted the ladle and brought it to my friend. "Here. Drink this." When she had drunk her fill. I took my sash and dipped it in the cool water, then placed it upon her forehead. She sighed in relief. "I am going to try my best to wash you."

The coolness of the rag and her quenched thirst made her more talkative. "If I was not so sick, I would find this humorous. The queen of Judah washing a mere servant."

"Not just a servant." I paused and made eye contact. "My very best friend. And Dinah, I am so sorry. I need to tell you before..." I stopped myself again.

"Before I die?" She coughed, and her insides rattled.

"No. Do not die. I forbid it." I washed her face and neck and worked my way down each limb with my soaked sash. "I will have to undress you. You have soiled yourself."

"If I was not so sick, I would be embarrassed."

"There is nothing to be embarrassed about. It is just I, Michal. And you have helped me more times than I can count. The least I can do is wash away the dirt and excrement. I asked for a change of garments for you. As soon as they arrive, you will feel much better."

"I already feel better. Thank you. It was thirst that made me delusional. May I have another cupful?"

I stopped washing her and brought the ladle to her lips again. This time she managed to push herself up enough to not lose any to the ground. She lay back down and closed her eyes. Before long, her breathing had evened out, and she slept. Her chest still rattled, and that bothered me more than I cared to admit.

While I waited for supplies, I did the best I could to clean and tidy the small back area of the tent. I found a dilapidated broom that worked well enough. I also found a nice, thick animal skin being used as a partition. I yanked it down, shook it out far away from Dinah, then stripped her down to finish her bath. There was nothing I could do about the disgusting mat now soaked from the bath water. I was embarrassed to admit to myself I had not thought this through. Then again, I had never bathed anyone.

I tossed aside her filthy garments, ripped another sizable chunk from my tunic, and tried to mop up the mat as best I could while she slept. I pushed her to her side, wiped up the mat from underneath her, then did the same to the other side. She shivered but still snored. "I am hurrying, my dear friend. But I do not want to put a blanket upon a wet mat."

When I finished, I stepped back and decided it was good as it could be under the circumstances. I lay the animal skin upon her nakedness and tucked it underneath her.

What water remained in the bucket had turned brown. I wrinkled my nose and picked it up, carrying it to the front of the long tent. I would have them dump this and fetch more water. I thought of how long I had already been in the tent. "Surely, their commander has made his rounds by now."

I paused when I heard the voices on the other side of the tent. There was a third! I nearly opened my mouth to address them from behind the tent's flap when their words stopped me.

"What is she doing in that tent?" The man seemed to speak above the other men, and a horse snorted.

"The king informed us it is her maidservant. He said she is to receive anything she asks."

"She chose to sully herself for a slave?" The commander scoffed. "Fine. I will send a girl out here with the supplies even if it is a futile endeavor. Anyone in this tent is sent here to die."

"The king is worried about that too. He nearly went inside to retrieve the queen, but we begged him to reconsider. An urgent message came right about then, which distracted him. He left immediately."

"I was told it is messengers from the king. The other king."

"There is no other king."

"I speak of Ishbosheth."

"What are his men doing here?"

"I do not know, but I heard from the tribe's elders that ever since Abner's death, Ishbosheth has been terrified that David is coming for him. There are rumors of night terrors and madness, much like what his father had."

"Maybe they come seeking peace?"

"I will inform you on my next round. If she asks, tell the queen that supplies will be provided soon."

I waited for the commander to be far enough gone before requesting more water. I set the bucket just outside the tent flap.

"The commander assured us that supplies are on their way," one of the guards said from the outside of the tent.

"Yes, I heard part of the conversation." I would have asked about my brother and his messengers, but these guards were as clueless as I was. "Thank you for the water. Call out to me when the supplies arrive."

Why would Ishbosheth send messengers? Would he really seek an alliance? I doubted he would abdicate the throne.

I sighed, knowing that I would not be able to find out for several days. I told myself not to worry. I had enough to worry about with Dinah's sickness and my precarious situation with David, but something inside warned me that the messengers did not come in peace. Ishbosheth may not have the strength and courage as my other brothers, but he was still a son of Saul. He would never hand over our father's kingdom.

A dark thought struck me. *What will David do when he has everything?*

He will have no use for you, the voice whispered.

32

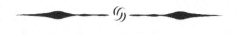

David

Hebron

1010 B.C.

I entered the throne room, trying to put out of my mind recent events with Michal. We were broken, but I was unsure how to fix us. A part of me still longed for her, and I loved her fiercely, but another part was angry, and that part grew daily.

Cush interrupted my thoughts. "They said it was an urgent matter for King David. They refused to leave until you spoke with them."

"Let us hope that Ishbosheth seeks the end this division of Israel. Send them in." I sat on the throne and held my head in my hands. Two young men entered. One carried a sack. Something about them sent my hair on edge. They did not wear the messenger sash. "State who you are and your reason for demanding my attention."

"Rechab and Baanah, the sons of Rimmon the Beerothite," One of them said.

Both prostrated themselves before me. "Long live King David."

"Enough. What is this message you bring? You are not the king's appointed messengers, so state your reason."

"We come with great news."

"And a gift," the other mentioned.

I motioned with my hand for them to continue.

"Ishbosheth, the counterfeit king who took what was yours, is now dead."

A sudden hush filled the room.

The two brothers seemed oblivious, chanting, "Long live King David!"

"Stop!" I yelled. "Are you telling me that Ishbosheth, son of Saul, is dead?"

"Yes, oh great king, and we can prove it." The one opened the sack and pulled out the severed head of Ishbosheth.

I shot straight up, shock and dismay hitting me like a javelin to my heart. "What is this? What happened?"

"Behold, we present to you the head of Ishbosheth, the son of Saul. The Lord has avenged you, oh great king, and has delivered you from Saul and his seed."

"Who did this?"

"We went to him while he was resting and killed him in the name of David. We brought you his head with our sworn allegiance."

"Not in my name. I did not order or ask for this. This is Yahweh's anointed. Who are any of us to touch what He has ordained?" The young men set the severed head down. I motioned for it to be removed. "What kind of coward kills a man in his sleep?"

The two men glanced at each other. One swallowed and stuttered, "W-We did it for you and for Israel. No more division among the kingdom. Is this not what you desire?"

"What do you think happened to the messenger who told me that it was by his hand Saul was killed? My men, in turn, took his life, for no one should touch the anointed. But you? You cowards. You dare to kill a king when he cannot even defend himself?" The more I thought about their actions, the more infuriated I became. It was more than my reputation to the Hebrew people, many of whom already considered me and my men barbarians. It was the idea that Ishbosheth was simply murdered. It was not supposed to happen in this way.

My guards already surrounded the two brothers. They pleaded with me, but I held up my hand to silence them. "You are wicked men who killed an innocent man in his sleep. For this wicked action, you too will die."

———————

"It is done." Joab entered my chamber. "Their bodies are now hanging over the waters of Hebron."

"Good." I shook my head. Two days had passed since learning of Ishbosheth's death, and I still had yet to fully process its implications. "What weak-minded, wicked men. I may not have thought well of Ishbosheth, but no one deserves to be murdered in his sleep."

"What will we do for Ishbosheth? He has servants and a harem that will need instruction and distribution."

I rubbed my face, knowing decisions needed to be made. I thought of those already in this compound living in close quarters. "We buried him at Abner's tomb. We will deal with the other decisions when I truly become King of Israel."

"Is it true the elders of the tribes have already sent messengers? I heard they look to you for leadership."

"Tis true." I set the papyrus leaf down. "When elders heard of Ishbosheth's death, they sought me out. They desire a strong leader."

"And they came to you?" Joab joked, a small smile pulling at the corner of his mouth.

Even in my exhaustion, I chuckled. "It is a wonder."

Cush entered and ushered in my evening meal. He greeted Joab and then bowed to me. "Forgive me for the interruption, but many here are concerned about the queen. I normally would not bring it up, but I do not want an uprising."

"Why would there be an uprising?"

"Rumors run like a gushing torrent that she is unclean, and you have done away with her."

"The rumors are false. I will deal harshly with anyone who spreads such lies," I said. Cush and Joab seemed to wait for me to continue. "She is with the sick, caring for her maidservant."

"The one she cast aside and threw in shackles?" Joab asked.

"Yes, that is the one. It is a complicated situation. According to her, the blame falls entirely at my feet, and I have been told emphatically to leave her alone to care for her maidservant." I sighed. "So, I have honored her request. When she is finished with caring for the unclean, she will separate and present herself to Abiathar for the cleansing ritual."

"Does she know of her brother?" Joab asked. He and Cush waited for me to answer.

"No. Now is not the time when Dinah is so sick. We will have the discussion when she enters back into the compound." I released Cush and sat down to my meal. To Joab, I said, "Come and sit. We must talk of Jerusalem."

Joab sat beside me, and we gave thanks, breaking bread together. "Is it time?" he asked, sipping from his wine goblet.

"Yes. It is not as much time as I would prefer, but Abiathar and I have sought the Lord, and Nathan affirms He is with us. The time to move forward is now."

"And the strategy? It is the same as our earlier conversation?"

"Yes. It was genius for you to sneak up the water tunnel. The first group of men will need to be a small enough number to securely make it to the tunnel's entrance without detection."

"We will need to eliminate the guards at the tunnel entrance. I doubt they have retracted their numbers."

"We are of the same mind. Our spies are still in position, or so they should be, from when we left. They can provide us with the locations of each guard. We will need one group to descend upon them simultaneously so that no one has a chance to sound their horns. From there, we will send another set of men."

"Timing is critical. When the sun comes up, all will be revealed. We will need to be in place."

"I am curious if we can accomplish this over the course of several nights. Our men need to be within city walls before any alerts take place. Once they discover their men are dead, they could close up the tunnel or even flood it."

"With small numbers, yes. Going undetected was easy when it was me alone. The more men, the greater the risk of detection." Joab swallowed a bite and took another sip of wine. "We surprise attack them, and we disguise ourselves in their attire. When the reinforcements come, we will already be in their assigned positions. We have surprise on our side."

"We kill the reinforcements."

"Without their horns for communication, they are at our mercy. The walls of the city are too high up for anyone to truly observe any disturbance."

"Especially when the disturbance happens at night or early morning." I lifted my goblet. "Let us meet with the elders, secure their allegiance, and then secure my city."

"It is time," Joab said, lifting his goblet.

"It is time," I repeated.

33

Michal

Hebron

1011 B.C.

The coughing concerned me. Dinah would cough so violently that she would gag and vomit bile. The rattle inside her never went away. I kept hoping she would cough, and whatever made such a raspy noise inside her would be satisfied. But after the second day, I was terrified to sleep, afraid that I would wake up and the coughing would have ended with finality.

Raja and a team of servants traveled the distance from compound to tent to deliver necessities and even some luxuries. No one ventured inside, and I was left to drag in the baskets, clean bed mats, blankets, and other supplies. I was no match for the manual labor, but still, I persisted.

At times she would be coherent and would sip broth. I tried to mask the concern as her skin felt like fire. She would want the blankets off, only to begin shivering and needing them again.

On this third evening, I stepped outside the back of the tent. Stepping outside the tent without being observed by the priest was strictly forbidden, but occasionally I could not help myself.

This evening was different. My lower abdomen cramped in fits and starts, but now, it came back with a vengeance.

I took in big gulps of fresh air, but I clutched my stomach as another cramp came. I had already come to terms with what this meant. I knew enough about pregnancy to know when a woman's body had accepted or rejected the unborn child.

Once the cramping subsided, I looked up into the night sky and felt so alone I had to turn away. A prayer halted on my tongue. There was no God. How could there be? How could any god or goddess allow such suffering and heartache? I wiped the tears from my eyes, desiring so strongly to talk to Him or to anyone who would listen. As the grief and heartache poured out of me, I stifled a scream into my newly-changed tunic, falling to my knees. The dejection weighed on me like the yoke on an ox. If there was a God, He had already chosen sides, and He had chosen David.

"Queen Michal."

I jumped at the sound of a man's voice. "Stay away! I am unclean. I have been in the sick tent, and I have yet to be purified."

The sun had mostly set, but I could still see the prophet approach. "I will be all right," Nathan said and closed the distance between us. "Just as you will be."

I pushed myself up from the ground and tried to straighten my garments, but I stopped, seeing the futility. "Please forgive my appearance. I have been caring for my friend."

"Dinah, is it not? That is your maidservant?"

"Yes." I awkwardly leaned on one foot and then another. I wondered if he heard my thoughts and denouncement of God. "Why are you so far removed from the compound? This is no place for the prophet. David will not be happy."

"I came to see you." The words were so simple, yet they moved something within me.

"Why? Have you not heard? I am the volatile queen who has *episodes*. You should avoid me." I heard the bitterness of my voice and felt heat rise in my cheeks.

"You are bitter."

"Yes," I said, not knowing what else to say.

"You have a right to feel upset. Life has not been kind to you. Then again, life is a struggle for women, is it not? You have no say over your life. You must be at the ready for the whim of your husband who in turn brought other women into his life. I would struggle with bitterness too."

I watched him with my mouth open. No man, save David, had ever talked so openly and honestly with me.

Then he turned to me. His gaze pierced mine. "But be careful, Michal. The bitterness will poison you. It has already taken hold, but it is not too late."

"Bitterness has become my companion."

"Then cut it off. It will kill you."

"I do not know what to do with the hurt and betrayal I feel. Then, there are the voices…" I stopped and covered my mouth. I could not have David knowing that I too might suffer from madness just as my father did.

"You do not startle me with your confession. Your father often talked to Samuel about dark thoughts."

"Then Samuel forsook him. Refused to even see him." I, once again, heard the bitterness in my words.

"Yes, disobedience comes with a high price. David's household will suffer too should he choose to disobey the ordinances of the Lord." Nathan paused, then continued, "Michal, there is much to do with David as king. He is far from a perfect man, but his heart toward the ways of Yahweh has led him to this place and will continue to lead him. But there is a place for you too. It is no mistake that you are queen. It is no mistake that you live. But you must choose."

"Choose what? I have little decision-making power. I am, after all, merely a woman."

"Choose forgiveness. Choose to follow the one true God in all ways."

"You make it sound easy when it is not. Unforgiveness.

Jealousy. Bitterness." I stopped talking and thought about how those negative traits had overtaken my life. How long had I been this miserable, wretched person? Then I felt defensive. "It is not my fault that I am this way. Others had a role."

"Life has been unkind, yet you have been most blessed. You do not have to keep holding on to bitterness."

"How can you say that? Was it a blessing to be taken from my husband all those years ago? Was it a blessing to lose my sister, then my father and brothers? Was it a blessing to be forced to leave the home I had grown accustomed to and loved? Where are these blessings you speak of?"

"Change your vision," Nathan warned. "Perception is everything. What you see as a curse, Yahweh meant as protection. What you see as denial, He meant as provision."

"I do not see it that way," I said miserably.

Nathan took another step toward me. We were so close I could see the gray hairs in his dark beard with only his small lantern providing light. "Change your vision, Michal," Nathan warned. "Before it is too late. Start by choosing the ways of Yahweh. Follow Him, and let Him lead you. Then choose to be thankful for blessings instead of stewing about what you lack."

I watched him walk away, and then I only had the night and the starlit sky as companions. I wanted to be angry, but I was too exhausted. Not only from the long hours I had spent in the sick tent, but exhausted over being so miserable. Staring up at the night sky, the words tumbled out. And the prayer was not for me but for my friend. "Please heal her. Her sickness is my fault. Please do not let her die." My words were met with the quiet breeze.

There were voices in the front. I had stayed outside longer than I should have, but I was not yet ready to go back inside and deal with sickness. The cramping was still present but had become a dull ache. I quietly walked around the long tent, staying in the shadows. Nathan must be talking with the guards. Only it was not Nathan, but one of David's men. He stood beside his horse, talking with the other two.

"You are not to speak of his death, per king's orders. Not while she is here."

"I feel bad for the queen. Ishbosheth was her last surviving sibling."

The commander shushed him. "Do not speak his name! She could hear you."

Ishbosheth? He was dead? I took a step back, telling myself I may have misunderstood. In the dark, I did not see the tent stake and tumbled to the ground.

"Someone is out here," the commander said. "Scour the perimeter."

I hurriedly pushed myself against the tent, using a hanging animal skin to partially conceal me. I held my breath and waited. It was then I saw the horse, completely unattended. Without thinking, I hurriedly moved to it. A ride along the trails would help clear my mind.

I took the reins, jumped on the horse, and snapped them. Just as the horse ran off into the night, I heard the commander yelling to halt.

"Set the javelin down," the guard yelled. "It is the queen!"

I turned back to see the commander holding his javelin. "I will return it!" I called back to him. "I promise!"

They continued to call out to me, but the horse was fast. Without a lantern to guide us, I was at the mercy of this large beast. This horse was twice the size of Eglah or Princess. How it could see in the dark bewildered me, but the beast ran without slowing down. Pulling on the reins did no good. It was too large, and it was not listening. It took me far, running toward the outlying forest. I pulled on the reins with all my might. "Whoa, slow down." It ignored me.

I tried not to panic, reminding myself that it was used to a man guiding it. I tried to remember the commands the soldiers used. "Halt!" I said, using a deep voice.

Suddenly, the horse stopped, but I was not prepared. It

catapulted me into the air, and I landed on the ground face-first. The pain was immediate. I screamed out, and I felt the warmth of my own blood as I fell into unconsciousness.

34

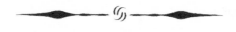

David

Hebron

1010 B.C.

I kissed the forehead of my newborn son and prayed another blessing. Turning to Maacah, I said, "I will be leaving in the morning. We hope to capture Jerusalem. I will be gone for some time, but when I return, it will be with another victory."

"We will be here waiting," she said, taking Absalom from me.

I stepped out of her chambers and made my rounds to the rest of the family. Abigail had prepared an evening meal and agreed for Ahinoam and Amnon to join us, so I could enjoy the meal with my two eldest sons. "You take care of the women while I am away," I said to Amnon and Daniel.

"I am the oldest," Amnon said to Daniel. "I will be their protector."

"Me too," Daniel complained.

I stayed until it was time for the boys to wash and prepare for bed. I kissed them both and prayed over them too. As I was leaving, Abigail stopped me. "How is the queen? We have heard that she is unwell."

"She is well. It is her maidservant who is sick. Michal cares for her."

"I will add her maidservant to my prayers."

I smiled at Abigail. "Thank you. Your gentleness and wisdom are a breath of fresh air in my life."

I walked Ahinoam and Amnon back to their chambers. I paused in the communal courtyard and took in the sight. This was my family. Each of them. How could I make Michal see that? How could I make her see she was a part of this?

Joab approached. He appeared winded. "Uncle, there is an emergency. Come quickly."

I followed him out of the courtyard, through the halls, and out the southern veranda. Abishai stood with three of my men. "What is it?"

One of them turned to me and bowed. "It is the queen. She is no longer in the sick tent."

"She must be showing herself to Abiathar. What of the maidservant?" I looked to any of them to clarify.

"The maidservant is still in the tent and is still among the living for the time being."

"Michal must have decided to leave her there." As soon as I said the words, I did not believe them. "Do you know where she went? Have you checked with Abiathar?"

The soldier glanced away as if guilty. "She stole my horse. The two guards will attest to the events."

"How did she steal your horse?" I could not mask my shock or irritation. "How do you lose a queen?"

"We heard a noise, and we went to investigate. She took that opportunity to jump on the horse and leave. She did call out she will return, but we wanted to let you know that she is on horse…unattended."

"And unclean," another soldier said.

"Who is at the tent now?" I asked, looking at the men who stood before me.

"The sick woman."

"You all left the sick tent unattended."

"We did not think the sick woman would go anywhere. We were more concerned about the queen."

"Who may well show up again!" I yelled. The two men bowed and left quickly. I turned to the other one. "What direction?"

"Southern forest," Joab answered for him. "I have already sent out men."

"Somebody get me my horse," I growled. "Do we have any indication as to why she stole the horse?"

One soldier could not maintain eye contact. "She may have overheard me speaking to the guards about Ishbosheth."

I slapped my hand to my forehead. Joab and I made eye contact. He must have sensed my concern because he reassured me, "Uncle, we will not stop until we find her."

I grabbed the other man and said, "She better be found alive and well, or you will pay for your wagging tongue."

As soon as my horse arrived, I pulled myself onto it and sped away. Any irritation at Michal's disregard for orders was second to the worry. I worried about where she was headed. I worried if she would be able to navigate the horse in the dark. I worried she would become lost in the forest.

The hours passed, and Michal was not found. The entire compound was lit up with lanterns and torches, and every available soldier and servant was sent out to find her. I searched the forest throughout the night. I called out with no answer, but the forest was vast and surrounded the mountains. "Where did you go?" I said under my breath.

Someone shouted, and then a series of calls broke out. I pushed the horse to move in that direction. Eventually, I made it to a small clearing near a brook. Benaiah appeared grim. He sat upon his horse, holding the reins of another. "We found the soldier's horse."

"No Michal?"

Benaiah shook his head.

Panic gripped my heart. "I doubt she would have willingly

gotten off to go by foot. And I doubt vagabonds would take her and not a horse."

Benaiah agreed. "These horses are much larger than what she would be used to."

Uriah approached on his beast. "She fell off the horse? I thought she knew how to ride."

"Riding in the dark with an unfamiliar beast is a dangerous concoction," Benaiah answered. "I venture she is injured."

"Oh, God." My insides flipped at the thought of Michal injured and terrified in the dark woods. "We keep looking, and we keep calling out. Let us fortify this forest. She must be here somewhere."

The morning light came with a rain shower. The gray skies and noisy raindrops against the leaves made the search near impossible. I knew the longer it took to find her, the more likely she would succumb to injuries. In frustration, I bellowed her name, "*Michal*!"

Had she been that desperate? The thought would not leave me alone. The news of Ishbosheth's death must have been the breaking point. She was all that was left of Saul's legitimate children with Queen Ahinoam. My heart broke for her, and the guilt of being angry at her made it hard to breathe.

I was angry at *her* when I was the one who ordered everyone to keep my activities silent. She already felt betrayed by me and my actions, and then I brought her closest friend into the deception. The betrayal had been too much. Why had I not seen that earlier?

Eleazar approached. "Those who search grow weary. Should we take shifts?"

I wanted to scream no, but without our senses sharp, we might miss a clue or her altogether. I nodded. "I will stay out and continue searching."

"You are soaked and have been up all night. We will come up with a schedule and oversee shifts. You are no good as king if you are sick or delirious from exhaustion."

"I will continue searching a little while longer." I saw Eleazar open his mouth to contest. "I am fine. My wife, on the other hand, is not. I want to continue the search."

Eleazar nodded. "We will find her."

"But will it be too late?" I could not hide the emotion in my voice.

"We are all praying for her safe return."

Shouts interrupted our conversation. "Over here! Over here!"

I lifted the reins and clicked at my horse, and we took off in the direction of the shouts with Eleazar right behind me. But the shouts not only increased, they seemed to come from several different directions.

"This way," Eleazar said, turning his horse to the right.

We nearly plowed into Uriah. "I was heading toward you," he said. "Follow me."

The journey to her weighed heavily on me, and I begged God to spare her life. I spotted several individuals clumped together, and they moved aside when they saw me approach. My mouth dropped when I saw her. Face first on the ground, so tiny among the trees.

I slid off the horse and sprinted to her. "Michal?" I looked up at anyone who could tell me anything.

"Her chest moves," Uriah said, coming up behind me. "And there is blood. The rain has yet to wash it all away."

I saw the blood stain upon her wet forehead, but more alarming, I saw the blood stain stuck on her apparel in her lower extremities. "Oh Michal," I choked back the sob. I rolled her over gently and got a better view of the head wound but took in a sharp breath over the extensive blood stains near her lower abdomen. "Everyone leave!" I ordered, taking off my cloak and covering her.

I shook with worry, but I pushed it aside. I picked her up, her frail body—how had I not realized how tiny she had become—and carried her in the direction of the compound.

"David, we will move faster on horse," Eleazar said. "Let us help you secure her."

But I was not listening. Instead, I moved as fast as I could out of the forest and began the long journey to the compound, carrying my broken wife.

———————

I took Michal's hand and held it in mine. She rested peacefully, but other than occasional moments of semi-consciousness, she had yet to wake up. The days and nights all melded together. I slept beside her. I helped clean her. I talked to her. I begged her to wake up. Because of the bleeding, the men stayed away, including Abiathar and the physician. The women cared for her, and I felt out of place amongst them. But I could not leave her side.

"Please, rest, my king," one of the women urged me. "Only God and time will heal her."

"But the bleeding." I choked on the words.

"This amount of blood is typical when a woman has lost a child, and it is a lot less than four days ago. She is healing as is her womb, so please, go and rest."

Several of the women who served as midwives notified me hours after I arrived with Michal in my arms that upon closer inspection, the blood contained fragments of what would have been a growing child. If I was not grieving enough, that was enough to rip my heart into little pieces. *Michal was growing my child? Did she know?*

I kissed Michal's forehead and left into the adjoining chamber. This allowed me privacy for washing, eating, and changing garments until I was purified from the blood. Shutting the door behind me, I wept.

I washed my face and changed my tunic, deciding on prayer instead of sleep. I was surprised when someone knocked at the door. I glanced outside and saw that it was not even close to daybreak. "Who is it?"

"Nathan. Open the door. I have a word."

"I have not gone before the priest."

"Open the door."

I opened it. Nathan stepped inside without an invitation. "You will have to purify yourself."

"I am not near the blood. I am here with you, and I have a word."

"Is it a good word?" I was not sure I could handle anything else.

"You are to purify yourself, and you are to go and secure Jerusalem. The time is now."

"I cannot leave my wife like this. I was not with her when she lost our first child. I must be with her for this loss."

"Why? The unborn child did not live. We cannot change that, but if you lose your focus on the immediate situation of securing Jerusalem, this window of opportunity will close. It is time to surrender to God's design and move forward. I heard you sent tribal elders away."

"Only until I am purified and seen by Abiathar. We will meet with them soon, but Michal—"

"She will live. You cannot serve your kingdom by her bedside."

"That may be true, but I can serve my wife. Is that not a higher priority?"

"You have served her. For days. You have mourned the loss of the unborn child. It is done, and the kingdom will not wait. Once you have secured the city, you will have time to devote to the queen. If there is anything left to salvage, that is."

"What do you mean by that?"

"Your marriage to Michal is broken. It was broken the moment Saul gave her to another man. The break continued when you chose to marry other women. She will still be Israel's queen, but the union may not be salvageable."

Even though Nathan's words hurt deeply, he was right. With Ishbosheth dead, the tribes of Israel looked to me to lead the way. Securing Jerusalem would establish dominance over the kingdom and loudly shout to other nations my strong kingship. I took a deep breath and accepted the decision. "Let us secure Jerusalem. But first, I need to send for Abiathar."

"He is here already. I brought him with me. Shall we begin the purification process?"

35

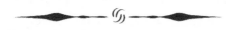

Michal

Hebron

1010 B.C.

When I opened my eyes, I expected to find David. I had heard him during those moments when I was semi-conscious, but it was Dinah who sat beside my bed.

I blinked and immediately questioned my senses. "Dinah?" My voice was raspy and sounded foreign in my ears.

She gave me a small smile. "Tis I. We have once again reversed who cares for whom."

"When? How?"

"You have been in and out of consciousness for several days. I went before the priest, and he concluded that I was no longer sick. I just arrived to you this morning."

I held out my hand, she took it in hers. "I am so glad for it. I do not know what I would have done if the deathly rattle would have stolen your last breath."

"Deathly rattle? From inside me? Yes, it was concerning. I too wondered if the coughing would be my end." She paused as if contemplating. "However, I woke up from sleep, and my skin no longer felt like fire. I called out for you, but you—and no one else for that matter—came."

"The guards did not do their nightly rounds?"

"They eventually did, and I was sitting up, asking for you. It turns out you had left for your own deathly adventure."

"Not purposefully. I took the horse to catch some fresh air and to process the news of my brother. The horse was huge, and it would not listen to me." I studied my friend. "It is a marvel. The last thing I remember before stealing that horse was hearing about Ishbosheth's death and praying to God to save your life."

"He heard you, and He answered. Praise Yahweh."

"And Ishbosheth? Is it true?"

"Yes. He was murdered in his sleep. David punished the guilty men by cutting off their hands and hanging their bodies over the Hebron waters."

I crinkled my nose in disgust. "Men are so gruesome, but I am glad David avenged my brother's death." We stayed quiet for a moment. "I assume I am no longer pregnant? If I ever was. I had severe cramps for days."

"You were pregnant," Dinah said quietly. "I am sorry. That is why you were struggling to stay alive. You lost a lot of blood. Just like last time."

I swallowed back the grief. "I suppose I should not be selfish and grieve the child when you stand before me as an answered prayer." Tears leaked from my eyes. "But without the child, my plan to win David's affections will not work."

"He grieved deeply. From what I was told, he wept often and never left your side."

"Where is he now?"

"He purified himself and met with the elders of Israel. They said they look to him to lead the nation."

"So, no more Judah separate from Israel?"

"No. It appears David has won over their hearts. We are one nation again. He is now with his mighty men on some military mission to secure a city. It sounds grand. It is a city high on a hill, surrounded by impenetrable walls. If David succeeds, it will be the capital for the nation."

"There is no 'if.' David *will* succeed." I did not voice my questions or concerns about where that left us because I already knew. I would take my place among many women. With Ishbosheth dead, David will inherit the harem. He will have his choice over any of them. Where did that leave me? The childless queen?

"I do have good news. David told his manservant, Cush, to see to you that you have whatever you desire. This morning, he asked me if there was anything to help your healing, and I mentioned Merab's sons. I explained that Adriel had chosen you to raise them, but you had yet to bring it up with the king. Cush said David had received a message several moons ago from Adriel about you taking Merab's sons, but David never responded because he was out on military duty."

"He is out again on military duty."

"Cush said that he would send word to the king, and then with approval, he can send for the boys."

"I suppose that is my lot in this life. To raise my sister's sons."

"There are worse fates."

"I agree." When I saw Dinah's widened eyes, I gave a small laugh. "Being close to death again is enough for me to see I cannot change my fate. I have tried. I have tried to win David's heart, to give him an heir from my womb, to keep him to myself. I failed. He is no longer mine. He has families with other women, and it will only expand with more women and heirs."

Dinah frowned. "I do not understand the ways of men, but I know David loves you in his way."

"He loves the memory of us. He said as much. I am not the bride he married, but he is not who I married either."

"What are you to do? It is our station as women to be subservient. They can have many wives. Women can only marry one man."

"I cannot dwell on it," I said tiredly. "I am not sure what I will do or how this will work out, but being around him makes it worse."

"I wish there were words of wisdom to offer, but I have none. He is king, and you are not. There will always be those who desire him."

"Nathan came to visit me. The night of my accident. He warned me not to become bitter. It will kill me. Then I went and jumped on a horse and nearly killed myself."

Dinah leaned over and rested her head against my arm. "I am glad you did not die."

"I am glad *you* did not die," I repeated to her. "I would not have been able to live with the guilt."

"What is your plan? Other than getting well."

I thought about all the years I had wasted longing for a man who could not offer me what I desired most. Him. The faithful commitment of a partner. "I plan to live life alone. I found some semblance of happiness with Merab's sons and my horses. I want to find that again."

"I think the days of you being alone are a myth. David will never cast you out."

"I will always be his wife. I cannot change that, but I closing my heart off to him. If I reject him enough, he will go elsewhere. Soon, we will be like strangers, living at opposite ends of a compound."

"That sounds depressing. You deserve so much more." Dinah gave a humorless laugh.

"I have all I need. In that way, I will be better off. You know, my mother pined after my father all the years of their marriage. She would be thrilled with the occasional occurrence when he would visit her. Then she would be horrible to live with afterward. She was constantly in a state of agitation and envy."

"Oh, I remember that. I was at the receiving end of her scorned heart many times."

I glanced over at Dinah and blinked back tears. "And that is what happened when I threw you in shackles. I became my mother.

I was so overcome with jealousy and anger that I threw my best friend into an underground cell. When you were sick, I vowed if you ever became well, I would do things differently. And I will. I vow to choose sanity over madness. That means leaving behind the emotions and the people who make me crazy."

"You mean David."

I nodded. "Yes, it has taken me years to finally figure this out, but to save myself, I must cut him off."

It took several more days before I felt like myself. My body needed to be retaught how to move, especially my legs and feet. A wooden cane was crafted for me to use during exercise. With Dinah and Raja, I would walk the garden paths of the compound each day. Days came and went, and I became stronger.

Three moons later, a knock at my chamber door renewed my strength. Ashvi barreled in. "Mimi!" he cried, throwing his arms around me. The other two older boys came rushing in, and all three piled on top of me, showering me with hugs and kisses.

Tears of happiness trickled my face as I kissed each of them. "Oh, let me look at you. How you have grown!"

The youngest set of twins walked inside, both acting unsure.

"This is Mimi," Ashvi told them. "Remember?"

Dinah had already picked them up and was hugging them both. They giggled while she tickled them. "They are no longer babies," she said. "How many years are you? Hold up your fingers."

They held up four fingers each.

"Too old!" I laughingly chided. I kissed each of their cheeks. "You were barely toddling when I last saw you."

For the rest of the evening, we laughed and talked and played games. My cheeks hurt from smiling so much. Ashvi whispered to me that he would pass his eleventh year soon. "I prayed and asked Yahweh to come back to you. That is all I wanted." He grinned and planted a kiss on me. "And He answered!"

He reminded me so much of Merab that it nearly took my breath away. I grabbed him and embraced him. "Yes, He did. He surely did."

36

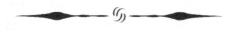

David

Jerusalem

1009 B.C.

S omething about climbing up a narrow water shaft will make a man contemplate his life. Many moons passed full of strategizing and spying, and we had finally made our move. As the days marched forward, my thoughts when alone often turned to Michal. I trusted the prophet's words that she would live, but I worried about what kind of life that would be. Without bearing children, I sensed her misery would only increase. Any irritation from before finding her in the forest had dissipated. But I could not dwell on her long. For the kingdom of Israel was mine, and that meant leading from a place of power. That meant securing Jerusalem.

"I see a light in the distance," Eleazar said. He climbed directly above me. My brothers Shammah and Eliab followed behind me.

We were the third company to use the Jebusite water system to enter within the walls of their city. The other two companies who went before us were led by Joab and Abishai and were now hidden in plain sight, waiting for the order from their king. This meant I could not let this narrow passage kill me.

Infiltrating the city took longer than anticipated because we refused to make a wrong move. My men could easily hide among the people. Others disguised themselves along the outer walls, waiting for the gates to open. And then there was the entire host of Israel's army waiting at varying locations for our trumpets to blow.

But the water shaft was longer than anticipated with several parts being vertical climbs.

"You are moving slow up there, old man," Eliab jibed.

"Are you not the eldest?" Shammah joked in return.

"I may be the eldest, but I would already be up there winning the battle by now."

"I can only go as fast as Eleazar," I said, joining in the camaraderie. "He is the old man."

"If I slip and fall, I land upon all of you," Eleazar quipped. "I do see light. Should I whistle now?"

"How close?" I asked.

"A couple stones' throw."

"We need to get closer. That way if there is an ambush, we can pull ourselves out and not drown."

Closing the distance between us and the well's opening, Eleazar gave a soft whistle to see if any of our men were nearby. We waited. "Again," I whispered.

After the third whistle, we heard their whistle in reply.

"There it is," Eleazar said. "It is clear. Should we proceed?"

Just then, a rope was flung from the other side of the well to us. "Go," I said to Eleazar. "I will be right behind you."

He grabbed hold of the rope and tugged on it. I watched as he climbed the rest of the way out of the well's opening. The rope was thrown back into the well for me. "See you soon," I teased my two older brothers.

"Hurry," Eliab said. "I am tired of smelling Shammah."

As soon as I was up and over the well's edge, I saw Joab in Jebusite apparel. "Hello, uncle," he said with a wry grin.

"How did you end up with their soldiers' garb? Or should I ask where did you hide the bodies?"

"They had men guarding the well. We surprised them when we

climbed out of it and had no choice but to attack. We were quiet, of course. They are not skilled fighters. They use these walls as their protection, but they fell easily. We put on their garments and dropped their bodies in another well."

I made a face. I did not like the thought of rancid, decomposing bodies poisoning the water source.

"It is a shallow well and no longer used, uncle. We will pull them out and bury them when the time comes."

"Not their water source?"

"No."

Once Shammah and Eliab were out of the well, we followed Joab to their hiding location. "This is the guards' station. All rotations start and end here, which is a big mistake for the Jebusites. Without any other commander or troop coming here, we have stayed undetected."

"Right under their noses."

"The well is beginning to stink," It is just north of us. We prayed you would arrive before we had to move to our next plan."

Our plan should any of us get stuck or caught in the shaft system was for the first group to simply go to the gates and open them. We have enough stationed along the outside walls to run in unannounced and do some damage. "Thankfully, we do not have to resort to another plan. At least not yet."

"Benaiah, Uriah, and Jashobeam are at locations with their core groups at the three main entrances. They are disguised and scattered to not draw attention to themselves. We need all three gates opened with little interruption or detection. We will go in pairs. The rest will follow but not too close. The objective is that when the Jebusite soldiers realize what is happening and attack those who opened the gates, they will be annihilated by those storming in and those on rooftops with good aim." Joab explained the plan to us, completely in his element. This was what my nephew did best. He led, and he fought for the kingdom. I was impressed and considered myself fortunate that I chose to forgive him for his wrongdoings. We needed him here at this moment.

"Does everyone understand their role?" I asked. "We move to our locations tonight. Too many of us are here now to be in this one position. Eventually, someone will call on these men requesting their reports."

"Dusk is upon us," Abishai said. "We are rested and ready to move. We were simply waiting on you to arrive."

There was a pause before most of the men began to quietly laugh. Abishai looked confused. "Are you saying I am slow?" I teased.

"N-No, I would never say that," Abishai stumbled over his words.

"I would," Eliab joked. "He and Eleazar move like old men."

"Are you not older than the king?" Abishai asked him.

While everyone continued to chuckle, I said, "Thank you, Abishai. No matter how old I am, I will always be the youngest of Jesse's sons."

"And my birth was mere days from David's, so the real old men should stay quiet." Eleazar slapped Eliab and Shammah's shoulders.

We reviewed several other plans should anything go amiss, then divvied up supplies and left in our disguises. I chose the location closest to the central gate that led to the heart of Jerusalem. I desired the quickest route when the time came to show their leadership that no one insulted Hebrew troops without punishment. Eleazar was with me, and Shammah and Eliab were close by, searching for another location at a different angle. The goal was to find a place on rooftops providing us a clear target at the gates.

Eleazar and I lingered amongst the local stall owners selling their wares. We discreetly searched for a back entrance or narrow passage between homes that could help us climb to a roof. Joab warned that there were not any Hebrew sympathizers that he and his group discovered. "These Jebusites are safe behind this wall. They do not need any other group."

I kept my head down and refused to make eye contact with the locals. My reputation as the golden-eyed warrior still made its rounds throughout the land, and it always surprised me when foreigners would make mention of it. I could not have anyone recognizing me here.

Eleazar walked past me. Without stopping, he gave a low whistle, indicating he found a place.

I put some distance between us and kept my interest on the stalls. As I perused fruit wagons and spice racks, I would occasionally peek out and see where Eleazar was. By the time stall owners were closing up for the night and packing away their product, it was dark enough that I moved more freely toward a darkened passage behind a pair of tied donkeys.

We waited for a sliver of moon to rise, and for the quiet of night to descend.

"We will have to scale these stones." Eleazar pointed at the jutted edges of stones used to build the residence. Scaling rock walls was easy for both of us. As former shepherds, we learned early on the importance of climbing a cliff or rock edge as quickly as possible.

Eleazar went first. Since this residence had only a second level. We made it up the stone wall without incident. "This will work nicely," I whispered.

"Do you see?" Eleazar pointed to the eastern gates.

I saw Joab, moving along the interior wall. Lanterns occasionally showed his shadow from one location to another. Soon, I saw those with him. Scattered in their formation, but knowing their mission, I found myself smiling. These Jebusite soldiers will never see us coming.

A brief horn sounded then was silenced, but that was enough to alert others. I saw shadows fighting shadows. Both atop the wall and on ground level. "I cannot see enough to assist them."

"We stay here," Eleazar cautioned. "Joab knows what he is doing."

But a large mass of soldiers moved toward our men, horns sounding along the streets. Suddenly, the gate opened. I breathed a sigh of relief. Joab will have reinforcements. I moved across the roof and saw the southern gate open. I saw my men rushing in.

The shuffle of feet brought me to my current situation, and I swung around to see two Jebusite soldiers lunging for Eleazar. I threw my javelin at the one while Eleazar sliced through the other. Both fell from the roof.

"Not good," Eleazar said. "We have been spotted."

An arrow flew past me. "Our cover is blown," I said, swinging myself over the roof's ledge. "We fight on the ground."

By now, lanterns blazed throughout the city. The Jebusite war cry sounded, and we were entrenched in the fight. Eleazar and I jumped down at a safe distance, using the dark passage as an aid. Even though I still preferred a sling and stone, when in tough situations, a bow and arrow were a guaranteed kill. Eleazar and I took turns shooting arrows at every soldier that ran past. They fell like flies.

The sound of someone landing behind us startled me. I turned quickly, but I was too late. The soldiers had their swords at our necks and pushed us out in the open. "We can jump from rooftops too," he said in broken Hebrew.

In one swift move, I knocked his sword from his hand and used mine to slice below his breastplate and knock out the other one's knee. Eleazar finished the move with a slicing of the head.

And just like flies, more were upon us. Eleazar and I fought back-to-back. But we were not alone for long. Eliab and Shammah miraculously appeared, covering me from Jebusite blows. "Get him out of here," Eliab ordered Eleazar. "We will finish this."

"Thank you, brother," I said in between blows to the opponents. "But I do not need protection."

A javelin whizzed at Eliab, and he expertly deflected it while using his sword against two enemy soldiers. "Just let your big brothers protect you for once."

But as Joab had indicated, the Jebusite soldiers lacked true fighting power. The four of us easily defeated the mass of soldiers who descended upon us.

"It is the Hebrew king!" A soldier shouted, running toward us. Another mass of men followed.

A horn blew from the top pathways of the eastern wall, and then another. These were our horns. The horns continued until I could hear the faint shout of the Israeli army emerging from the forest. It hit my ears like a sweet bird's song. I smiled as I fought.

I stood on the balcony of the small palace of their king. This would not work as it was not much larger than other residences. Even my Hebron compound was more expansive. Still, it provided a gorgeous view of the city. My city.

Not just mine. Not just Judah's. But the victory was Israel's, handed to us by Yahweh. This victory was ours.

All the years of running, of trying to prove myself. How many times had I questioned whether or not Samuel had gotten it right? I closed my eyes, took in a deep breath, and remembered the way the oil felt when it ran down my face and neck. My family had been shocked, as was I. A lonely, shepherd boy anointed King of Israel? Now here I stood as king.

And I finally felt I had made it *home.*

Epilogue

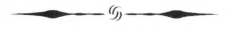

Michal

Jerusalem

1008 B.C.

"I suppose congratulations are in order," I said, above the cheers of the crowd. "You have everything you ever desired." My gaze skimmed the large grouping of women David had inherited from Ishbosheth and the Jebusite king. Before, it would have broken me, but no longer. Still, I gently pulled my hand from his. Now that I had closed my heart to him, the chasm between us felt vast and cold.

"Is it not everything you hoped for?" David grinned at the crowd; his arms thrown out to them. He truly seemed to be reveling in this moment.

"Not everything, but I am happy for you. Enjoy the celebration."

"Will you not attend? My queen must be at my side."

The last place I desired to be was at a vast banquet full of drunk men and dancing girls. Being with my boys was my only wish. "The celebration is for the men, but I can come to greet them if you desire."

Suddenly, David turned to me. I continued to keep the façade in place and admire the crowd. When I could take it no longer, I turned slightly and glanced in his direction. "You are different," he said.

"You have said that to me before. That I am not the woman you married."

He acted pained. "I should not have said that. But this is different from even that. You seem…distant. Is everything all right? I know the Jebusite palace is small, but I already have plans for a vast palace. It will be beyond your dreams."

"That sounds lovely, but I am content here with my boys by my side."

David's expression remained unreadable. "I am glad you have your sister's sons. I would have discussed arrangements with Adriel earlier had I known."

"They are with me now." I spotted them in the crowd with my maidservants, and I waved at them.

"You are different. It is something. I sense it. What can I do for you? Tell me, and I will make it happen."

"I explained to you when I first arrived. When someone comes close to death, it changes her perspective. That is all. There is nothing for you to do but enjoy your celebration."

He paused for a moment, before saying, "You arrived several days ago, yet I have not received an invitation to visit." I heard the hurt in his voice.

It is better this way, I told myself, and I truly believed it. By choosing to accept my lot in life, I had found some peace. I could not open my heart to the heavy, exhausting emotions that festered and oozed from unrequited love. Even with David professing his love, it was severely limited. He loved me, but he also had a harem of women to attend to his every need. I refused to be a part of the fray. To him, I said, "Forgive me. There has been much to do." Unable to help myself, I indicated the other women. "I am sure you understand."

"Trust me when I say they are not the one I desire."

Oh, the words dripped with feeling, but I simply sighed and waved at those beneath us. I would play this part, and then I would go and be with those who truly loved me. My true family. "Wave to the crowd, David. They desire their king."

The End

Author Notes

This book, just like the first two of the series, came right out of the pages of the Bible. If you are curious about what is fact and what is fiction, I encourage you to read the Biblical account. It is found mostly in 1 and 2 Samuel and 1 Chronicles. This section includes the author's discussion on some interesting facts about this story, along with what was plain ol' fiction.

1. *Michal raised her nephews.*

   According to Scripture, Michal raised her sister's sons. Merab birthed five sons, and she must have had an early death (detailed in the second book of this series) because Michal raised them as her own.

2. *David's marriages to other women.*

   David married while in Hebron, and when he moved to Jerusalem, the Bible details that he aquired many more wives and concubines. In this story, I focused on the marriages in Hebron: Michal, Ahinoam, Abigain, Maacah, and Haggith. These are their actual names as recorded in Scripture. The Bible also details that Maacah was a princess and Haggith was a dancer, so I chose to create their stories from these details.

3. *David and his men conquered Jerusalem by climbing up the water shaft.*

   Yes, David and his men conquered Jerusalem by climbing up the water shaft! Check out 2 Samuel 5 and 1 Chronicles 11 for more information on this amazing accomplishment! Ancient Jerusalem was impenetrable with its walls. It truly was a city on a hill. Scripture records the Jebusites insulting

David and his men, so that scene is in this book too. Joab played a big role in securing Jerusalem for his uncle.

4. *David's nephews and their role in David's life.*

    Joab, Abishai, and Asahel are all in Scripture as serving under David. Joab is David's commander. Scripture shows him as an excellent leader but a bit of a hothead. In Ancient Israel, it was common for kings to have their families in important roles to preserve the bloodline. A fun fact: Abner and Saul were related, which is why Abner was Saul's commander and why Abner was determined for the kingship to stay in the family.

5. *Michal's marriage to Paltiel.*

    Saul handed Michal to Paltiel in marriage as an insult to David who was on the run. In Saul's mind, David was as good as dead, but mostly, it was considered a low blow for David. That said, there is nothing in Scripture that points to Michal consummating the marriage to Paltiel. Jewish history explains that consummation did not happen and that David actually sent a bloodied sword to Paltiel as a warning not to touch his wife. This is explored in book two of this series.

    Scripture does describe Paltiel's emotions when Michal is taken by Abner for David. He truly did weep and follow the entourage. Considering Michal was with him for nearly a decade, this makes sense. Michal's reaction to the events is not specifically recorded in Scripture, so artistic liberty was taken.

6. *Abner, Ishbosheth, and Rizpah.*

    There was a falling out between Ishbosheth and Abner, and yes, it had to do with Rizpah. Abner became so angry over Ishbosheth's accusations that he severed ties with his cousin and offered an alliance with David.

7. *Abner and Joab's conflict.*

    According to the Bible, the war games happened, as did

Asahel's death by Abner's sword. Abner did tell Asahel to turn back, but David's nephew did not listen. Joab, in turn, murdered Abner in retaliation. This entire situation hurt David's precarious relationship with the other tribes, especially the tribe of Benjamin at first. But when Ishbosheth found out about Abner's death, he was terrified of David, and it ultimately led to his own death.

8. *Michal's friendship with Dinah.*

Dinah is a fictional character. She is not in Scripture. Artistic liberty was taken to describe Michal's character arc and to illustrate how she can go from loving princess to resentful queen. Dinah's character helped elevate the humanity of Michal.

9. *David's manservant, Cush.*

The stranded Egyptian slave is described in Scripture when David and his men seek information on the Amalekites while in Ziklag. However, his name was not provided, and he was never recorded as becoming David's manservant. Artistic liberty was taken.

10. *Michal's miscarriages.*

The Bible states that Michal had no children until the day of her death. Some scholars feel she is recorded as Eglah in 2 Samuel, which was David's pet name for her. However, for the purposes of this story, Michal's struggles with pregnancy only aided in her struggles with jealousy and comparisons. That said, there is nothing recorded in Scripture that she had miscarriages.

Author Acknowledgements

This book series has been a labor of love, as well as some tears and venting sessions. Historical fiction is difficult to write, and I think Biblical fiction is harder yet. The research must be painstaking and meticulous. Often, I questioned if I should ever write the tale of David and Michal. How could I ever compete with the Word? Scripture is the best book in the universe, and it is literally the inspired Word of God. But I kept writing. I wrote these three books not only because David is such a captivating character from Scripture, but because Michal's story compelled me. She is usually seen as a "bad woman" because she was bitter, but I felt drawn to share with readers what may have made her that way. What took her from a loving, loyal girl to detesting David in her heart? So, I delved deep into the Scripture. I researched Jewish history. Through all of that, I found her story. That is what you read on the pages of this 3-book series.

To all of you who have been along for the ride since book one, thank you. And to my Heavenly Father, I thank you most of all.

Thank you for your purchase!

If you enjoyed ***The Anointed Heir,***
Read the first two books of the David series:

The Secret Heir
The Runaway Heir

Visit the author online at www.janicebroyles.com

Made in the USA
Las Vegas, NV
28 March 2024

87877676R00184